BAD BARGAIN

A SPACE RULES ADVENTURE PART 1

IAN CANNON

First published 2019
By NKBooks/IanCannonBooks
DFW, TX, U.S.A.

Cover design by www.DerangedDoctorDesign.com
Edited by www.FadingStreet.com

 Created with Vellum

ACKNOWLEDGMENTS

O Captain! My Captain!
our fearful trip is done,
The ship has weather'd every rack,
the prize we sought is won.
~ Walt Whitman ~

Thank you Captain James. T. Kirk,
Captain Solo, and Captain Malcolm Reynolds
for turning reality
magically into dreams

And the captains of the Indie Ship American Inklings for
turning dreams
back into reality.

CHAPTER ONE

—————

"HE'S BEHIND YOU, babe, six o'clock." Her voice came through his headset.

"I can't get a visual."

"Of course you can't. I said he's behind you."

"Very funny. You tracking him?"

"Just keep moving. He's coming fast."

"Yeah, but are you tracking him?"

There was a giggle in Ben's ear. A giggle. Made him snarl. She said, "You still don't trust me, do you, babe?"

What a ridiculous question. He trusted her with his life, with his very soul. She was just razzing him now. Not a good time for razzing. "Of course I trust you. I just..." The jump booster on his atmo gear hit full charge with a...

Beep.

Boom!

He blasted off.

The ground dropped from under his feet very quickly. Weightlessness became inertia, made him grit his teeth. He tapped the toggle pad in his gloved hand and a secondary vent in his bio-suit hissed spinning him around. He could see the asteroid drop away beneath him.

And there he was. Rogan. His pursuer. What a bastard. Not too bright, either.

Tawny had been right. He was close. Now the man stood below looking up helplessly angry. Made Ben laugh. "See you, sucker."

His automated suit voiced in his ear, "Ben, your trajectory is deteriorating. I would suggest..."

"Yeah yeah," he said spinning himself back around in mid-flight. The overlay showed on his visor, green optics targeting flicking to red, the target asteroid slipping to the left. Yep, he was off by several meters. "Adjusting." He toggled gently. Vents hissed. He felt his vacuum flight adjust. The asteroid came up quick. His pre-calculated landing zone centered making him grin. But his velocity was too high.

"Babe, you're coming in hot!" Tawny called in his headset.

"I know!" he said through held breath jerking the toggle up and reversing the jumper vents. Too late. The preordained landing zone—a nice, safe, comfortably smooth spot between crater impacts—went by below. He watched it forlornly through his visor. He totally missed it. Then he looked up. A stone spire approached, coming fast. His eyes went big. "Oh, this is going to—"

FROM TAWNY'S position several vacuum miles away perched on her own little asteroid, Ben's impact looked like a tiny puff of dust ejected into space from the vertical side of a stone tower. But she knew better. That was a man colliding with an asteroid. That was her husband. Her heart stopped, mouth dropped, eyes went doughy. "Babe?" she whispered, and waited. Nothing returned. "Benji!"

A bearish groan issued through her headset. "I'm okay. I'm... okay."

She sighed relief, half pissed off and half overjoyed.

"You copy, sweetheart?" he said.

"Yeah, I copy," she finally said, "you big dummy!"

"What's his position?"

She swung her M-209 solar collection plasma weapon back down toward the previous asteroid, zoomed up on the visor overlay. The weapon was a body-mounted, long-barreled sniper cannon—a beast with a charge pack connected to her back. A digital reticle narrowed in on her target. Her eyes became slits.

There he was. Rogan. Dumbest man in the system.

He was toggling switches of his own and lowering into a squatting position.

"He's preparing a jump, Benji."

"Figured that. He's welcome to join me if he wants. But it's going to hurt. What's his distance?"

"Three hundred meters."

"Copy. I'm on the move."

She swiveled her weapon further downward, adjusting her view. Another asteroid showed. It was a big one. Huge. A small moon. This was the primary. Every asteroid field had a mother—a worldlet from which the others broke away in their endless pirouetting. This field was ancient, creating a sea of debris that trailed off into the star-speckled fjord. But the rock she viewed through her visor overlay known as Hominus IV was by far the biggest, taking up the entire lower periphery.

"Your destination is straight below you."

"Preparing to drop. How far is..."

"Oh babe, he just jumped!"

BEN, clinging to the side of his tower, twisted around searching for his pursuer with the naked eye. He caught him, a man-shaped dot in the distance arcing silently through space, zipping from one asteroid to the other. He was coming up quick, going to land below him, cut him off. "Oh hells!"

He kicked way out from the side of his mountain tower and punched his toggle control. Jets boosted him into a straight-down nosedive. He watched Rogan get nearer and nearer. Collision course.

"Benji!" she called in his ear.

"I know!"

"You're going to..."

"I know!"

Ben whipped his dual pistols out, held them at arm's length. Rogan did the same, unleashing his own blaster, the two human projectiles closing the distance fast, one coming from below, one coming from above. Their paths crossed in a heartbeat, barely missing. Ben spun around, keeping Rogan in his gun sights. The man rasped his free hand at him trying to grab him, but their velocities were way too fast, and just like that, Ben watched Rogan go shrinking away, once again looking down at him helplessly furious. Ben snickered. "See you, sucker."

"That was close, babe."

"Tell me about it."

"Why can't we just shoot this moron and put him out of his misery?"

"Rules, baby."

"Oh yeah—like he follows the rules."

"He didn't shoot me, either. We got to give him that."

"That's only because he knows I'm out here tracking him."

"Then maybe he's not as dumb as I thought. You're probably right, though. Landing." The surface of Hominus IV zoomed up at him. He reversed his jets, came down hard. The surface declined and he slid along kicking up loess, not from gravity, but the inertia of his landing. He growled, grinding himself to a stop. Once on stable footing, he moved his way up the incline and stood at the edge of a canyon bowl. The place was enormous—like a moonscape below, the night sky speckled with rotating tonnage above.

"Can you see it?" she asked. "It's located at the bottom."

Ben's visual instrumentation sought out his target destination, found it, zoomed it in. There was a vacuum shack at the bottom of the canyon, a gray building sealed against the vacuum of space. Four hundred meters. "Yeah, I see it. Making my approach. What's REX telling you?"

"Activity. Ten guards."

"Great."

"Be careful."

"That's why I got you," he said.

He heard her groan through his headset. His life was in her hands now. Her expertise would be the only thing to save him, especially once the hermetic door opened on the garage below and a trio of moon vehicles emerged, each with two operators—a driver, a gunner—kicking up moon dust. Here they came. Headed straight for him.

The first plasma bolt came raining down from the dark sky like a streak of orange light burning a stripe from above. Tawny's salvo. It pounded the surface. The explosion down in the bowl was brilliant, a shower of searing debris bursting like a fountain into space, and the first moon vehicle was gone. After a moment, Ben could feel the impact blast strike him. At this distance it was tiny, but he could imagine the lives below being shaken to their core. "Nice one, hot shot," he said.

"Re-charging. Get moving."

Time to go. He went bounding down the decline in great, sweeping strides, the gravity here being a smidgen above weightless. Laser fire came his way from down in the bowl. They were shooting at him. He could see the shots approach, light streaks zipping toward him, whip-quick. He nose-dived into the ashy moon surface. The rock before him blew apart into chunks. "Tawny!"

"Firing!"

Another bolt came down from her asteroid hideout, just a speck among the specks. Another salvo from his wife. *KABOOM!* Another moon vehicle blew into trans-axels and big, bouncy tires. Ben peeked up. The other buggie spun around, bugged out.

Four guards out of comish.

Two more fleeing for the hills.

That's six.

Four left in the shed. Bad odds. But he'd faced worse. Much worse. "Nice job, honey."

"Just get moving."

"Roger that." He was up again making headway toward the vacuum hut. As he approached he kept his visor readout scanning the building's top, around its sides. No movement. Yet.

He reached the door already having unzipped his disable unit. The plug went in. A series of digital symbols flashed. His device read the pad lock's system language. Ben gave it a curious look. He didn't recognize the language.

The symbols stopped flashing.

A thunk. A click. The door scooted open.

He stepped back, gun up.

A hallway with lights.

Stairs at the end.

No one home.

He sprinted forward, checked the stairwell, went to the first landing. Still no one. He made it to the bottom level. There were no technicians. No workstations. No nothing. This wasn't a headquarters. Not even a control hut. This place was here for one reason. And that reason was behind door number one at the end of the hall. He was certain.

"Outside secure?" he asked.

"So far," Tawny responded. "Did you find her?"

"Think so." Ben went to the door, inspected his surroundings. Had to move quick. There was no lock pad. It was old school—good old bolt lock. He unsheathed a plasma cutter, lit it up with a tiny yellow plasma blade, jammed it into the doorjamb, started working it. The surrounding alloy pulsed red. Something gave and the door jiggled. Ben stepped back and kicked hard. The door swung open.

There she was standing in the corner, tall, chiseled, late teens, a powdery blue tint to her skin, dressed in the Orbinii casual attire she'd been kidnapped in. The look on her face was of a young woman ripped from a life of exotic pampering and thrown into the alien confines of her cell. Horrified. Shocked. Pissed off at everything. A seasoning of arrogant annoyance, as if she'd been wondering for the last several day cycles exactly who her captors thought they were, and now who the hells the bio-dressed Ben thought he was as he looked at her through a mirrored visor.

This was the second heiress and fifth in line to the Orbin throne.

Target acquired.

Ben zipped the mirror finish on his helmet away showing his face. "I'm here for you, your Highness. Get in the vacuum coffin. I'm getting you out of here."

She flashed a look to the capsule sitting on its grav cushion—an atmo transport tube. "I will not!" she barked. "I am Heiress Orona, and I will not get back in that thing!"

Ben looked behind. The passage was empty. "Your Highness, I'm rescuing you. Get in the capsule."

"I—" she stuttered, "I do not fit."

This was true, to a point. The Orbin were tallish, comparatively speaking, having grown on the nineteenth planet from Ae'ahm and being less affected by the sun's gravitation than their inner-solar kin. This one was six feet tall, plus. Nevertheless, there was no time.

"Curl up," Ben shouted. "I'm leaving with or without you."

She gave him an incensed look, which quickly turned to horror. Ben noted this. Some one was behind him. He drew his gun and spun around as something came down hard across his forearm. A lance with a curved blade at its end, like a scythe. His weapon dropped, slid across the floor and came to a rest by Orona's feet. She reacted only by screaming in an odd Orbinii dual tone.

Ben's attacker was bigger than him, and he lifted him off his feet by his scruff. He flashed a knife in his free hand. Ben reached down, engaged the creature's arm. The knife deflected. His attacker growled, reeling him back and throwing him across the cell. He smashed the wall, but was free. Back on the attack, Ben came in low, wrapped the guy up and took him down. The man-thing was too strong, though. Ben was thrown off him and sailed back across the cell, landing flat on his butt. He smashed Orona off balance.

She wheeled toward the vacuum coffin still screaming, caught a leg on the edge and went crashing inside.

For the first time, Ben observed his attacker. The thing was a hulking green-skin from Malybur, a no-necked lizard creature with nothing but muscle, dressed in vacuum armor with reticulating pauldrons that ran down both arms, a paneled breastplate and space helmet with a straight visor. The smooth crown showed an insignia, the mark of its affiliation—a red square with three dots placed in a non-linear fashion. Ben jerked back. He'd never seen this marking. This was something new.

The man-thing drew its scythe back, the tip of it glowing with some menacing combat technology. "Before I kill you, you will know my name. I am Ravekk, you Guilder wormdog, and I will end you," it snarled.

Ben's plasma pistol sat between his legs. Lucky lucky. He snatched it and fired in quick succession. His attacker blew back through the doorway flat on its back, unconscious.

There were footsteps in the corridor. The others were coming fast.

Ben sprang to the capsule and slapped the close button. The thing sealed in a flash turning Orona's screams into angry muffles. He wrenched the thing fully around, weightless on its grav cushion, and shoved it into the corridor, charging forward. Three men faced him, and they were armed. Ben roared, firing like mad. Tracer rounds lit the passage, throwing sparks in blinding showers. They all ducked, hitting the floor. Ben plowed them over with Orona's capsule, smashing one to the wall and shouldering past another. He hit the stairs jamming the capsule along banging it off walls and railing, jolting the heiress inside.

She was certain to find such treatment utterly intolerable, rescue or no.

On the upper level Ben slid the capsule through the exit way with one mighty heave and out into the vacuum. He came to the exterior lock pad, punched the button and slammed the door down, then shot it in a rain of sparks that died in the vacuum. Catching back up to the capsule, he slapped a mag tether on it harnessing it to his person. The wrist panel on his arm showed a full jump charge. "REX, you reading?"

"I got you, Cap. I'll guide you in."

"Here goes noth—"

Tawny's voice screamed in his helmet, "Benji, look out!"

Something landed only feet behind. He could feel the vibration through his boots. He spun around and everything froze, shoulders dropped in disbelief. He said, "Rogan..."

Rogan had him dead to rites, gun poised for a kill shot. With his free hand he tossed a small comm disc. It went thump against Ben's visor attaching itself and patching in an audio signal. "Hand over the goods, fly boy."

Ben said, "What?"

"Huh?"

"You called me *fly boy.*"

"What do you mean?"

"You said the words *fly boy.*"

"Yeah?"

"Then I said *what?*"

"Yeah, so!"

"That's the best you can do—*fly boy?*"

"Huh?"

"I said the best you can do is to call me—"

"Look—just hand over the goods."

"What goods?"

"Huh?"

"I said *what goods?*"

"What do you mean *what goods?*"

"You don't know what *goods* means?"

"Huh!"

"Look, I'm not handing over the goods, moron," Ben said at the end of his patience.

"I have a gun, Ben!"

"Yes, Rogan, that is a gun."

"I'll make it shoot you."

"No you won't."

"I won't? Wait—yes I will!"

"And get kicked out of the Guild for shooting on one of your own? Go ahead. They'll hunt you down, and you know it."

"With this kind of payoff," Rogan responded, "maybe I take that problem."

"You mean chance."

"Huh?"

"Nothing, dummy." Ben gazed up at Tawny's faraway perch. Tawny had been right earlier. She had Rogan lined up for a plasma kill from miles away. Rogan knew it. He wouldn't fire.

Ben grinned superiorly. "Hot shot, you tracking this buckethead?" There was no response. A stitch of concern crawled up his spine. His grin melted. "Tawny," he said sharply. Still no response. That only meant one thing. Tawny was in some trouble of her own. He looked back at Rogan, had to think of something to say, quick. "You pull that trigger, we both die."

"That's no guarantee. But if I don't pull this trigger, I lose out on nearly a million yield bits. That is a guarantee."

"No, you're wrong, Rogan. We both die. That's the truth." A lie.

Rogan's eyes glanced up toward Tawny's asteroid. It was somewhere up there in all that tumbling mess. He was being scoped right now. He knew it. Made him nervous.

Ben grinned at him. "You should really get a sniper. They're awesome."

Rogan hardened. "Doesn't change a thing."

"I just told you, we'll *both* die," Ben insisted.

"Maybe. Maybe not."

"Oh bi-lords, Rogan," he said, then adjusted his footing to face him square. "Then stop your squawking and get to it, see what happens."

He could see Rogan breathe under his bio-suit, shoulders rising, then falling. The gun adjusted in his grip. Ben tilted his head. Was he calling his bluff? Was he actually about to shoot him? Jeez—where was Tawny?

An explosion wrenched the hut door into shreds. The impact blast fanned out, knocked them both off their feet. Ben landed, looked up. His friends from the hut were back. And they were pissed. Tracer bolts stitched back and forth, he and Rogan both yelling into the comm device and firing away at the hut. Blasts pelted the surface all around Ben, throwing lunar pebbles everywhere.

He got to his feet, pounded the ignite button on his suit. The jump boost went *BOOM!* He rocketed straight up painfully, grunting against the sudden jolt. The mag tether yanked against his flight pulling the capsule up with him. He looked down. The firefight raged, but Rogan looked to be giving them Ae'ahm hell. Fine, forget Rogan.

He looked up, directly up, through the asteroid field and beyond. REX was up there somewhere in all that space. "REX, you got my signal?"

REX said, "Yeah, Cap. Locked on."

"Where's my wife?" He couldn't block the frantic note in his voice.

"Well, she's going to meet us at the secondary rendezvous."

"What's wrong?"

"There's trouble, Cap."

"Okay, fire everything up. I'm coming in hot. And I mean *hot!*"

TAWNY DIDN'T KNOW who they were or how many there were chasing her, nor did she know where they had come from, but she suddenly found herself on the run. One second she was operating solo. The next second, she was hauling narse. She only knew she was running out of places to go. Way out here on the edge of the corona tail, there were only tiny rocks, not much more than boulders, a few tons each, hardly large enough to land on or launch from. Leap frogging from one asteroid to another was getting difficult.

Plus—she wasn't the only one with a midrange weapon. They'd already proven that, blowing her footing out from underneath her not a second after she jumped. The blast propelled her out of control through space. Now, she crashed into a ten-ton—*"Ooph!"*—bear hugging it like mad.

"Rear imaging!" she called breathlessly. Her visor overlay rotated one-eighty. The asteroid field displayed at six o'clock. "Track movement!" Three red highlights popped up tracking her pursuers, each showing a few hundred meters distance.

Her bio-suit said, "Images are best-guess displays. Too much motion in the field, Tawny."

"Fine. Jump status?"

"Twelve percent. Eighty-seven seconds to full charge."

Eighty-seven seconds. She was being shot at. That was an eternity.

She crawled onto her knees feeling the asteroid try to spin under her motion. "Gun!"

The M-209 swiveled on its arm back to firing position. It wound up, an indicator showing a charge.

"Locate and target motion, quick!"

Three reticles populated, each struggling to lock onto their targets. "Oh, come on!"

"Incoming!"

She looked up, saw it, a light zipping through the rock field. She screamed, fired on impulse. Her beam pounded a rock not twenty meters from her position. A few tons of oar pulverized. The explosion swallowed the sky, blinded her. She flinched. A second explosion thrust her off her rock. Screaming, she floundered through the vacuum until she crashed into another boulder, hard. Felt like she'd broken her back. A siren wailed inside her helmet.

"Breach!"

She groaned, "Stable... ize."

Her suit emitted floxa-foam around the tear in her lower back sealing off any atmosphere leak. It would save her life, but restrict her capacity to jump.

She blinked, shook her head. What had happened? Best guess—she blew the rock into bits creating a screen for the incoming plasma bolt, which in turn, struck the screen and erupted. Lucky lucky. But...

Where was REX?

Where was Benji?

She was running out of time. Needed help.

Had to keep moving.

Ignore the pain.

Her jump status showed twenty-nine percent. It was enough to get her off this rock. She looked out at the field for a place to land, frantic.

"Enemy target approaching," her suit said.

She didn't bother looking back. It would take too many valuable seconds. She needed a landing site.

There! Straight below. Four hundred meters. A big one. At least big enough to land on. Through a sea of spinning stone. She could jump, let the frictionless environment do the rest. If she made it at all.

"Jumping!" she screamed.

"Up, baby, up!"

It was Benji's voice in her headset. She looked up. REX roared overhead, thrusters glowing hot. The ship was nearly a thousand tons of RX-111 cargo vessel, a forward cockpit, squared fuselage with heavy armor, and long mag-spires rotated to the up position like huge vertical fins. Auto cannons blasted away. Lasers stitched the sky casting a blinding light down on her. Explosions highlighted targeted hits, small boulders exploding... and a few enemy pursuers. He thundered by in a big, fat streak.

She jumped straight up leaving the asteroid belt below and moving headlong into open space.

BEN POUNDED the emergency thruster control reversing their flight. Too late. The entire ship sank into the asteroid field. He didn't care. He was saving his wife's life.

And in doing so, he was saving his own.

Rocks thudded hard against the hull—*boom bang boom pow!*

REX went, *"Ouch ouch oooh ouch!"*

"Sorry, REX!"

"I'm breached. Starboard mag-spire control hub."

"Okay, sealing now." Ben wheeled around, punched the proper commands in the overhead panel. "Yeah, that'll be a repair." He looked forward. "Do you see her?"

"Yep. She's floundering."

"Stay on her, REX. We're getting out of this mess."

Boosters jetted. REX ascended the rock field, spun about. "Yeah, I see her," Ben said. His wife was a dot, spin wheeling off the bow. It made his heart surge in his chest.

"I'm grabbing her," REX said. Tow cables fired from the underside fuselage. "Got her. Go meet her in the ..." REX noted he was suddenly talking to no one. Ben was already gone. "Nevermind," he said.

DOWN IN THE primary cargo bay, the airlock thudded open. Tawny was on her hands and knees. She'd already unharnessed her gun. It lay at her side.

"Tawny!" Ben cried barreling toward her. He hit his knees initiating her helmet release. It folded back. There she was looking at him with those fierce, Raylon warrior eyes, and that Raylon fire-hot red hair falling free. He threw his arms around her, kissed her face, kissed her eyelids, kissed her cheeks, kissed her lips. She did the same, started to laugh. There was no humor, just relief and gratitude.

He looked at her, nose-to-nose. "Are you okay?"

"I'm okay," she said.

"Are you hurt?"

"A little bruised but okay, babe."

He grabbed her face, hard. "Are. You. Okay?"

"I'm fine, I'm fine."

He took a big breath and let it out. Everything went lax.

Then he got to his feet and shouted, "Good, because I was *freaking out!*"

She laughed at him. Everything stilled. She got to her feet.

"What happened? What didn't we see?" he asked.

"They had sentries. REX spotted them. They were closing in."

Ben looked up. "Thank you, REX."

"You're welcome, Cap."

Tawny looked up. "You okay, REXY?"

"Yeah, Boss. It's just a few bruises."

"Sorry about that."

"It's cool."

Tawny looked at Ben. They shared a moment swimming in the cool-down. The action was done. Danger evaded. She said, "So, how's the cargo?"

He made a face, stepped aside, presented Heiress Orona's capsule still hovering on its grav cushion. She was inside angry-faced and wide-eyed, mouth moving a hundred miles an hour, soundlessly yelling commands and cursing ad hominems. Tawny nodded, tight-lipped and muttered, "Yep, she's a royal."

CHAPTER TWO

AT TWENTY LIGHT minutes from the Hominus IV asteroid field, the trip back to Orbin would take a few hours at two-max inner-warp. After their escapades, they were in no big hurry. Ben entered in the coordinates and speed calculations, compared them to the local, current traffic reports and set the course. REX reviewed it through his nav-circuitry and said, "Looks good."

"Okay," Ben said. "We're set and met and the systems are go. Burn, pal."

The inner-warps thrummed through the bulkheads. They could feel the gentle tug of acceleration against their artigrav support field as it adjusted, and they were off.

Ben lifted himself up from his snug pilot's seat and onto the elevated rear cockpit deck, then cleared the pilot's station into the central passage corridor of his craft. His feet clicked along the steel/alloy grating as he passed two passenger quarters to the left, two to the right. They were always empty.

At the end, a stairway led down into the main hold, the crew lobby. It wasn't a large area, but homey, comfortable, especially for a crew of two. Alcoves to the right and left offered privacy seating with rounded viewports, each with a cosmic view.

Ben stared at the port alcove. His wife had personalized the area with her private effects—incense candles, soft overhead glow light, small collection of wines on a shelf—all the essentials one needed for hours of reading. She liked a large assortment of literature, from the romance adventures of Molta-Danora to the military docu-dramas of Malybur to the mystery thrillers from the non-partisan planets. He smiled to himself. She was a playful woman, always chiding him, poking him where his personality had buttons to poke. And she was impulsive, very emotional, always looking for a laugh. Sometimes a fight. She could even be reckless. It's what attracted him to her initially. When he discovered her mind was also capable of the solitude required to absorb prose and narratives for hours on end washed in the peaceful, star-speckled vista of space, he fell in love with her. She was a multi-faceted woman. She was a dream for any stoic, half-lonely realist like himself, ready to be a part of something small and intimate, yet cosmically big. Like love.

His smile turned to a frown. He'd almost lost her today. It pulled emotions from him he wasn't used to showing, wasn't prepared to express. It scared him. Horrified him. He took a big breath and moved on.

At the far end of the lobby, an open utility lift lowered him down into the main cargo hold. He jammed open the gated door and stepped into the moderately-sized space, more narrow than wide with bulkhead ribs at the sides. To the aft was a ramp that led to a large vehicle hatch, there was an airlock chamber to the starboard, some hefty tie-down netting draped across the port wall, and a side-mounted, heavy-duty gantry crane that suspended their All-Terrestrial Vehicle overhead and above the center. The thing was mostly all frame and suspension, big heavy steel shock absorbers and fat rubber tires with a large flatbed on the back. Ben had made his share of alterations to it, not the least of which was a dual-barrel top cannon on a swivel.

He and Tawny rarely used the cargo hold for hauling goods. That was reserved for the twelve big storage units that sat outside the ship secured to the mag-spires—a pair of two-hundred foot long appendages—by a series of high-yield electromagnets. The big spires were tucked into their downward position giving the ship an extreme vertical configuration.

The place was empty, except for the heiress' capsule. It looked lonely sitting off to the side. Ben approached it cautiously, not sure what he'd find staring angrily back at him from inside. But no one was there. It was empty.

"Starboard One," Tawny said from behind. He turned, looked at her a bit blank. "She locked herself in while you were playing with REX. Insisted on being left alone."

Starboard One. Passenger quarters.

"You let her out?" Ben asked.

"Just didn't seem right." Tawny still had her bio-suit on, peeled down to her waist and dangling toward the floor.

"What is she doing?"

"Huffing and puffing like an Imperium princess would."

"Mmm. I'm surprised she doesn't want the company after what she's been through."

"Oh, she does," Tawny assured him. "Just not ours. Dirty pirates. Filthy spacers. You know, all that good, friendly, thanks-for-saving-my-life kind of stuff." She put a tool away in its chest with a thud, shut the door.

"Ah. So much the better, then."

She moved to him, put her arms around him. He

enfolded her. They stared at each other, she looking directly up at him, he looking directly down at her. "That's why we chose this life." They kissed.

Ben sighed, discerned.

She squinted. "What's on your mind?"

"I didn't choose this life to see you in that kind of danger. It scared me," he said.

"That's why I have you."

"I'm serious."

She rose up on her toes, kissed him again. "I'm serious, too." She pulled away, went toward the lift. "Come on, babe, time to check the list—get it over with."

THEY SAT at the center table in the crew's hold with an optics diagram projected over the surface. A numbered list with sub-bullets displayed. It wasn't an extensive list, but they had added to it over time. Now, there were ten items. These were their Space Rules.

Ben brought up a secondary window. It flickered a light blue, hovering in the air. He pulled it toward him reclining back in his seat, feet up on the table. "Okay, our contract papers for this job."

"Oh, boy," she said.

He read, "Use any and all resources at your personal and or Orbin disposal to search for, locate, retrieve and rescue Heiress Orona. Upon her safe delivery to the Orbin homefront your compensation will be as agreed upon and yadda yadda yadda." He looked over to his wife. "And that's it. Minus our payoff, we've completed the job. Now for the fun part."

He dismissed the window with a flick of his wrist,

leaned up and pulled their Space Rules over to him. "Rule one."

"You may have to translate," she murmured.

He looked at her ridiculously. "Sweetheart, these are our rules. We wrote them. We agreed upon them."

"They change all the time," she rebutted.

"They don't change. We just add to them from time to time."

"Just shut up and do it," she said.

He chuckled. "Okay, sweetie." He continued, "Rule one. No actions will be taken to directly affect any war effort in the carrying out of combative measures." He looked at her. "In other words, did we blow up, shoot at or otherwise destroy any military installations to fulfill this contract?"

She gave him an insulted look. "No."

"Okay, then we're good there. Rule two. Did our contract require us to..."

"Babe," she said. This was the part where she always got bored. He'd have to hurry things along.

"Okay. Rule two. Assassinations. No. Rule three. Espionage. No. Rule four. Arms deals. No. Rule five. The delivery of military technologies. No. Rule six." He paused, looked at her, said, "Oh boy."

"What is rule six? Is that the politician one?"

Ben said, "Yep." He read rule six, "We will not accept personnel as cargo as it relates to the military or political tactical transport of either side." He scooted the window over. "When we got this job from Sympto, we deemed the contract in alignment with our rules."

"Things changed," she said.

"And now?"

"We're definitely transporting a political figurehead," she said.

Ben flicked his lips with his finger—up down, up down. He did that when he concentrated. It was a Ben-ism. He looked up. "That's true, but what kind of sway could she possibly have in any political body? She's just a kid."

Tawny gave him a corrective grin, said, "Uh, no sweetie. That's a woman in there. Young, maybe. But definitely a woman."

"I didn't notice." He cleared his throat. "If she is a politician, that would be a breach of our rules."

"She's a royal. Does that make her a politician?"

"I don't know how they do things on Orbin. I'm sure she's got huge cultural clout. An Orbinii royal? A teenager?"

Tawny agreed, "She's probably a global celeb. Little Orbinii teeny-boppers probably watch her every move in packs and herds."

"Yeah, but that doesn't have anything to do with the war effort. How involved in Orbin strategy could she possibly be? They have whole war councils for that."

"Okay," Tawny said, "so let's assume she's *not* a politician."

"Then we're good," Ben declared.

"Unless," she said.

"What?"

"Maybe her kidnapping had some political significance to the Underworld cause. Maybe the Cabal had political intentions, and here we are—interfering with their cause. That would be a breach, wouldn't it?"

Ben leaned forward in the chair, put his elbows on the table, hands together, thinking. He gave her a severe look. "Is that how you feel? I mean, the Cabal are your people.

Would they consider kidnapping an Orbinii royal as a political maneuver?"

Tawny's face melted into a frown. This was where hers and his ideals clashed. She was Cabal. He was Imperium. They were supposed to be mortal enemies. Now they were soul mates. The Cabal would definitely consider kidnapping a Royal as a political maneuver. They were a hard grouping of interplanetaries, often ruthless. But did she herself? Was she that ruthless on the inside? She knew her husband would disagree; he would consider kidnapping a crime, period. She smiled, said, "No. This was kidnapping. War or no war, this was a crime. I believe that. And honestly, we don't even know if the Cabal was involved."

"Agreed. From now on, we should never consider it a direct breach of our rules to save a girl from a ransom, politician or otherwise."

"Absolutely," she said. "But then there's another problem."

"What?"

"Rule seven."

Ben pulled the window back over to him, read on, "Rule seven: There will be no contracts of a law enforcement nature, especially those pertaining to the adjudication of war crimes." His eyes went up to her. "You think this was a wartime law enforcement contract?"

She gave it a moment's thought staring off to the side, then said, "Nah."

Ben swished the window away. Rules eight, nine and ten all dealt with delivering certain supplies, wartime communications and the ethics of their services. They had nothing to do with saving an Orbinii heiress. He said, "Fair enough. So in short, this job neither benefited nor obstructed any war effort for either side—your Underworld Cabal…"

"Or your Imperium." She over enunciated the words playfully, "Per-fect neu-tral-i-ty." She walked passed him drawing a hand across his shoulders.

"Where you going?" he asked.

She went to the stairs leading up to the top quarters, the master suite, and said, "We're on our way to meet the Orbin Royal Council. I want to be presentable. I'm taking a shower." She stopped at the steps and turned her head to say seductively over her shoulder, "Come join me."

HOT WATER SEETHED across their skin, steam furling up from their feet. Ben lathered her down starting with the back of her neck, then her shoulders, down her arms, around front. Her body was immaculate. Fatless. Hard. Slender. Even her scars seemed oddly pinkish, as if they were uniquely joyful to be gracing her contours. And there were plenty of scars. She had one on her upper arm. A bayonet. Two low on her abdomen. Shrapnel. A few others. He thrilled over them. They were no different than his own. He had been an infantryman in the Golotha 501st, high altitude jumper squad. Landing behind enemy lines was a bitch, always worth a few scars.

But she had a few he didn't thrill over. The ones crisscrossing her back. He hated those scars, didn't like what they represented. Those scars made his stomach churn. It turned his thoughts to their current situation.

He breathed in the moist, hot steamy air and said, "We'll be at Orbin in an hour."

Her head tilted, her red hair pasting against her back. "Yeah?"

"How do you feel about that?"

Her tiny, hard shoulders shrugged. "I've seen stream pics. Looks like a beautiful planet. Pretty horizons. Everything's yellow."

"It's Orbin," he reminded her.

"I know what you're saying," she said. "I've been to planets in the Imperium before. A few Imperium moons. An Imperium colony or two. If you'll recall, I was even at an Imperium prison once."

He blinked, a bit stung. His eyes went down to those scars peeking out from under her soaking, matted hair. He said, "Don't remind me. Not exactly my shiniest moment with you."

She turned around, put her hands up on his chest. His hair turned black when it was wet. His eyes like blue ice. Their look was a serious one, as if she'd breached some uncomfortable topic. Her tiny grin soothed his nerves. "Don't kick yourself. You weren't even there. We didn't even know each other."

His eyes rolled. "Still..."

"Look, my husband," she said. "Just because we were technically on opposing sides of the war..."

"They were my people," he snapped, his self-loathing showing.

Her hands went to his face, guided his gaze down to hers. "It doesn't mean it was your fault. It happened. It's over. This is better."

He marveled at her. She was strength, beauty, darkness, brightness, all wrapped into one. She was the whole package. She had every reason to hate and loathe every Imperium soldier that ever lived. But she didn't. In fact here she was, showering with one, calling him husband. He capitulated to her, nodded, thought—*Ae'ahm, she's a strong one.*

She turned her back to him, pointed at her shoulders indicating more lathering. He started lathering. She said, "Look, me going to Orbin is no different than you going to planets in the Underworld. Remember Lexxum? How about Molta-Danora, remember that?"

He couldn't help but grin. Molta-Danora, a night planet, everything crystal clear, the air crisp, the lights stark, black water oceans, tepid breezes. They'd made love in the mountains of Molta-Danora, on the beaches, everywhere they could. Yeah, he remembered Molta-Danora. However ...

"Molta-Danora's not in the Underworld."

"Whatever," she said. "Look, as for my escapades in the war, what about you and the moons of Sarcon, hmm?" she said.

He'd taken combustion frags to both legs, even lost one from just above the knee. It got blown into meaty smithereens. But they grew it back, patted him on the butt, sent him back to the 501st. He said, "Mmm, yeah..."

She turned back around, faced him. "Where was it?" she said guiding her hand down his midriff, across the planes of his pelvis to his inner thigh. Found his scars. "Was it here?"

He smiled. "Yeah."

"Here too?" she said moving her hand higher, finding another scar.

He smiled bigger. "Yeah."

"Want me to kiss it?"

"Hurts sometimes."

She grinned like a devil looking up in his eyes and said, "I'll make it feel *all* better."

CHAPTER THREE

BEN TROTTED down the main corridor securing the top button on his nicest shirt, a beige workman's long sleeve. It complimented his dark spaceman's jeans. He came to Starboard One and slapped the button. The door slipped open. The heiress sat on the edge of the bed looking as comfortable as an Ae'ahm priestess in a Wi'ahr cathedral. He smiled, said, "Your Highness, I thought you'd want to know…"

"I am an Heiress," she demanded.

"Ah. Heiress. Well, we're approaching the Orbin system."

She snapped, "Well, tell me when we are there. I cannot wait to get off this bucket."

He nodded, still grinning. "Oh, me too. I'll let you know." He thumped the button and the door shut. Tawny met him on her way to the cockpit. "I'm thrilled to have that one on board," he said.

She gave him a weary look, and they entered the cockpit. Orbin was a yellow disc still a hundred thousand miles distant. Two Orbin state cruisers slid toward them bearing the prototypically over-designed look of an impractical people. They were large yet oddly sleek with blipping running lights and visible viewports.

"REX, how we looking?" Ben said swinging down into his flight chair.

"Looks like a greeting party. They're hailing."

His eyebrows went up, impressed. "Oh, well..."

Tawny brought up the hail and a three dimensional image of their caller holoformed over the comm pad. He had the blue-hued skin of an Orbinii with a head and features elongated a few percentile from the standard humanoid.

"This is Captain Dash of the private transport freighter REX. Hello," Ben stated.

The head looked around as if to take in the cockpit, looking both of them up and down. "I am Security Viceroy Orsic of the Orbin Royal Council. We have been informed of your approach. Do you have the heiress in tow?"

"We do. Preparing to deliver the package upon payout."

"Package," he said less than enthused.

"The heiress."

"I do not see her."

Ben looked over at his wife, then back. "She doesn't seem to want to come out of her compartment."

"Compartment?" Again, less than enthused.

"Quarters."

"Is she unharmed?"

"No worse for wear, I'd say."

"I assume that means she is well."

"Uh, yes, correct, sir."

"Hmm. Proceed to *Orbiter One*. Once there, you will be briefed. Afterwards, you will be escorted to the palace."

"The palace?"

"That is correct."

"We'd prefer to collect the payout and be on our..."

"You will be escorted to the palace."

Ben and Tawny shared a look. Ben said, "Perfect," less than enthused.

ORBITER 1 WAS AN ENORMOUS, multi-decked frame, housing an endless row of vessels—cargo transports, interstellar corvettes, personal vessels, private and public. The frothing planet of Orbin was directly below shedding a brilliant yellow light on all the station surfaces. Ben was assigned a slot and told to relinquish control of his ship. Hesitant, he did so. REX was guided slowly by tractor beam until he came to the designated spot, stopped and lifted into place. There was a thud and the systems wound down.

"REX, we good?" Ben said.

"Ask me this time tomorrow, Cap."

"Right." A long passage umbilicus extended forward telescoping until there was another bump. The inner air lock hissed down in the cargo bay and husband and wife gave each other a look. "Well, let's go greet the greeters."

"I don't know much about the Orbinii," Tawny mentioned as they moved down the passage.

"They're temperamental," Ben said. "Friendly, but stay on their good side."

"Yeah," she agreed.

He punched Starboard One's hatch release. Before the door was fully open, Heiress Orona came whisking gracefully from her room, prideful chin in the air, turned and headed away. They followed patiently. Once all three were in the lift, they stood in silence as it lowered toward the cargo bay. Orona seemed determined to ignore their presence, so it came to Ben as a shock when she murmured simply, "Thank you." The words seemed very much against her will, but he'd take what he could get.

"You're welcome," he said.

Viceroy Orsic stood front and center in the bay, an armed team of royal guards, all wearing military blacks, stood behind. His greeting to Orona was extremely formal. She walked to him and stopped. No touching. "Welcome home, my Heiress," he said.

"Yes," she replied.

He motioned to the guards to lead her back through the air lock, down the umbilicus. Next, Ben and Tawny stood before him, both looking up. He stood a characteristic seven feet tall, had long, narrow limbs to match his elongated head. "We of the Orbin Royal Council are indebted to you."

"Oh nonsense. The debt was already agreed upon. After we get paid, I'd say we're even," Ben said with a cargo runner's grin.

"Payment will arrive immediately by yield account deposit. Come with me."

Not wanting to, he said, "Okay."

They moved down the umbilicus and into the station thoroughfare. Long windows showed the awesome sight of hundreds of ships lined out as far as the eye could see. Ben eyed REX among them. The mag spires were angled down, the cargo haulers tucked between, making it the tallest ship out there, but as they moved away, he had a sinking feeling. That was his home. It was his wife's home. He didn't like leaving it under Orbinii care.

They followed their escort through the station busied by a handful of differing species, from the dwarfish, power-fully-built bipeds inhabiting the Dornan moon Tremus, to the slick-faced Stothosians with their vertical forehead ridges, to the cat-faced people from the jungle moon of Saltu. Orbin had a lot of visitors. Ben even turned and gawked at what he thought was one of the mythical non-gendered no-names-without-origin of some distant star, a tall, faceless being that didn't even have eyes.

Eventually, they entered a security sector and went to a private office. The room was large with a panel of Orbin magistrates and administrators behind a table. Ben and Tawny were instructed to stand before them. They did so, Tawny offering a good-natured wave, Ben saying, "Hi there."

Viceroy Orsic took his place standing next to the center Orbin, a stoic looking fellow whose face seemed incapable of a smile. The guy said, "I am Supreme Viceroy Olan, Administer of Internal Defense. You are here for our assessment. Mission details."

Tawny and Ben stood silently, waiting for something, not knowing what. Finally Ben said, "Oh, you want us to speak?"

Supreme Viceroy Olan nodded once, slowly. A yes.

"Oh, uh, well—the mission was pretty simple. In and out. There were complications. Nothing we couldn't handle." He looked at Tawny for affirmation. She nodded.

"Was there danger involved?" Supreme Viceroy Olan asked in his even, droning voice.

"Uh, yeah. Yes. I suppose so."

One of the other Orbin councilors said, "There will be no added compensation for your inconvenience."

They looked at each other. Ben said, "We didn't, uh, think there would be."

Supreme Viceroy Olan said, "And the heiress. Was she endangered at all?"

Ben said cautiously, "Depending on the answer, will it *cost* us any compensation?"

They all looked at each other. Viceroy Olan said, unamused, "No."

"Maybe a little," Ben said.

"Who were they?"

Ben said, "We're not too sure. One of them was named Ravekk. He was kind enough to introduce himself before trying to kill me."

Viceroy Olan said, "And he was not successful?"

Ben paused, surprised at the question. He looked down, scanning himself to check for life, and said, "Uh, no he was not."

"And did you kill him?"

"I can't be certain. I shot him with a plasma gun. He was wearing armor. And he seemed very happy to be wearing armor."

"We are curious to know who is responsible for this crime against the Orbin royal family."

"I assure you, we are too," Ben said.

Tawny offered, "We'd never seen them. They were new, someone we'd never encountered."

One of the Orbin snuffled at the sound of her voice, a notion of disgust.

"Could've been pirates or some for-hire clan," Ben said.

"What was their nature?"

Tawny and Ben exchanged a look. "Decently equipped."

"Very tactical."

Ben said, "I would prefer not coming across them again."

Supreme Viceroy Olan said as evenly as he'd said everything else, "I would prefer to eviscerate them into Molosian shark bait."

Ben's eyes widened, surprised at the remark. He said, "Wow. You don't seem... nothing."

"And they have no known association?"

"They had markings. We didn't recognize them," Ben said.

Tawny finished his thought, "A square. Three dots."

Another snuffle.

"Which means one of two things," Ben said.

"What would that be?"

"They were either very low-profile operators. Or very high."

One of the panel members assumed logically, "They targeted the heiress. Somebody from the Cabal. Somebody with political motive."

"Or..." Tawny said.

They all switched eyes to her.

She continued, "I wouldn't be too quick to assume they were on the other side."

All eyes went back to Ben. Olan said, "What does she mean?"

Ben looked at his wife feeling a tad guilty. He responded with, "She means they could have been one of your own, maybe an enemy within the Contingent. Do you have any? Enemies within the Contingent, I mean. Political enemies."

They all switched eyes murmuring amongst themselves. Supreme Viceroy Olan said, "None that would stoop to kidnapping. To whom might the female be referring?"

Ben sighed. "They were tall. Maybe... Orbinii. I don't know."

"That is absurd!" one of the panel members shouted.

Viceroy Olan turned his head to Ben, stared at him with seriousness.

Ben said, "We're cargo runners, sir. We're contract operators. The last thing we are is investigators."

Tawny said, "We're afraid you'll have to rely on your own intelligence for this one."

A round of snuffles cleared the entire panel. Disapproval.

Viceroy Olan pointed a slow finger at Tawny. It was long, menacing. "Is she Raylon?"

Ben closed his eyes. Their secret was out. It must have been her Raylon red hair, or her slightly rounded accent, or perhaps her gleefully bad attitude—all Raylon. He said, "Yes, she is."

"She is part of the Cabal! What is she doing here?" cried one of the panel members.

"Last I checked, she was retrieving your kidnapped heiress," Ben said logically, in her defense.

The council calmed. Everything settled, except the tension.

Viceroy Olan finally said, "She cannot enter the palace."

Ben clapped his hands together allowing for some brevity in the room. "Right. Understood. We think that's a great idea. Hey, thanks for everything, it was nice doing business with everyone. We'll just see ourselves back to our..."

"Hold!" Viceroy Olan called. He lifted a communicator to his mouth. Someone was speaking.

Ben leaned forward, couldn't make out the words. His gaze drifted over to Tawny. She mouthed the word, "Sorry." He shrugged back at her.

Olan lowered the comm device. "You will follow your escort."

"Where to?" Ben asked.

"You will follow your escort."

"Okay."

THE ESCORT TURNED out to be a pair of Orbin royal chaperons, each dressed identically in shoulder to floor gowns—very sliming for narrow, seven foot tall creatures—and visorless helms, topped with massive, fine-feathered crests. They strode like proud Molosian peacocks leading the way, until they reached a drop ship. Tawny and Ben lowered into the small main hold with their ever-present chaperons, where an Orbinii male sat awaiting them. He was dressed in contemporary sytle with dress clothes, a jacket and even a tie of sorts. The man said without shaking hands, without so much as changing his facial expression, "I am O'aba, King Oto's planetary emissary. I am here to escort you to the palace."

Tawny and Ben switched a look.

O'aba continued. "You are about to be in the presence of the supreme. Act accordingly and you will be treated as such. Because you were not invited ahead of time, your current dress will be sufficient for meeting the great King Oto, and afterwards you will be escorted to your palace suite where you will be provided more appropriate dress."

"King Oto?" Ben asked.

The man nodded his head.

"Okay."

Up front, a single pilot detached the drop ship from the orbiter and lowered them gently through the atmosphere. They felt the bounce and sway of a tumultuous sky before the view opened up to the Orbin world twenty thousand feet below. It was a magnificent world, shattered by mountain ranges and endless flatlands. They zipped over a mammoth ridge of peaks opening a view to an ocean sparkling with yellows and brass, and stretching toward the horizon. Orbin had an abundance of molecular aurum, the solar system's natural deposit of gold, causing its seething color of beauty.

They approached the palace compound and swiveled around. The building was a collection of tall skyscrapers, each rounded at varying heights built into a mountainside. Endless water falls cascaded between the structures adding a euphoric grace to the entire vista.

The drop ship landed and O'aba led them out onto a golden grassy tarmac with the escorts in tow. Two, single file rows of palace guards awaited them, bringing them to the steps of the palace, a broad stone stairway leading up to an open reception space. There, the king and his queen stood looking powerfully down at them. The king made a subtle nod and the palace guards quarter turned, a thunder of boots snapping to. He held out his hand and the chaperons began ascending the steps, leading Tawny and Ben up and up.

O'aba said, "You will bow upon introduction. You will speak only when spoken to. You will make only brief eye contact, and only during an exchange of words." He paused and turned to Tawny and said, "And you will stand only behind me."

They arrived at the top of the steps. The king was tall, handsome with his bluish tones, dressed in an oddly simplistic formal wear stitched with embroidery. The queen on the other hand, wore a layered gown and large collared headpiece. It was an impressive show.

O'aba said with his eyes to the floor, "Your royal highnesses, may I introduce Mr. and Mrs. Dash of the Guild." He gave a flourishing gesture to Tawny and Ben in introduction. They each bowed at the head looking as comfortable as a porcupine in a Molosian tar pit.

The king eyed his visitors. He moved to Ben standing before him and put both hands on his shoulders. "You have the thanks of a grateful world, a grateful people and a grateful king for the return of their heiress." He scanned his gaze to Tawny. "Both of you. Now, if you would, come."

They entered a massive cathedral-style lobby shimmering with oranges and yellows. The Orbinii did nothing small. They went to a chamber door where the king turned to address his guests, specifically Ben. "I would like to speak to you, alone."

He looked at Tawny, said, "Your gracious graciousness and royal king," he tripped over his own words. "I don't go anywhere without my wife. And I don't keep anything from her. Not one thing."

O'aba insisted, "No Raylon has ever set foot on the palace steps, nor entered these doors."

"She's an independent. Every planet has independents, even Orbin." He looked at the king and said, "And, she's my wife." He offered a tiny bow.

"Raylon is still under Cabal influence," O'aba said.

"She's not," Ben said. He could feel his wife basking in her own unwelcome. She was strangely comfortable, almost gloating.

"Let me ask," the king said. "Is she a defector?"

Ben frowned. "We don't get involved in interplanetary issues—politics and that kind of thing. She was free to leave her homeworld. So she left."

A voice boomed from the far end of the lobby, "Ha!"

They all looked over. An Orbin moved toward them powerfully. He was clearly military, dressed in ceremonial armor with a half cape flowing behind. "Free to leave. Fleeing for one's life hardly implies a freedom to leave."

The king took a big breath and said, "This is General Ona'Oona. I must warn you, you will not meet with any degree of candor where the Cabal is concerned."

Tawny stiffened.

The man stopped before them, his large, round eyes never leaving Tawny. "Anyone seeking freedom from Raylon does so with their life at stake. Or any Underworld planet for that matter."

Ben cleared his throat. "If that's true, then she's more an ally than most."

Ona'Oona offered the characteristic Orbin snuffle at that.

The king put his hand on Ben's shoulder and stepped to the side with him. "Forget politics, forget the war. You are of the Contingent. She is a member of the Underworld Cabal. These are facts. How is it possible that you two have come together as man and wife?" his question smacked of curiosity, not accusation or judgment.

"We make it possible," Ben said, frankly.

General Ona'Oona snarled, "We do not allow red-hairs of Raylon in the palace, much less the antechamber of kings." His gaze narrowed on Ben, his eyes becoming slits. "Your acquaintance with her makes you a suspect of the Orbin state."

Ben forced a grin and said, "Yeah, I completely get that. Look, we have no intentions of interfering with protocol. We thank the royal court and all, and this..." he let out a whistle, "is one heck of a house you got here, but maybe it's best if we just shoved off, what do you say?"

"No," the king snapped. He turned, paced, turned back. "What you did for my family creates the ties that bind." He took a breath and said, "I would be honored to have you—both of you—join the royal dinner this evening to celebrate the safe return of our junior matriarch."

"Your Royalty!" Ona'Oona said. "I advise against that. How will it look, a Raylon at the royal table."

The king said simply, "It will look like a Raylon at the royal table."

Ben laughed nervously, said, "Uh, your Royalty, I hope you don't take any offense if I decline your offer. It's very gracious, but there's no need to stir the pot."

"Stir the pot?"

"Oh, it's a saying. We say that on Golotha. Stir the pot—it means kick the hornet's nest."

"Kick the..."

"Hornet's nest. We don't want to make any inconvenience, is all."

The king nodded, considering his words. "Give me a moment with my advisor." He led Ona'Oona into the antechamber. Ben looked in as the doors were closing. The king was already conversing, pointing a finger and talking fast. He had a point to make, and Ona'Oona was listening grimly, nodding his head, frowning, arms crossed, and then he started to speak in return, but the door closed and Ben couldn't see what happened next.

"Huh..." he said.

"You pass up dinner with the royal court on Orbin for me?"

He turned around to see Tawny smirking up at him.

"I'm flattered, Mr. Dash," she said.

"Oh, stop it."

She walked around him in a circle, chiding. "No Orbin brown sauce on Orbin pork flank with Orbin pine relish?"

"Love, I said stop it," he warned.

"No Orbin fruit curd or Orbin sugar pastries?"

"Tawny!"

She giggled and said, "I love you more and more, Mr. Dash."

They stood in long silence, staring at the door to the king's chamber. Several seconds went by. Ben finally admitted, "Makes me fart."

She gave a hearty laugh.

The antechamber door shoved open and King Oto stepped back out. He strode to them and stopped. "No one has ever declined an invitation to sit at the royal table."

Ben gestured with his hands. "Like you said, sir. The ties that bind."

"Then there will be no offense. We accept your request to dine."

"Uh, but, wait a minute..."

"Your chaperons will show you to your palace suite. There, you will freshen up, and afterwards, you will join me in the palace hall for dinner. We dine at seven evening time." King Oto nodded and the royal entourage moved away down the hall before either of them could respond. Ben gave Tawny a *well-that's-that* look, and followed their escort, moving in the opposite direction.

THE PALACE SUITE turned out to be a palatial apartment unit with a recessed sleeping area, a bed designed to house the much longer Orbinii, a huge stone balcony overlooking a water fall from across a vast drop off with the golden ocean crashing against a mountain shore far below. It was beautiful, soiled only by their tenuous welcome.

Their chaperons had apparently decided not to guard the outside of their apartment, but rather stand guarding the inside. They stood to either side of the large door looking in. How awkward.

Ben went to his wife giving her a vague, apologetic stare, put his arms around her and pulled her toward him giving her a long, intimate kiss. Once her confusion slid away, she reciprocated. The kiss was a particularly loud one—lots of slurping and smacking that turned to moans and purrs. Lots of tongue, too. It was visible and shimmery. When they parted and looked over, the chaperons were gone.

She chuckled and said, "Tell me you're not just teasing me."

He gave her a notion to wait a second and hailed REX, pacing briskly back and forth across the stone floor. REX said, "What's up, Cap?"

"You tell me, REX. How are things?"

"Boring. I'm just sitting here."

Ben stopped pacing a moment. No news was probably good news. Then REX said, "Well, there is one thing."

He groaned, "What's that?"

"They've tethered me."

"Oh great," he said, pacing again. "What's it look like?"

"Mag straps. We're locked down. There's no leaving until they let us leave."

"Okay, well—see what you can do."

"Uhh—I just said, there's nothing I can do."

"There's always something, REX. I have faith. Out."

"Oh, well thanks a—"

He ended the transmission and shared a thin look with his wife, both sighing uncomfortably at the same time. Ben looked over at the entrance. The chaperons had not returned, obviously standing outside the door. He looked back at his wife. "I don't fully know what to expect out there, but I figured the less you say to them, the more they won't snort and snuffle. It would probably be best just to say nothing at all."

She looked at him, challenged. "Oh you do?"

"Don't you?"

She gave him a cross look.

"Truth?" he said.

She grimaced, said, "Truth."

"You fought against the Orbinii. You fought for the Underworlders. If they knew half of what you've done, well, the roof on this palace isn't high enough, know what I mean? Now you're about to sit down to dinner with their royal party?"

She huffed. "Babe, I'm not going to assassinate any royal Orbinii today."

"No, it's not that. I just—I know how you are. These people are politicians, Tawny. They're ideologues. They're going to talk. They're going to say things you won't like."

She put a hand on her hip. "And you think I'm going to pop off and go blah blah blah. Is that it?"

"Yeah, exactly. That's exactly it."

"And what gives you that idea?"

He laughed uproariously, defensively, and said, "Uhh— how about that time on Triggo Four when you beat up half the bar because someone said that thing about Pendulosi chicks looking like Molosian pugs."

"Oh please."

"And that time you went off ranting about the Cabal-god for twenty minutes in front of those lunar aristocrat kids."

"Hey," she said leading with a finger, "that kid was waaay out of line."

"Tawny, that kid was four years old. You traumatized them. And how about that time on Cedillas when you called that judge a narse-headed little—"

"Alright, okay!" she shouted. "I'll keep it buttoned."

"You promise?"

"I promise."

"Okay." They looked at each other, Ben appearing the slightest bit apologetic. He said, "Why do I feel like I'm about to punch a king?"

"I don't know, but you get very sexy when you're upset."

His eyes rolled, forcing patience. "I'm not upset."

"Yes you are."

"No—I'm not."

"Yes you are."

"No, sweetheart, I am not upset, *okay?*"

"See, right there! Very sexy," she said with that devil's grin of hers.

CHAPTER FOUR

THE ROYAL DINING hall was no less spectacular than the rest of the Orbin Royal Palace, an immense room with an oddly articulated table that crawled through the space at differing levels and right angles. A hundred dignitaries and their spouses occupied the space, all dressed in formal wear, all there to catch a glimpse of the honorary hero and his Raylon wife, maybe even share a word or two.

Viceroy Olan made an appearance with what Tawny and Ben assumed was his wife. She had the blue skin of the Orbin, and as it seemed standard, she bore a single tuft of hair grown from the very back of her skull falling down to her lower back. She was an extremely pretty female. But blue.

Feelings were mixed at the table and dialogs were shared by everyone in attendance, some gratuitous and heated but most in politeness, whether disparaging or otherwise.

As Ben looked around marveling at the sight, he wondered if he shouldn't have doubled the price given such pomp and circumstance. Still, a million yield bits was a beautiful take—not enough to make a man and his wife rich, but certainly enough to eat off of for an indefinite period. Speaking of that wife, he kept giving Tawny glances. They were subtle, but meaningful, as he continuously tried to read her. From time to time, he'd touch her leg or brush his knuckles across her forearm just to remind her of his presence, let her feel his support.

As for Tawny, every moment was a chance to smile, nod, mention a note of gratitude—or otherwise. She couldn't help but put her internal alarms on overdrive. She'd fought these people, gone into combat against the Orbin forces in a war that still raged hot throughout the solar twin system. She had to wonder if the words of thanks that flittered her way were of a noble genuflection, or shadowed grins from a hateful bunch.

And then the food came.

It was a feast like neither Tawny nor Ben had ever seen. They were showered with spiced meats, great dishes of shimmering flesh sliced and filleted and left steaming in an orgasmic aroma of delicacy, sweet indigenous vegetables, steaming pots of soup, varieties of side dishes from Orbin pastas and bean salads, to shell fish from a golden ocean, all served on the silent whisk of automated grav bots busying about. They ate like they hadn't eaten ... ever.

The dinner wound down after dessert was served, each member of the royal entourage choosing from sweet custards, moist pastries, dishes of Orbin ice cream or simpler delicacies—either candied bits or cookies.

And the whole time, General Ona'Oona rarely took his eyes from Tawny, as if he glared at her with a combined sense of distrust and bigotry, the monster of his paranoia constantly lurking behind his large, expressionless eyes.

The different factions of the entourage began

dismissing themselves, shuffling off into the reception area through a long sky bridge that would take them to the far side of the palace complex. Tawny and Ben looked at each other, their bellies utterly satisfied, both betraying the want to return to their vessel. Ben nodded to her. It was time to dismiss themselves, go home.

King Oto approached gracefully and powerfully. He seemed quite comfortable hovering above his royal party members without the constant shadow of his guards lurking at his sides. But as he approached Tawny the red-haired Raylon, and Ben, here they came—four sleek, handsomely garbed Orbin guardsman not allowing him to get too close to the Raylon guest without their constant presence at hand. Silent killers. Ever-present warriors.

Ben greeted him with a smile, getting to his feet and extending a hand. The king stopped before him, confused by the gesture. There were no handshakes on Orbin. It was an odd tradition. Ben recoiled with a grin and said, "Your Highness, we don't know how to..."

"Nonsense. Did you enjoy the meal?"

Ben nodded and said, "I've had meals before. This wasn't a meal. This was something else."

The king gave him a bewildered tilt of the head.

"I mean—it was a compliment. The meal, yes, it was fantastic." He exchanged a glance with his wife. She shrugged.

"Excellent. Come with me. We have something to discuss." The king looked over at General Ona'Oona who stared back from across the broad table. Ona'Oona headed for the door as did the king with his guards in tow.

Ben groaned, wondering if they were about to discover the true reason they were invited to stay, something unexpected, a ruse. He looked at Tawny.

She said, "What now?"

"I guess we follow them."

THEY STEPPED out of the dining hall, moved in silence down a wide, tall passage and up a broad stairway, and, eventually, into a long meeting chamber. The far wall had an expansive window revealing an ocean vista at night that took their breath away. A sea of calm, undulating water below, a sea of twittering night sky above. Big, bold mountains broke the shore line up to the west.

The doors closed behind. They both turned. The guards were at the door, four silvery lances in hand, the king standing before them, Ona'Oona lurking to the side, those eyes always cast at them.

The king moved to the window and stared out at the ocean. There was a deep love in his gaze. A threatened calm. He said, "Orbin is a great and wonderful world. Do you know our history?"

Ben said, "Only what I was taught. I grew up on the Golothan lunar front. Orbin was always so far away."

The king looked at Tawny as if to present her the same question. She cleared her throat, said, "The Orbinii can fight like Wi'ahr hellions. That's all I know."

The king made a one sided grin, as if her remark came as a compliment. He said, "We used to be a planet of nation states. Separate. Warlike. It is not like that anymore. Do you know why?"

Ben said, "No."

The king inhaled as if beginning a great tale. "The war has united us. There was conflict. There always had been. When the Solar Twin Wars began we were hesitant to take sides. Did not want to fight. Had enough of that amongst ourselves. But then the war came to us. The Cabal was first."

"The Underworlders are a hideous lot." Ona'Oona's voice hailed from the flanks. They each looked over, Tawny preparing for the worst. But the general continued, unhindered. "Reprobates. Blood thirsty, raging ideologues. They have no faith except in a god system that would have them burn entire peoples, destroy and ravage. Slavers and usurpers, all. I do not care which planet they hail from—Solaptra, Omicron Prime itself or any other, when the Underworlders are gone and we have erased their ways, we will be free of tyranny. The Wi'ahr. Damnable evil."

Ben reached for Tawny's hand, took it, calmed whatever storm might be raging inside her.

King Oto cleared his throat, a long, veiny trunk, and said, "I will not restrict the general's speech. We are free to express ourselves as we will, as are you, and I believe the truth will only unite. Nevertheless, the Underworlders believe in peace through might. We do not. So we resisted. We did not stand a chance. Their entire planetary cabal was pitched against our one planet. We suffered a choice—not as divided nations, not as a separated people, but as one. One single voice. Join the Cabal in their fight for bi-solar domination, or join the other side—become the eleventh planet of the Contingent and recruit their help. So, that is what we did. We joined the Imperium. The Cabal failed here, but it cost us. For twenty years our lands and our cities and our people burned in the flames of war. That united us, brought us together. A common enemy, a common cause. Cultures were redefined. Societies joined together. Religious codes were rewritten, and all the ideals of before turned away from hate and bigotry. We rebuilt, together. That was three hundred Orbin years ago."

"And since, we have fought," Ona'Oona grumbled. "One planet is ravaged and the war moves to the next while the other rebuilds, but the ravaging goes on."

"Sometimes it comes back. Whole societies raised to fight. Whole generations bent on killing. Entire planets lost," the king said.

"There is no better example than Denubis."

Ben exchanged looks with his wife, each looking daunted. The planet Denubis was the sight of hot contention, each side vying for its abundant ore resources. They both knew what had happened there, and history would tell two tales, one from either side of the conflict. Yet Ona'Oona continued with his own version, "I was there. I saw it happen. I sat on the planes of the moon Heptis and watched. Have you ever seen a planet set loose from its axial seat? It rips itself apart. Seeing something so rich die under the machines of war will touch inside you a toll of terror you thought did not exist. It will reach inside you a deeper place than you thought possible. And the Underworlders called it a victory." His glimmering eyes went to Tawny and he spat, "Disgusting."

Moving the conversation forward quickly, King Oto said, "Fortunately, Orbin is on the outskirts. We are placed abreast of the conflict. But now we know better than to turn our eyes away from it. It will come back, Benjar Dash. We fight now to keep it abroad."

Ona'Oona spoke as if to no one in particular, casting his gaze out on the dark night of his world, "How many generations have been lost? How many more must there be?"

King Oto glided toward them, came closer than he had before. "We need your help. One small part in a greater plan, and we will take a mighty step toward securing our planet."

Ben cocked his head, looked at him interested.

"The enemy launched a frontal maneuver against Golotha—primary world of the Contingent. Our capitol. Your homeworld. They failed."

The General's chest rose, his chin lifting to the sky as he said, "They couldn't breach the Golothan defense systems. We pounded them back, column after column. Defensive bombardment was too heavy. Our net caught them, forced them to retreat back to the oblivion from whence they came. The comm streams were glorious."

"But," the king said grimly. "It was a ruse. The frontal assault on our prime world never had a chance. It was a diversion for their true plan."

Ben listened closely.

The king said, "While our interplanetary resources were occupied, they moved a smaller force against the outskirts. Now, it is the moon rim of Stathos that is under contention. Stathos is our neighbor. A mere two light minutes away. She hangs in our sky to the east. If their moon rim falls to the Underworld Cabal, Stathos will fall. If Stathos falls, we will be next, Benjar Dash, and the war will have come back to our shores, our skies."

General Ona'Oona said, "The Cabal has already taken Menuit-B, the smallest of their three moons. They have secured it. Reconnaissance has delivered intelligence. There is an Underworld construction effort. Resources are being shuttled under heavy guard from the Underworld planets Iot and Zet." Ona'Oona went on, "The moon is small and remote, which makes it tactically unimportant. But it also makes it easy to weaponize."

The king put a hand on Ben's shoulder, locked eyes with him. "They are turning Menuit-B into a long range interplanetary pounder. A cannon platform."

Ben couldn't help the edge of horror that creased his face. The king was describing a deathblow that the Cabal was preparing to deal. Those old wartime feelings scurrying underneath years of repression tried to resurface. It made him frown.

Ona'Oona said, "From there, they will be able to launch planet killers at Stathos, and if they get under our own planetary defenses, even at us. It will be Denubis all over again," Ona'Oona growled, his voice rimmed with the sadness of memory. "Only this time, unlike Denubis, Stathos has civilization. Billions will die at the hands of those Omicron slum rats."

Ben glanced impulsively to Tawny, reading her. She showed nothing—no emotion at all. But he knew his wife. Her values, her system of belief, her very childhood was being bombarded with insult. This was usually the point in the conversation when she started flipping over tables, taking pot shots, putting people in hospitals. He wanted to hold her, wrap her up in his arms and protect her. But he couldn't. They'd see it. They'd know their allegiance was toward each other, not the war. So he blinked, looked away.

King Oto sighed heavily. "It is a playing piece in the game of war. If they are successful, they will split our front in two. Our planets will fall, and with them our peoples. Stathos will be first. Orbin next. Then others."

Getting down to business, the king continued, "But there is a counter-plan, a mission. We must think surgically. An all out assault would only bring their armadas. As such, we have developed a plan. It is intricate, very secretive. We will deliver a payload to Menuit-B. The Cabal subcontracts with privateers regularly. We have the proper downloads, suppliers handles, access codes—everything. The chosen pilot will get through their security measures, deliver the goods to the construction effort. The cargo itself will look harmless. Packaged alloy gel for heavy construction. But with an added, little ingredient."

Ona'Oona said with a grin, "Our military science teams have worked tirelessly to perfect it, and it will be foolproof." He put his chin back up and proudly declared, "Senex-1B-1. Mol bots. Military grade. Undetectable by surface scans. Designed to destroy. They will invade their systems, eat them from the inside out. Destroy their moon weapon."

Ben looked at the king and said, "Sabotage."

King Oto said, "Arrangements can be made conveniently, but the more time that passes, the more secure the moon site becomes. Time will soon be of the essence. This is a contract job, Benjar Dash. It is what you do."

Ben's eyes bugged in shock. He melted into nervous laughter, put his hands up in a show of neutrality. "Guys— your Highness—I wasn't exactly prepared to discuss further contracts."

The Orbin looked at each other, then back to Ben. The king said, "The General and I have discussed it. Given your talents, and given your..." he looked at Tawny, "... partnership with a Raylon female, it makes you quite possibly the perfect contractor for this job. They would not suspect your intentions. I consider your presence here to be a matter of great fortune." He looked sternly back at Ona'Oona and said, "Despite the general's candor."

Ben swallowed hard, almost painfully, and said, "The Guild wouldn't like it, us taking outside jobs. It breaks disclosure acts and privacy clauses and sensitive information agreements and the whole deal."

"I am the Orbin king. The Guild is an underground, black-market haven for piracy and bounty hunting. Corruption and crime is rampant. I can bypass the Guild. This would be a two-party contract. We cannot risk a middle-man. It would be strictly between you and me, the Orbin king."

Ben flicked his lip, concentrating, and moved to the great window. He looked out, pondering the situation at every angle, diving into the character of the room, the temperament of all involved.

What to do?

What to do?

General Ona'Oona blurted, "Come on with it! The time to decide all things is upon us. You are Contingent. With whom does your loyalty lie—with us, or a hoard of power mongering murderers bereft of value, blinded by evil, determined to stamp out all that is good in our solar system?" And on reflex and impulse, he motioned toward Tawny with the flick of a wrist.

Her face went tight, anger seethed. She flushed an angry red, something the blue-skinned Orbin could not read. Her fury simmered to the top like an Omicron volcano, ready to explode. She opened her mouth to rebut and Ben blurted, "We'll do it!" Her mouth closed. She looked to her husband with bolts of fire and swords and explosive plasma balls seething from her eyes. He nodded with great certainty, and said to King Oto, "Get the contract."

"Excellent!" Ona'Oona said.

"Wonderful," the king agreed.

Ben looked at the general. "We'll need approach vectors. Authorization codes. Equipment and info inspec-tion data. Every piece of information on that station that you can feed into my onboard intelligence processors. That includes the Underworld contract protocols for freelance operations, access codes, everything. We will *not* go into this job blind, understood?"

Ona'Oona's face broke into a severe, convicted grin, and he said, "I will have my data team begin downloads right away."

Ben looked at the king. "We'll return to our vessel and begin preparations, immediately. When I return in one hour we discuss payout."

The king nodded.

"And your Highness," Ben said, "This had better make us rich."

"You will be very pleased, I assure you."

"I don't want to be pleased. I want to be rich."

The king nodded with understanding. Rich it was.

Ben looked at his wife with hard, unmoving eyes, shocked at her cutthroat stare, and said, "Let's go."

THE ROYAL ESCORT took Tawny and Ben back to the shuttle tarmac where they loaded up and boosted skyward like a flash. Within minutes they bounced through the atmosphere and watched *Orbiter 1* approach, the whole time Tawny fighting to contain herself. She reeled with the searing, hot resignation of fury, and yet there was also the gut-dropping hurt of betrayal. Her husband had turned against her. Everything they stood for, the years of trust and mutual bonding they'd built up, he'd just slapped in the face. For this very day was why they'd developed their Space Rules; to preserve each other's ideals, to bond them closer together through their differences.

And now this.

And now this?

She looked at him with hate in her eyes. *Oh—you just*

wait until I get you alone. Wait until we're back on board our ship. You betray me like this and expect no consequence? I'm a soldier, a warrior of the Cabal. And you have fanned an old, cold flame back into life. You just wait, mister.

The pod connected to a multi-port airlock. There was a thump and the door opened. They stepped into a small white compartment. The royal guard nodded to them wordlessly and hit the button. The hatch swung shut and went thump. They were alone.

Tawny spun to him letting loose an open-handed slap —*pow*—right across the cheek. It surprised her as much as it did him. He looked at her, rubbing his face with the back of his hand. The opposite door opened into the passage umbilicus. He said, "Oh, don't be so dramatic," and stepped out, headed toward REX's air lock, double-timing it.

"Benjar," she snarled pacing quickly behind. "What the hells are you doing? This is a clear breach in our agreement —transporting weapons grade technology, taking combative measures, even espionage. You're stepping over half our list!"

On the move, he waggled a finger at her, half-angry for the smakaroo to the face. "I knew you knew our list better than you were leading on."

"And what about you accepting a contract to haul military weapons!"

Still pacing rapidly, he said, "Oh for the love of— we ain't hauling nothing but narse, baby. We're getting the hells out of here."

"Wait—what do you mean?"

Still walking fast. "Look, I had to agree to the contract back there. If we'd turned the job down we never would have made it past the palace gates, not with this information. Were you listening to them? Did you hear them talk?

Especially that general. Do you think they would have just let us go? Oh no—we'd be sitting in some cushy palace cell right now waiting to get our happy little mindwipes. No thank you, baby."

"You lied to the king?" she asked.

"You're damn right I did," he said thundering into the ship. Her mouth dropped. She was wrong. He'd been bluffing. Of course! Benji would never betray her like that. How could she even think that? She felt suddenly and immediately guilty. Indescribably guilty. And kind of horny, too. My god, she'd slapped him. She'd never even conceived of such a thing, slapping her husband. And all he was trying to do was protect her. Now she was going to have to make it up to him. Yeah, she would have to get seriously funky on him.

Seriously.

Funky.

But not yet. Right now, they were getting the hells out of orbit, preparing to haul some serious narse.

"REX, what do you got, baby?" Ben called moving through the crew's hold.

"Do I smell more trouble?"

"Lots and lots, buddy. Give us good news." Sprinting down the passageway.

"Well, there's no breaking their mag tether. But they're mag locked to our cargo haulers."

"We can detach them." Swinging down into his pilot's seat.

"Well, yeah, but... we'll lose them. We kind of need them."

"I don't care. We'll get more. Plot a course to..." he looked at Tawny, thinking, and said, "to Omicron Prime." He started flipping switches, firing up systems.

"That's the heart of the Cabal," REX said.

"They'll never follow us." Now flipping switches overhead. "No time to prime up. It's going to be a cold burn at top speed, buddy. Can you handle it?"

"I'll try to stay in one piece."

He looked at Tawny. "Strap in."

REX said, "Oh. We're leaving *now?*"

"Yes. On my mark." Grabbing the cargo release lever above.

"Oh boy. This is going to give me a headache, isn't it?"

"And... detaching cargo units!" He slammed the lever forward.

Outside the ship, the mag-spires cut power to their electromagnetic generators and separated. The cargo units inside their clutches began tumbling free of their hold. The tether holding REX at bay slackened, no longer controlling the ship.

"I hope you got that plot laid out, REX," Ben called.

"Uh. Umm."

"Uh umm? What do you mean uh umm?"

"Yes. Okay. Punch it!"

"Hang on!" Thrusters boomed. Systems pounded into life. They lurched forward, squeezing through the narrow orbiter frame. But parked ships approached.

"Down down!" Tawny screamed.

Ben redirected on the fly. They dropped straight toward big, yellow Orbin. He corrected and looped away, back toward open space, everything shifting around them.

"There's a hail," Tawny called.

"Yeah, I bet."

The *Orbiter 1* commander holoformed into view looking critical. "This is *Orbiter One.* You do not have clearance to..."

"Shut it off."

Tanwy did so. The head holodissolved.

An emergency klaxon wailed.

"They're targeting us," REX screamed.

"They won't shoot. They wouldn't dare."

Laser bolts from *Orbiter 1* crisscrossed overhead making Tawny and Ben gasp. "Yep—I'm wrong, I'm wrong," Ben admitted through gritted teeth. "We need inner-warp, REX."

"In a minute."

"Look!" Tawny screamed pointing directly forward.

Two ships. Destroyer cruisers. Big ones. Four thousand feet long. Probably more. Headed their way.

"C'mon, REX!"

"You said cold burn. No time to prime. This is a cold burn. No time to prime."

"Then give me whatever top speed you can."

"Okay. Okay. You got it."

Ben punched it forward gaining speed. The cruisers grew and grew. A collision course.

"They're going to trap us in," Tawny cried.

"Oh, no they're not," Ben said flipping a series of overhead toggles.

Outside the ship, the long mag-spires began shifting apart from one another, each one on its respective turnstile, until they flattened out becoming long, narrow wings, two hundred feet to the port, two hundred feet to the starboard.

"Hold on!"

"What're you doing?" Tawny asked.

"Spinning the monkey, sweetheart."

Ben initiated a boosted spin maneuver. The vista of space began swirling all around them, turning REX into four hundred feet of rapidly spinning iron, like a demented spiral blade approaching fast, ready to mulch anything in its way.

The cruisers reacted, each initiating evasive maneuvers and angling away from each other. REX shot between them, very fast, whirling at a blinding speed, enough power to pulverize asteroid mass.

"We're clear! Stabilizing," Ben called. The ship leveled back out, balanced itself.

"Inner-warp ready, Cap."

"We're outta here!"

The inner-warp engines grew into a blue hot glow and they were a dot in the distance—*BOOM*—gone.

EVERYONE LET OUT A UNIVERSAL SIGH, even REX. Ben melted back into his seat, shook his head, relieved. That could have been a lot worse. They had surprise on their side. It was the only reason they weren't stopped, captured, or destroyed. He had to act fast. It worked. They were free and clear.

But now he had a wife to contend with. He might have been better off staying with the Orbinii. "Look," he said, "I know you're angry. I'm truly sorry. I didn't have time to discuss the—"

He never finished his sentence, never even got to complete his thought.

She tackled him right there in the cockpit, right there in his captain's chair, started sucking on his neck, chewing on his lips, ripping clothes off. There was nothing he could do. She was too fast, too powerful ... too hungry.

REX muttered, "Oh boy..." and shielded his eyes experiencing a computerized version of awkwardness.

CHAPTER FIVE

———————

"DO you want the good news, the bad news, or the interesting news?" REX asked.

Ben moved through the main hold putting a shirt on. After Tawny basically ripped all the buttons off his best shirt, he traded it for his favorite—a flowing, Golothan red, long sleeve pullover with a loose v-neck and rolled-up cuffs, tucked in at the waistline. Ahh, he was home again. "Give it to me in that order."

"Well, the Orbin home front is long gone, and there aren't any signs we're being tracked or followed."

"Looks like our getaway was clean."

"Yeah."

"How long until we reach Omicron Prime?" Ben asked.

"Eighteen hours, approximately."

He checked his watch, said, "We're making good time. So, what's the bad news?"

"Our cargo haulers are gone."

"All of them?"

"Yeah, Cap. Every last one." REX said this with a hint of obviousness, as if to prod him.

Ben figured they hadn't had any other choice. It was a minor inconvenience compared to sitting it out in an Orbin jail cell. He just shrugged. "We can always get more haulers from Norg. So, what's the interesting?"

"Get this. We received a number of downloads before we left. This is some interesting stuff, technical readouts on what looks like a Cabal military project. This has got to be classified information, Cap."

Ben froze, his pacing coming to a dead stop. He looked up as if to reference the life form of his ship, whatever that might be, and said, "Menuit-B?"

"Yeah, how'd you know?"

"Heh—that is interesting." He punched an inner-ship comm link, said, "Tawny, you out of the shower?"

"Yeah, what's up?"

"We need to talk about something."

"Let me dress. Be right down."

THEY SAT at the holotable observing the hovering diagram of the data download from General Ona'Oona's lab. Long windows displayed scrolling data in streams. The central image was a rotating, three-dimensional schematic. The moon was accounted for in shimmering lines. The cannon had a thousand subterranean parts, not to mention ventilation towers and defensive batteries all over the place. A central blast generator showed as well. The thing was going to be miles big.

Ben whistled, said with whispered awe, "Look at all this data. This thing's massive. They're going to kill a lot of people with this thing."

Tawny gave him a sad look. He was talking about the

Stathosians. Maybe even the Orbinii. They were Imperium. They were Ben's people. She said, "Benji?"

He snapped angrily, "It's none of our business. We're not soldiers anymore. We're through fighting."

Tawny sank down, just said, "Okay."

Ben calmed. He spun the diagram three hundred sixty degrees, eyeballing it. "If there's one thing I can say about the Cabal, they're an organized bunch."

She eyed him, not sure how to breach the next subject. She said, "This data could be worth a lot of yield."

He thought for a second, said, "Only if we sold it. Technical information on Menuit-B? No one's going to want to touch this information. They'd be crazy to come within a warp minute of it." He squinted, tilted his head. "Unless we sold it to the Contingent. They'd purchase it."

Tawny said, "They already have it."

"No. Orbin has it. They're only one small part of the Contingent. There are other parties. They're not all friendly with each other either, trust me. Take Cedillas. They don't necessarily get along with Orbin. They'd jump at buying this information."

"And what if they used it to blow up a bunch of Cabal freight haulers on their way to Menuit-B, or destroyed their resource facilities? Those are *my* people, Benji."

He inhaled, nodded. "You're right. Rule three. Espionage. I'm getting ahead of myself. Okay, no selling to the Contingent. They'd only use it to their military advantage."

"But we could sell it to the Cabal. They'd want to know it's secure."

Ben snorted laughter. "Oh yeah, we show up on the Omicron Prime war consulate front stoop and go, *Hey fellas, look what we got. It's nothing, just top-secret data on your little moon baby. You know that big planet killer you're building over there on Menuit-B? Yeah, we got all the data we need to blow that sucker up.*" He gave her a discerning look and said, "Not smart."

She rebutted, "Orbin, then."

He gave her a sudden, interested look. "What?"

"We sell it back to Orbin. They know we have it. They don't want us to have it. So, we sell it back. It's got to be worth something."

He pondered it for a few seconds and settled on, "Mmm, they'd consider that blackmail. The Orbinii hate our guts as of about an hour ago, remember? They're probably launching bounties on our heads through every channel from here to the Xylon system as we speak."

"Then what does it matter? Let's at least make the offer."

"It wouldn't stop the bounty. We'd still be criminals of the state. They'd still hunt us." He stood up, walked over to the viewport, stared out into space, then turned around suddenly, a finger in the air. "But I have a better idea. A good faith exchange. We send it back to them. Say we're sorry. This belongs to you. Not interested. Yadda yadda yadda. And by the way, how's Heiress Orona? Hope she's well. Have a nice life. Leave us alone. That kind of thing."

"You think that would stop the bounty?"

He groaned and flapped his hands on his thighs. "I don't know. Probably not. There's no way to tell."

"So would we rather look over our shoulder the rest of our lives because we *don't* know if we should be looking over our shoulder—or—would we rather look over our shoulder for the rest of our lives because we *do* know we should be looking over our shoulder?"

Ben sat heavily back down. "Either way, we'll still be looking over our shoulder."

"Exactly," she said.

"Then we do what we've always done. Nothing. We disappear. It's the surest thing."

She grinned, said, "Then we should probably stay away from Omicron Prime."

"You mean that big, blue planet that we're currently speeding toward?"

"Yeah, that one."

"The one with the rings?"

"Uh-huh, yeah."

"Right. Good idea. REX, full stop. Course correction, buddy."

CHAPTER SIX

Outer Commerce Routes
The Planet Speculus
Non-partisan space region

REX ZIPPED out of inner-warp and into standard drive like a blink from nowhere. And there they were.

The planet Speculus sat below perfectly black, like a slice of space hidden from view, save the starless, round field that it produced. It was an airless planet without atmosphere or moon—just a sphere of obsidian four thousand miles in diameter. Those in the region called it the mirror planet for its invisible qualities. They espoused that if you stared at it from superorbit, you would see only yourself in its void. The place would speak to you. And then it would know you. It would whisper tellings of your own death. Most thought it ridiculous. The more superstitious regarded it wearily.

Other than that, the planet had no indigenous life. But

it was surrounded by the coming and going of thousands of craft, all of them crisscrossing its featureless face in lines of commerce giving this region of space a shimmering frenzy of motion.

"We've arrived," REX said dolefully. "The Guild."

"Relax, partner," Ben said spying the nav screens, looking for an opening in the traffic at superorbit. It was sporadic at best. There. He spotted one.

REX continued, "Why is it every time we come to this place we arrive peacefully, yet every time we leave it's at top speed?"

"We got friends here, REX."

"Oh, yeah—friends. Is that what you call them?"

"Hey, at least there's no Cabal."

"Or Imperium, for that matter," Tawny said stepping into the cockpit.

Ben acknowledged her with an agreeable look. She was back in her usual attire—blue Raylon combat vest, low cut, tight-fitting undergarment, utility suspenders studded with ammo, belt and holster over flesh colored tights and buckled knee-high boots. Fiery hair back in a ponytail. She stepped forward and put her hands on Ben's shoulders, both looking through the viewport. He glanced up at her to see that burning, wild stare. She was a warrior and a half, with blood that always ran a few degrees hotter than most. He didn't know if it was her Raylon blood, her seasoning as a battlefield killer or a need to constantly be back in the saddle. He figured it was all three. Nevertheless, she stared forward at *Station Oficium* willing to get it on. He shook his head privately. Twinkling lights bit stark against the pure black backdrop.

"Lowering into superorbit." Ben initiated the

commands and the vessel slipped gently into the highest orbiting line of vessels. "Okay, REX—"

"I know, Cap, already spotted it."

"Going to auto. Bring us in, buddy."

"Yeah, yeah. Hub one-oh-four, dock twelve, upper platform. Do they even know we're coming?"

He looked up at his artificial intelligence with a sly smirk. "Of course not."

"Was afraid of that."

"Come on, where's your sense of—"

"I don't have one, thank you."

"Right." He looked at Tawny. "What about you, sweetheart?"

"Oh, you know I do," she said.

"Heh. Okay, let's go." They got up and headed for the upper airlock.

REX meandered slowly through the curving line of traffic toward *Station Oficium*, a massively long space station primarily consisting of a docking strip segmented by large social hubs, each of varying levels. Ships from every make in the solar twin system were attached, their occupants engaged in the gaming, dining or transacting that went on at *Station Oficium*. Most of it was corrupt to one degree or another, either under the table or straight up illegal. As REX veered free from their traffic and headed for hub one-oh-four, Tawny and Ben knew what to expect. This place was one of the system's deposits for villains and assorted scum. Not even the warring factions of the Ae'ahm and Wi'ahr patrolled here. This place was far from the war, yet action was around every corner.

They slipped in under the endless frame and came to a gentle stop. REX pivoted himself around and lifted toward a crane arm. There was a thump when connection was made, a second thump as the extending umbilical reached out. A hiss as atmospheres matched.

REX called up to the top airlock over the comm and said, "Good luck, you two nutjobs."

"Oh, stop scowling," Tawny said as the door rolled away.

As REX noted their absence and the airlock sealed back, the cargo security cranes down in the main bay crossed—REX crossing his arms, pouting.

THEY EMERGED into the upper main thoroughfare of hub one-oh-four to a mass of foot traffic. Every group in the system was represented from mining outliers of the Nubus IV moon system to station spellsayers constantly hawking for the next weenie-minded sucker to con, from freighter crews searching out their favorite cantinas to refugees escaping colonial establishments ravaged by the war. Personnel auto-carriers navigated the traffic beeping and honking while slave droids hustled along with their masters' belongings.

Tawny and Ben had to pause to allow a group of Golothan women to stroll by, each wearing some semblance of green or red denoting their cultural sway and clutching shopping boxes on handles. Moving in the opposite direction were a trio of *Station Oficium* blue collars, all male, with their large, ribbed protective body covers folded back into collapsed packs on their shoulders, each eyeing the Golothan women and smirking devilishly.

Tawny and Ben themselves were independent contractors arriving on the station to secure another contract. They expected to run into one of their own at any moment. The meeting could mean camaraderie and drinks, or quite the opposite—fist-a-cuffs and brawling. They were ready for anything. They always were.

A kiosk set into a station alcove welcomed them as they approached.

"Welcome to *Station Oficium,* you two. Are you checking in?"

"Yeah," Ben said. "Slot twelve."

"An RX cargo unit?" There was a pause. "Is that Mr. and Mrs. Dash?"

"Yeah, Oh-One, it's Mr. and Mrs. Dash."

"How you two been?"

"Busy."

"Here for some down time?"

Ben gave Tawny an impatient look, said, "Actually, we need minor repairs."

"Oh dear. What's the issue?"

"Breach in the starboard control hub," Ben said.

"Okay, hold. Ah, here we go. We have two options. There's Fexx Pol's vessel and equipment repair at hub one-two-nine or station service at the main promenade."

"We'll take Fexx Pol."

"Are you sure? Station service offers impeccable customer satisfaction while Fexx Pol's customer rating is lower than satisfactory."

Ben chuckled. He knew the truth. *Station Oficium* ran the customer report streams. Of course they rated themselves highly whereas they shorted the privateer shops. But Tawny and Ben knew Fexx. He was a gregarious sort, very Pendulosi, hardworking and honest—with only the slightest penchant for undercutting his clientele—and they'd done him favors in the past. They'd get better work out of him for a smaller price. Ben said with assurance, "We'll take Fexx. What's the schedule?"

"We'll have your vessel escorted to one-two-nine within the hour. REX, right? Leave him on auto and we'll see you there after repairs."

"Thanks, Oh-One."

"Of course. Anything else?"

Repairs on REX aside, they were actually here to see their Guild contact, Sympto, and they were never too sure if he was friend or foe. Now they had reason to believe he was the later. They had questions for him, and they wanted answers. He said to Tawny, "Should we let him know we're coming?"

She said, "You know what I think."

He gave her a pressing look.

She said, "I don't like him."

"Tawny..."

"I don't trust him."

"He's our contract liaison."

"I don't care. He's given us too many jobs that went wrong."

"They didn't go wrong, per say," Ben said.

"The Janus affair?"

"That wasn't Sympto's fault."

"Aligon?"

"That didn't go as planned, but it doesn't mean it went wrong."

"And now," she said, "with Rogan showing up on one of *our* jobs?"

Ben capitulated to her. Sympto had given them plenty of reason to be skeptical. He said, "Okay, you win. Let's surprise him, get the truth." He looked back at the kiosk and said, "Nope. That'll be all."

"Okay. Enjoy your stay here at *Station Oficium*."

They moved away from the kiosk, blending into the crowd.

"What do you think he'll say about Rogan?" Tawny asked.

"I think he'll lie," Ben said. "But I think we'll see it."

"What if we don't?"

"Then he's probably not lying."

"And you think Sympto would ever tell the truth?"

Ben shrugged weaving through oncoming traffic. "Well, he's not afraid of me, but he probably has nightmares about you. If we press the right buttons, we'll get the truth out of him. So just be ready."

"Oh, I'm ready," she said. Ben started to chuckle, but stopped abruptly. Tawny flinched, curious. "Babe?"

Ben spun around. The crowd was thick, but there was one that stuck out like a sore thumb. An Orbin male. He was several paces behind moving toward them. He stood above the others, easily a seven-footer. They made eye contact. The Orbin stutter stepped, but it was subtle, controlled. Ben nodded. He knew it. They were being followed. He could feel the eyes on him.

The Orbin approached as if carrying on with his own business and strolled uneventfully on by, carrying on down the walkway. They followed him with their eyes. He was dressed in civilian clothes, but they were tight to the skin, and he carried a holster and pistol, utility vest, boots. This was no tourist. This was an Orbin pistoleer.

Tawny and Ben looked at each other, concerned, exchanging an entire conversation silently. The bottom line: They'd have to stay low-key, operate in the shadows.

THEY APPROACHED the entry point to hub one-oh-four.

Over the archway in plasma-neon letters were the words: GUILDER'S MIX.

This was *Station Oficium's* entertainment hub, a real red-light district for drinkers and gamblers. This was where the station's mongrels came to find downtime. That usually meant corruption, violence and heathenry. Security personnel were sparse. Its supervision was unofficial. Hired thugs kept the peace, but more than not, they also stirred the chaos. And overseeing it all were the invisible eyes of the Guild, a solar twin system-wide fraternity of pirates, smugglers, independents and goons. The Guild's presence was no secret here, but no one talked about it. *Station Oficium* rented the hub to them, collected their fees and turned a blind eye. Beyond that, it was Guild business.

The place was a massive labyrinth of gaming floors, cantinas and private spaces for VIPs, all overlooking the large social courtyard below. It was business-ready solar time or lunar, always with the mirror planet below ever-present, as if waiting for its fortune to be whispered over the frenzy of a thousand haranguing voices.

Along the large periphery were entrances into the establishment. Tawny and Ben made their way to an entrance-way. To the right a group of ruffians were being escorted out gruffly by large goon types. To the left, some opportunistic prostitutes watched, waiting for their chance to take advantage of a few frustrated egos. One of the females had the smooth blue skin of an Orbinii and stood a head taller than the others. She caught Ben's eye. He watched her closely. She winked at him with the oversized, golden eye of an Orbinii beauty queen. Very lusty. He ignored and punched in a request for Sympto, Guild admin and contract allocator, into the kiosk. His request came back. Non-data.

"Figures," he said. "Looks like we'll have to ask."

They stepped into the establishment and were immediately greeted with the whiff of multi-worldly scents and exotic wines. Some strangely non-syncopated music from the Pendulosi ring colonies played. Runner lights zipped and blinked across the architecture giving the place a kinetic atmosphere. Revelers stood around gaming tables clapping their hands, slapping each other on the back, sloshing their ales about. A thousand different sounds swirled together in a confusing mix. Alien cigarillos left a thin haze in the air. Drinks glowed.

Toward the center was a service bar in-the-round. A dozen tenders hustled about pouring drinks. Service bots supported them. People congregated.

Tawny smiled up at Ben. She was first, plunging into the bar goers. She was particularly small, good at slipping through crowds. Ben followed with less luck. Eyes diverted angrily toward him as he bumped and plodded through —*sorry, excuse me, my bad...*

He met her at the bar. Immediately next to them was a figure dressed in some sort of vacuum suit. It was difficult to immediately discern the man's species under his helmet and full visor. But whatever he was, he drank from a closed growler mug that breathed steam—a boiling hot drink, maybe a sulfuric-based liquid—through a helm tube. Ben had never seen one of these people before. He acknowledged his presence. The guy returned the gesture with a slow, stoic nod, then turned back to his drink.

The tender approached. She had the dual vertical forehead ridges of a Stathosian female. "Watcha want?" she said.

"We're here to talk to Sympto," Ben said with a serious edge in his voice. Everyone knew Sympto. This was where he operated. It was as much his home as anywhere else.

The tender grinned chomping on bubble gum and leaned onto the bar with an elbow. "Who's asking?"

"Old friends," Ben said with a sideways grin.

"Yeah, right. I don't know where Sympto is."

"Hey—" Tawny started.

Ben interrupted, "We're not here to kill him. We just have some questions."

She gave him an untrusting look.

"He'll be happy to see us," Ben said, easing her doubt. He looked up toward the top of the bar a hundred feet above, where the VIP windows overlooked the space below. "Which one is he in?"

"Wait here," she said and left before they could rebut.

They looked at each other a bit deflated. "There goes our surprise," Tawny said.

"Maybe," Ben agreed before noticing the helmeted character at the bar was gone. He'd disappeared back into the crowd. He wondered if Tawny had also noticed. Ben tended to be the one that picked up on ambient details. Maybe he was just paranoid.

"Benjar Dash!" came a voice that sounded like it had come from a gullet twice the depth of the average humanoid. Tub'Num approached, following the female tender. He was one of the dwarfish Tremusians hailing from the life-giving moon Tremus. Caught between the dueling gravity wells of two planets constantly shifting the moon's orbit back and forth between them, the planetoid had been crushed into an oval, just as its people had been crushed into squarish creatures. Tub'Num was no exception, save the fact he was particularly large and wide, even for a Tremusian. At five feet tall he weighed a small ton, too —thick and dense and stronger than a Molosian mule. Ben was glad to be friendly with him.

"What's up, Tubs?"

They shook hands, Ben wincing in pain. Tubs turned, gave Tawny a hug. She winced also, squeezing the Tremusian incredibly hard, her affection hardly being felt at all.

"You know them?" the tender asked.

"Yeah, they friends," Tub'Num said dismissing her politely. She went back to her position. "How was heiress job, make fat?" He rubbed thumb and fingers the size of beer bottles together indicating money. Cash.

Ben avoided the topic, patted himself on the belly. "Not hardly, Tubs."

"Ha!" the Tremusian barked. "Not what I hear."

"You weren't supposed to hear anything."

"You know Sympto. Boy is secretive as busted comm buoy."

"Speaking of which, he's why we're here."

"That what I hear, too." He rubbed his broad chin with an equally broad hand. "So why you not notify ahead of time?" Tub'Num was chief security for Guilder's Mix. That included the contractor admins. That, in turn, included Sympto. It was a question he was obligated to ask.

Tawny leaned forward cutting into the conversation. "Thought we'd surprise him, Tubs. He likes surprises."

He squinted an eye at her, smelling the lie, and then laughed at the remark.

"Just friendly business," Ben said.

Tawny added, "If we were here to kill him, he'd be dead already." That was the truth. But it made Tub'Num grin at her. He appreciated her sense of humor. They weren't here to kill the man. If they were, they wouldn't have come to Guilder's Mix.

"Well, if he do something to piss you off, I guess he need good tongue lashing. Follow to me."

. . .

TUBS LED them away from the bar and toward a lift tube at the end of the courtyard. It took them up to the top level and whisked open into a balcony area with holotables and sports broadcasts on stream consoles from the interplanetary media system. It was darker up here, quieter. The people here were high-profile privateers, either top dog contraband smugglers who'd gained favor with the Guild's top management, or owners of large yield contractor groups. Whatever their professions were, these were the high rollers and big ballers. This was the hub's upper echelon.

As if in punctuation to the room's status, a secondary lift sat in the corner that only went up to the uppermost room. No one went up there without formal invitation from the Guild leadership. No one. Not ever. Most people even wondered if there was a room up there at all, or if it was a ruse to create some mythical presence over everyone in the hub.

Tub'Num took them past a pair of Triggan poker tables to a stairway at the back and up to the VIP rooms, down a rear, plushy carpeted hallway and to a smoked glass door. The music and commotion of the lower social deck was all but muted up here. He swiped his security badge and the door opened into a dim room where a courtesan greeted them wearing long, sweeping robes leaving her rock solid midriff bare. She noticed Tub'Num with familiarity, then gave the two guests an up/down once-over. Tawny and Ben were clearly not VIP material, yet the courtesan made an intrigued little grin at Ben—tall, lean, very handsome. Tawny rolled her eyes. "Welcome," she said, "to the Opulence room."

"Leequa, one of the VIPs got guests," Tubs grumbled.

Leequa waved them in with a graceful notion and they entered. The far wall was an observation deck overseeing the entire establishment. A private bar was off to the left, lights glowing dim and blue with bubble tubes gurgling softly. The music was tamer here, and lower, creating a gentler, more seductive atmosphere. In the room's center was a trio of lunar belly dancers shimmying and undulating, each curve a well-chiseled display. To the barely lit back of the room there was a lounge area. A couch with a dozen figures relaxed, sipping on yellow and blue glowing drinks, a few of them making out with hired pros, others chuckling amongst themselves.

There he was. Sympto. He sat in the shadowy corner with a hookah pipe plugged into his mouth, its long glowy tube curling into a central fluid jar. Smoke curled up from his head as he exhaled, grinning.

Ben nudged a chin toward him. Tawny noticed, eyes going into slits. She started off with a head full of steam, but Ben halted her. "Sweetheart, let me do this. You hang back by the bar."

She gave him a severe look. "You said I should—"

"Just be my backup. If I need you to beat him up or break his legs or whatever, I'll let you know." He gave her one of his wily grins and said, "Trust me on this."

She pouted, "Alright, husband," she said nonplussed. "I'll follow your lead, but don't give me half a chance. I'll clear every buckethead in this room with a smile on my face."

"I know you will," he said. She meant every word. He'd seen her do it before. She moved off toward the bar.

Ben cleared his throat and made his approach.

Sympto sat on the couch with his legs crossed at the knees, one hand propped up on the armrest with a lazy grin on his gaunt face, his eyes half open as he watched the dancers. He was an interplanetary mutt from the sister planets Iot and Zet—an Iotian father, a Ziotian mother. Or vice versa. No one really knew. But he had the broad facial features of one with the scrawny, bulb-jointed frame of the other. His ears protruded from the sides of his head like donkey ears, drooped into a lax position. It gave him a strangely unique look, kind of like a Molosian muskrat. Ben's shadow fell over him. At first, he didn't even notice, then he looked up. Surprise crossed his face. It was congenial, happy to see him, not panicked as Ben had expected.

With a broad smile showing gapped teeth, he said, "Well, well, Benjar—alive you are!"

Ben opened his mouth, but Tawny's voice beat him to the punch. "No thanks to you, hookah nuts!" she yelled out from the bar. Ben closed his eyes forcing patience. That was not the kind of thing one would want to yell across the Opulence room at Guilder's Mix.

Sympto looked over showing sheer and sudden fear. "Why she is here, Benjar?"

Ben muttered to himself, "I don't know," then louder, "Because she's my wife, Sympto."

"What she means by this?"

Tawny strutted across the room hips swinging, with one hand resting on her blaster. Even Tub'Num seemed nervous watching her move. She stopped at the couch and said, "We bumped into Rogan."

"What means this?"

"We were on the job."

Sympto shot a panicked gaze at Ben, then back, said, "You save the heiress, yes?"

"That's beside the point," she snarled. "He was on the job, too."

"Who?"

She scoffed meanly, leaned down and yelled, "Rogan, you double-crosser!"

Ben reached for her arm, placed his hand there gently.

Sympto shrugged, innocently. "What you do mean this?"

Ben said, calmer, "He was on the job too, Sympto. The *same* job as us."

Tawny said, "One job, one contractor. That's the rules."

"Send him for the heiress, I did not," Sympto said.

"Then who did?" Ben said.

"How I should know? The contract came from the Orbin royal family, it did. It must have gone out to every black marketer and contract operator this side of Haptus. Control this I cannot."

Ben eyed him, reading. "You didn't send Rogan after the heiress job?"

Sympto said, "No, I give to you."

"What job did you give Rogan?"

"See Rogan I have not."

"You haven't even seen him?"

"No."

"In how long?"

Sympto shrugged, said, "A Speculus cycle."

Speculus didn't have cycles. It meant a long time.

Ben inhaled and took a step back. His mind raced. Rogan had been at Hominus IV. He'd had Ben dead to rites. Someone had sent him. But who?

Ben eyed Sympto closely, looking for the lie. There was none. He was telling the truth. The Guild hadn't sent Rogan. But that answered exactly zero questions. He shared a glance with Tawny. Her thoughts were the same. Sympto hadn't double-crossed them. Tawny looked downtrodden.

She wanted to pick a fight. She wouldn't get the chance today. The mystery would remain a mystery... for now.

Ben said to his wife, "Wait for me."

She threw her hands up and moved back to the bar. It was time for a drink anyway.

Ben sat down across from Sympto. "So I guess you heard."

"Heard what about?" Sympto said.

"The heiress."

Sympto gave him a grin that was halfway between sneaky and proud, and said, "Oh yes, I heard I did. Rich you two are, yes?"

"You got your twenty percent."

"Yes, but..."

"We're just saving up for retirement, Sympto." He admitted, "It was a good take." He leaned forward, said, "Thanks for the job."

Sympto laughed at him. "Retirement suit you does not. I know better of you. Everyone know it now—hero save princess. All over the interplanetary comms it is." He gave him a curious look. "But no names?"

Ben reached into a bowl of nuts and threw a handful into his mouth. "That was the agreement, my friend. No names."

"Oh yes?"

"That's right. We made a deal with the Orbinii. We wanted pure anonymity."

"Don't want hero status, eh?"

"You know how it is. Our line of work? Please. We'd prefer not to have any status at all."

Sympto settled back starting to relax now that Tawny was across the room ordering at the bar. "Fair enough it is," he said. "And what is next for you, then?"

"We were hoping you could tell us."

Sympto's eyebrows went up, shocked. "Already for next contract? No time off for you, then."

Ben gave him a ridiculous look. "And do what?"

"I have idea or two."

"Yeah, I'm sure you do."

Sympto leaned forward. "Take no more contracts, at least for a while."

Ben rolled his eyes, grabbed another handful of nuts. "That's what we do, Sympto."

"Have baby!" he blurted.

Ben's eyes bugged. He nearly choked. "Ha!"

Tawny looked over, curious, saw nothing was amiss and went back to her drink.

"No have baby?" Sympto said.

"I appreciate the sentiment, Sympto, but we're here on business. What do you have?"

Sympto inhaled big, said, "Okay, I try I did. I have something. Very simple, it is. Easy pay off. I save especial for you."

Ben looked at him from the side of his face, wearily. "Should I be worried?"

Sympto exploded with laughter—"No, *hahaha!*"—making Ben cringe at him. It wasn't *that* funny.

"So what is it?"

Sympto settled. "Aqua run."

"Simple," Ben said. "You mean boring."

"That is what you said you want, no?"

"Boring's perfect," Ben said.

Sympto gave him a knowing grin. "If excitement you want, you should have baby."

"That's what I hear. We'll stick to aqua running. What's the payout on this one?"

Sympto pulled his palm admin device from an inside jacket pocket and thumbed it. It beeped and burbled showing the details of the contract. "Four-five-zero-zero," he said.

"Forty five thousand," Ben repeated.

Sympto said, "And my take at fifteen percent."

"What are our expenses?"

"The price of water."

"How much water?"

"One hundred thousand gallons by Imperium measures. For reimbursement, of course is."

"Speaking of Imperium measures, we're going to need new ident loads."

"Why?" Sympto said irritated.

"Like you said, we're all over the interplanetary comms. One little leak on our current ident loads and we're sunk."

Sympto groaned, "Okay, I have my team make another for you. Cost it will."

"How much?"

"Fifteen."

"Fifteen!" Ben blared.

"It is important tool," Sympto argued. "Not easy for fabrication it requires. Must counterfeit the data. Takes talent. I have your man, but expensive is he. Must have current ident loads."

Ben gave him a cross look. He was right, though. He settled back thinking about price. Forty-five minus Sympto's percentage, minus cost of water, minus fuel, minus cost of new ident cards. He muttered, "Doesn't leave much."

"No threat. No danger. No pay. But you stay very busy, you will, my friend."

"Heh—we stay alive."

"Yes, but boring."

"We'll settle." He leaned forward. "We like breathing, see?"

"So very married you are," Sympto said and brought the hookah up to his thick, wet lips. Pinching the hose between his teeth and smiling big, he said, "So so married."

Ben sat back, thinking. The job was small time. A low payer. But very easy. And after the heiress job, they didn't want to jump into any potential action. It sounded perfect. "We'll take it. What's the delivery detail, more cloud miners?"

"No..." Sympto said blowing a mushroom cloud of smoke out into the room. "Lunar outpost this time, yes. Mortus moon. They solid miner facility they are. No water. Need water."

"Mortus, huh? The place is a wasteland. There's nothing there but methane."

Sympto shook a finger at him, said, "Nickel ore too, yes."

"Yeah, but who mines nickel?"

Sympto shrugged, still clearing his lungs of his last hookah hit. "Not know. Not ask. Not care."

"Mmm—wise philosophy, Sympto. Okay, let's look at that contract."

CHAPTER SEVEN

HUB one-two-nine where REX had been auto-escorted for repairs was several hubs away through the main thorough-fare of *Station Oficium*. It was a long stroll, perhaps a mile through the gently curving station. Tawny and Ben opted against taking the whisper train, which ran along an exterior railway below the footpath. They figured the stroll would be nicer, and REX wouldn't be flight ready for several more hours. Besides, the view through the universal window wall to the right was hauntingly breathtaking—a black on black backdrop of Speculus sitting in an ocean of stars. They were right. The stroll was better. It was unhurried, relaxing, just the two of them wandering lazily along amidst the occasional crowd of scurrying station goers.

They entered one-two-nine and took a lift down to the sub level where Fexx Pol's Vessel Maintenance garage was. The viewport down here showed an enormous bay cluttered with meticulously placed craft, all hanging from station cranes with vacuum crews hustling parts back and forth, all of them grinding, cutting or attaching parts and pieces to the vessels with vacuum torches and laser rivet guns. Some even cranked away with good old wrench devices.

REX was easy to spot, his enormous mag-spires were in the downward position like legs stretching toward the black planet far below. A crew had already removed one of the starboard bulkhead plates showing his internal guts to the passers by. Progress was being made nicely, but anytime a ship experienced a breach necessitating exterior replacement parts, timelines tended to stretch. They were probably going to have to manufacture the right part in the machine shop. This could take a day. Maybe longer.

Fexx's operation office was through a set of greasy slide doors and through the large waiting lobby. At the far end was a reception window where a bored looking engineer sat with his feet up on the counter picking his dirty nails with a tool, the intricate bald pattern on his head betrayed his specie—he was Pendulosi. Fexx preferred hiring Pendulosi. He was one himself. Not the best tempered people, but a hardworking lot. Ben approached getting the guy's attention. He hardly reacted, just said, "What ship?"

Ben said, "The REX cargo vessel."

The guy didn't even look up. "It ain't done."

"We were hoping to catch Fexx. He around?"

The guy shrugged a shoulder, kept digging on his nails. "Somewhere."

"Mind checking on him? We're old friends."

"Everybody's a friend. Wait." As if inconvenienced, he chomped a bite from a half-eaten sandwich and punched a comm button. "Fexx."

"Yeah?"

"Got a guest. Two guests. One's Raylon."

Ben and Tawny switched eyes.

"Is that Tawny and Ben?"

The engineer scrunched his face, said, "I don't know, Boss. They're just two people."

"Yeah, yeah, be right up. And get your feet off my flubbin' counter, ya scum-wagger!"

The guy grumbled and dropped his big boots down to the floor. "So I guess he'll be right..."

"Benjar Dash!" came a voice from the nearby door as it swished open. Fexx approached with a vacuum suit peeled down to his waist, its arms dragging the floor.

"What do you know, Fexx?" They shook hands the Pendulosi way, yanking each other's shoulders nearly out of their sockets at the forearms. Ben found it menially painful.

Fexx turned to Tawny and opened his arms. "Well, well —the beast has a beauty." They hugged, despite Fexx's greased-up, sweaty appearance. The Pendulosi weren't ones for politeness, nor the eccentricities of civility. To them, dirt, sweat and grime were badges of hard-earned honor to be shared daily. Tawny disagreed, yet her interspecies respect for protocol was rock solid, especially where useful friends were concerned. So, with a tight face, she hugged him back. She'd much rather be drinking with him. Pendulosi were great drinking buddies.

"It's been a long time," he said, "though I'm sure REX would disagree."

"Yeah, we'll hear all about it."

"I knew I'd be seeing you two humanoid dogs before too long. Soon as I got a busted up RX-one-one-one in my shop I thought, yep—that's Tawny and Ben's handy work all right. What'd you two do to the old boy, bounce him off a few space rocks?"

Ben sighed, "Something like that. What's the damage?"

"Couple of impact shields need replaced. Internal diagnostic seems fine. Bulkheads held up. Tough ship. Pretty standard fare around here."

"What's the real damage?" Ben asked.

Fexx laughed. "Twenty thousand yield ought to do it. Get you out of here and back into trouble in half a day."

"Perfect," Ben said. "Can we board?"

"Yeah, go ahead. Just stick to internals, leave externals alone. You know the drill."

"Of course. Thanks, Fexx."

BEN SAT in REX's lower bubble turret watching the workers buzz along his ship's undercarriage. The starboard mag-spire control hub, a tiny space accessible only through REX's engineering crawl holes, was open to space, but the crew was closing it up with a piece of new shielding. They were a well-oiled machine. His old buddy was in good hands.

He sighed, half bored, and looked down. The entire bay was open to space and there below his feet, as sinister as the stories he'd always heard about Wi'ahr, was Speculus. The planet was impossible to see as it blended perfectly with the vacuum, just a see of black so crisp, so pure, it boggled the senses, redefining that blend of all colors until it became like staring into absolute nothingness. It took Ben's mind, made it go toward those stories of Wi'ahr. He'd grown up with them, wives' tales and childhood myths about an ancient people and an ancient god inhabiting those faraway dots of light, eternally shifting around that far faraway sun—those faceless, nameless people always staring back through the eternal distances with greedy, envious eyes. It made Ben the boy always wonder why they had to share such space with those people, those believers in Wi'ahr. Somewhere inside him, he always knew those tiny planets and that one distant sun were never so far away as he was led to believe. He knew that one day he would discover they were much closer, in fact, and on that day the war he'd always heard heroic and harrowing stories about would come to him. And he was right, for one day the peoples of Wi'ahr—praying to that wrong god and rumbling through neighboring space behind their war machine—came to his home. His childhood nightmares had come true. The Golothan moons Golot Prime and Golot Qued burned. He could see the twinkling in his night sky, watch the battles play out, see the lunar churners churn and hear the screaming in his ears. Those myths of his childhood were no longer myths.

The true myth was his childhood itself. Gone. Wasted.

From that day forward, he'd marched. To where, he did not know. But he marched. And marched. And then he was a man, scarred, beaten, always driven by the flog of combat, jarred to the bone until his pain numbed his mind, and his heart became like lunar glass—cold and icy. And then there was nothing left, nothing but him surrounded by a storm, standing amidst flame, always casting his eyes toward the next piece of horror. Just him. Alone. In a void. He could see it. He looked into himself until there was nothing left. Nothing but him. Nothing but emptiness.

"Benji!"

He jerked back, threw his arms over his head defensively. Tawny drew her arm away looking worried. His heart thudded inside his ears. He heaved momentarily like a Golothan marathoner slowly bringing himself back to calm, recollecting all his pieces. He shook his head, looked down at that black planet. It all made perfect sense—the superstitions, the stories about Speculus. They were all true.

The mirror planet.

"Are you okay?" Tawny asked.

"Yeah," he said. "Just go up."

He groaned lifting himself up out of the bubble turret and following her up the ladder and into the cockpit where he swung the hatch shut as if shutting away that strange planet beneath him. He moved down the passenger corridor and into the main hold with Tawny pacing behind eyeing him, worried.

She put one hand on his arm, one on his shoulder and leaned her cheek into him. They stood in the silence momentarily, not saying a word. She finally murmured, "Is it the war?"

He cleared his throat, said, "You know how it is."

"Yeah, I do."

He took a big, cleansing breath and moved to the table, sat down recuperating. The moment was over. Let it pass. Let if fade. He shook it away, took another breath, looked at her. "I was thinking about the Orbin offer; the Cabal planet pounder they're building on Menuit-B."

She sat across from him. "You're not having second thoughts are you?"

"No, not at all," he said reassuringly. "But it does bring up an interesting question, doesn't it?"

She looked at him interested. "Like what?"

He picked absent-mindedly at a stain on the table surface. "Well, what if we were offered a contract to carry some payload, maybe perform a service job, anything, that could save, perhaps, thousands of lives." He looked into her. "Would you do it?"

"Of course, I would."

"Even if it breached our Space Rules?"

"Our rules..."

"Right."

She got up, paced around. Had to think about it. She said, "That was the whole point of making those rules, to stay away from the war. We're done with the war, Benji. It's over for us."

"I know. But what if it could be over for *everybody,* and it was our call?"

She squinted at him. "What do you mean?"

Ben leaned back in his chair arranging his thoughts. "What if we got a job that could end the war? Would you sign the contract?"

"Of course, I would."

"What if it meant..." He looked up at her deeply, and said, "What if it meant defeating the Cabal—your people, ending Wi'ahr, everything—would you do it then?"

The slightest look of insult crossed her face. She paced back, then forth and stopped, said, "No."

He nodded his head accepting her answer.

She continued, "We talked about this. We went over it and over it. That's why we have our rules, remember? So we don't end up benefiting one side over the other. It's... what'd you call it?"

"Sacrosanct."

"Yeah, that."

"You wouldn't break our rules; not even if it meant ending the war?"

"And kill the way of life I was brought up into? No."

He frowned, said, "Huh."

She grinned flatly, her insult now showing clearly. "Would you do it? I mean, if it was the other way around and it meant the Cabal taking control of the system, and it meant the end to the Imperium—your side, your belief system, your way of life, all gone—to end the war, would you do it?"

He had to think about it. Her scenario was a dark one. The Imperium would die. His history would be erased. His culture would be over. His society would be rearranged, redefined, even reworked entirely. Nothing in his past would matter, not tradition, not convention, nothing. Even his system of belief would wash away with the turning of the stars. His very god would die and Ae'ahm would be replaced by something lesser. He looked up at her with glistening eyes and said, "No."

She made a resolute gesture. "See?"

"You're right, Tawny. There's the war, and then there's us. We have to put it behind. Simple as that."

She sat down, suddenly fatigued. "Why do we even talk about this stuff?"

"It's philosophy, sweetheart."

"I hate philosophy. It's stupid. It just reminds me of how different we are."

He chuckled at her compassionately. "I think it shows how alike we are. How deeply we can love something. How much we belong to something greater than ourselves. How far we'd go to preserve those things. We're exactly the same thing, you and me."

She looked at him. A question burned inside her she dare not ask. But she had to. "And what about our hatred?"

He blinked, leaned back, absorbed her question like a shot to the mouth. He grinned sadly and said, "The truth?"

"Yeah, the truth."

He inhaled big. "Okay—I hate the Cabal. I hate it. I know you love it. I love the Imperium." He reached across the table, put a hand on her face, felt her hot blood beneath her skin. "But I'd destroy the Imperium a thousand times over if it meant your life."

She smiled uncontrollably and pressed her face into his

palm. They swam inside each other's gaze for a moment, then he relaxed, pulled his hand back, came back to reality. "The war's too big, anyway. No single outlier like us would stop everything. And certainly no contract job."

"Ha!" she blurted getting back to her feet. "Don't tell that to General what's-his-face. He seems to think the Menuit-B job is the answer to all the troubles of a hundred billion people."

Everyone in the system, thirty livable planets, twelve Imperium, fifteen Cabal, the others neutral. A hundred billion lives.

Ben nodded in agreement. He said, "His hate is no different than his enemy's. When I was in the Golotha Service in the Contingent—the Imperium—we were given a motto, forced to repeat it, forced to believe it." His words were glum, low. He recited his 501st motto, "Kill every last one of them, or die to the very last man." He grinned with a sad version of pity and said, "I guess it didn't stick. I mean, I fell in love with one of them."

She smiled at him. "We had one, too. Well, it was unofficial."

He looked at her interested. "What was it?"

"Screw 'em." They grinned at each other, fiery and hot. She said, "Guess mine stuck, eh?"

He leaned his head back and gave a tremendous laugh. "And that's why I love you."

The mood lifted. It was their superpower as a couple— turn a downtrodden moment into a reason to fight, live, feel joy again.

She sat down leaning toward him, smiling with that characteristic fire in her eyes. "Hey, you know what I want to do?"

"What?"

"Have some fun."

He tilted his head, squinted at her. They were stuck here for the next few hours. Stuck at *Station Oficium*. Nothing to do. He grinned. "Guilder's Mix?"

"Oh yeah," she said.

He got to his feet and declared, "That's a great idea, let's go." He headed for the airlock but stopped and turned. "Better bring your gun."

CHAPTER EIGHT

———————

THEY STARTED with a game of Yakuna down in the gaming courtyard. It was a lover's game developed off the shoulders of Molta-Danora. Guessing each other's sexual appetites based on conceptual shapes hovering in the air, they flipped cards denoting their player's challenges. Each round's winner was offered a pressure pop of endorphins. Painless. Harmless. But thrilling. Unfortunately, Tawny and Ben knew each other's secrets too well. Each round ended in a draw. No endorphin shots. The game was designed more for newcomers on the cusp of a one-night tussle. They'd be drunk on lunar liquor before getting buzzed up on the game's offerings. Disappointing.

So they proceeded to the dance area where the music had segued into an upbeat alien mainstream pop-style rhapsody, loud and encumbering to the senses, the pounding beat syncopated to strobes and steam jets. It was crowded. Too crowded for Ben.

Paxxians and Lexxians from the twin Lyndo systems gyrated in groups. They were a sexual lot, dashing males and shapely females with bronze-colored skin hailing from deep in the Cabal. To the side, a pair of Golothan females sipped drinks, spying back at him. Ben had a homeworld in common with them, but he looked away with a congenial grin. Even an Ionian entrenched in its symbio-tank was present—an odd uni-gendered specie that breathed semi-solids in thick, lava-like gelatin staring out at the crowd from its tank.

Tawny held firm to Ben's hand, urging him onto the floor. He was reticent, wincing against the trilling digi-tech, thrumming in a vortex of sound. He was way too sober yet to be caught shimmying on the dance floor. He resisted her, shook his head, content to stand off to the side while she gave him a show of oscillating hips, and snaking limbs, drawing her arms up through that shimmering, red hair. She was beginning to feel the light-bodied effect of her drink. It made Ben laugh at her. She giggled embarrassment and they stepped away.

At the bar, they ordered another round—his a Golothan ale served in a tall, narrow carafe that glowed, hers a Molta-Danoran wine. She sipped and said, "Let's go up." Ben knew what that meant. It meant up to the public gambling tables. He shook his head trying not to grin. It was a bad idea, but how could he ever say no to her?

So they proceeded to the gambling parlor one level up carrying their drinks with them, both laughing and sipping. Standing at the edge of the floor, they scanned a dozen tables abuzz with commotion. Intergalactic gamblers living on the edge. Dealers and boxmen flipped cards or placed bets, some initiating their 3-D hologram game elements. The place was raucous, being fed from the carnivorous frenzy from below.

Ben gave her an ominous look. She only grinned that devil's way and nudged her chin toward the Bakka Faro. He knew it. Girl was a sucker for Bakka. The game was fast and rowdy, very energetic, requiring little in the way of study and patience. It wasn't the five card games of his homeworld of Golotha. More like the chance and chit games of her more impulsive homeward of Raylon.

"Why do I feel like I'm going to regret this?" he said.

"Oh stop," she snorted. "There's no crying in Bakka, babe."

The remark actually stung. He just laughed it off and said, "Thank you, wife." Groaning, he led her to the table. There was a spot at the end for her, a spot at the opposite side for him, with several gamblers between them.

Ben made eye contact with the dealer announcing his presence. The guy was seasoned at his job, constantly sharking for cutthroats and cheaters. Despite the reverie at his table, he was as stoic as a statue. Ben exchanged a mutual nod with him. Ben was no cheater; would rather lose fair than win crooked. Tawny on the other hand... yeah, Ben had learned to keep an eye on that one. She had been trouble at the gambling tables in the past, occasionally prompting a hand-in-hand full-tilt ass hauling from one establishment or another, debris being tossed their way— like knives and shocker bombs and such. It made him tense. But he loved her too much to correct her nature. Besides, the girl was just too damn fun to deny.

Ben scanned his wrist chip across an eye-reader on the table and collected a flow of chits as they fed through. He stacked them with a seasoned notion at the table. He had to avoid elbows from his surrounding gamblers as they tossed coin or collected pay. The table was crowded.

Bakka Faro was a simple game. The dealer presented digital card insignias on the table surface and waited. The punters would make their bets by placing their chits on the insignias they hoped would stay hidden, then the dealer would start flipping cards. With each card flipped, one's odds shrank. But the stakes grew. At the end, someone would win big—usually the house—and everyone else didn't. With an onslaught of side betting accompanying each round, there was never any want for noise and energy. Ben took a big drink. A big one.

Let the betting begin.

The first round was lucky. He won on his original thousand yield bits. Chits were shoved toward him. He looked over at his wife across the table. She was frowning, looking glum.

Uh-oh. A loser.

Another round, another win. The punter to his right shook his hand on a job well done, celebrated with him. Ben was beginning to feel the night lengthen. Refusing to leave a heater, he was willing to stand there flipping chits as long as he could. Players came and went, most of them scuttling off like scolded Molosian dogs. But not Ben. Shoot, he was up almost three thousand yield bits before he knew it.

He looked over again. Tawny's chits were all gone. She mouthed the word, "Sorry," and gave him an exaggerated shrug. She was out of yield.

He nodded at her—*It's okay, sweetheart.*

She was good at most anything she attempted. Not gambling. Ben felt sympathy for her. No matter how much she wanted to, she just couldn't read a table, couldn't feel the heat, sniff out the right time to bet. Her combat specialist's impulses were always in kickass mode, always wanting to go in for a kill, never willing to seek out an unknown target. He always warned her gambling took patience. She didn't have any. It was probably why she was known to cheat. It's how she won. In combat mode, there was no cheating. There was only winning. Combat and Faro were two different things, as it turned out.

She sank back leaving the table, allowing another punter to take her place. Ben knew where she was headed. The bar. He'd meet her there soon enough. And she'd probably be three-sheets-to-the-wind.

A bump to the left nearly knocked his arm into his stacks of chits scattering them across the table. A new punter stepped up next to him. A tall guy. Ben ignored. Didn't even bother looking at him. Why start trouble at a winning table?

The next round wasn't bad. Ben found himself winning in the midrange. He'd take what he could get. A disgruntled voice to his left muttered, "Heh—way to go." It was snarky, unfriendly.

Ben ignored.

Another round. Another win. Damn—he couldn't lose!

That voice again: "Loser's luck."

Ben bit his bottom lip, took a big breath forcing patience, demanding against his own fortitude to ignore the guy, but making a deal with himself: *This guy pipes up one more time, we're having words.*

The dealer ignited the next round of card insignias randomly across the playing surface. Ben spied them, feeling for the lucky combination. That one. That one. And... that one. He placed his chits. The playing started. Cards flipped. Voices raised. Side bets passed back and forth. The dealer made it half way through the deck. Ben's picks were still alive. His heart started to pound. This one might be a big one. More cards. More luck. He rubbed his hands together. Strangers started betting on his luck. Another card. Three more. Two more. A final. Boom. Winner!

Everyone cheered around him winning money. They slapped him on the back. A few flipped gratuity chits at him. He rejoiced momentarily with them, then the table settled, began preparing another round.

A big, heavy hand whopped him across the back from the left. That voice said in its smarmy undertone, "Never be poor again, will ya."

Ben shot him a glance and sneered, "There's no crying in Bakka, bub!" Tawny's words coming right out of his mouth. She was a terrible influence, always with the attitude check. And before Ben knew it, he stared directly up at the Orbin pistoleer he'd encountered earlier, made eye contact with, knew he was following him. He felt his breath catch in his throat.

The guy's blue face was pitiless, no emotion, just an undercurrent of something ominous. He said, "Especially not with that new million yield."

Ben's blood chilled. There was only one way he knew about that. The Orbin contract. This guy was a bounty hunter; and he was there for him and Tawny. Ben played it off well, simply looked him dead in the big, gold eyes and said, "Buddy, I don't know what you're talking about."

The guy turned square and faced him. Suddenly there was no Bakka Faro table, no crowd, no gaming. Just the two of them staring at each other, coldly. The Orbinii said, "I knew that is what you would say."

Ben smiled at him, laughed, then kicked him swiftly in the balls. He turned to run, but the Orbinii snatched the back of his scruff and slung him across the Bakka table. Chits and coin exploded. The punters howled in displeasure. Ben looked up and threw a blind punch hoping for traction only to have slap cuffs whipped around his hands. He was bound tight.

The Orbinii growled, "Where is your little female partner with the—"

WHOCK!

A bar stool smashed the back of his head knocking him on top of Ben. Ben kicked him away unconscious and Tawny stood before him, getting him to his feet.

"She's right there, narse-hole!" Ben yelled.

"Let's go!"

They scurried from the table and toward the stairs with Ben's hands cuffed at his waist. Ben cried, "I got almost seven thousand yield on that table!"

They both stopped, looked back. There was a small riot at the table as everyone scurried for his winnings.

"Oh, screw it," he said. It was easy come, easy go at Guilder's Mix. They took off down the stairs.

Once they reached the bottom it seemed they'd escaped the party above. Down here, no one had seen the commotion. They weren't running from trouble down here. They slowed down and headed for the crowd on the dance floor, blending in, Tawny in the lead holding Ben's bound hands. She was hells-bent on the exit, bumping cantina goers out of her way. Her mind worked from point A to point B. Simple. Focused. They exited the dance floor losing the crowd behind them. Ben's mind was more obser-vant. He pulled her to a stop. She looked back, followed his gaze.

Another Orbinii. The female prostitute. She was at the entrance, and she looked angry. A hip-hugging holster was slung low with one hand on her pistol. She spotted them, locked eyes.

"Can't go that way," he said.

"I can take her."

A second Orbin joined her, then a third, both males.

"There's too many. We can lose them here," Ben said. "Let's go." They faded back into the crowd.

Dancers bumped and shimmied as they reversed their direction. Even Tawny found it difficult to move freely. Intermittent light and dark made it hard to truly see. Sound deafened them toward danger.

A hand snatched Ben's shoulder from behind. He turned and saw one of the Orbin males digging his way through the dance floor. Ben whipped the hand off him. But his hands were still cuffed, couldn't punch back. Tawny sensed the motion, spun and came in low. She took the guy's feet out from under him slamming him down and taking a swath of party-goers with him. People started screaming, some in surprise, others in euphoria. Tawny unleashed her weapon. The laser blast was hardly noticed above the music and strobe effect. She whirled her blaster back into its holster.

One Orbin pursuer—down.

Ben scanned the crowd. The other two Orbinii pursuers were tall, easy to see. They stood above the crowd moving around the periphery of the dance floor. "The exit!" he yelled. They headed that way, shoving, pushing, bumping.

They made it to the cocktail area. There was more room to operate. They sprinted to the neon-lit archway. Ben glanced back. They were spotted, like it or not. And they were being pursued. "Go, go!"

A figure appeared at the entrance seemingly from nowhere, wearing a full bio-suit and helmet. One moment he wasn't there, the next he was. Tawny slid to a halt on her feet reaching for her weapon prepared to take him down, but he leapt high over them, flipped and came back down behind, separating them from the approaching Orbinii. A glowing lance emitted in his hands and he went into a combat artist's flurry, the long wand hissing and streaming as it arced. The first Orbin went down holding a severed arm, screaming over the crowd. His gun (and hand) dropped to the floor.

Mystery guy swung low, fully around, perfectly seamless in his motion, taking the other Orbinii off her feet, her boots flying away in opposite directions. She fell, howling in pain. No feet.

A laser blast zipped across the entire courtyard just over everyone's heads. Mystery guy was too quick. A hand-emitted force shield absorbed the blast as he summersaulted in mid air. From way across the space the first Orbinii stood sneering at them halfway down the stairs, gun raised. He'd recovered at the Bakka table and had come running down stairs. Big mistake. Now, he faced this unknown assailant from across the dim space.

Mystery guy sent a bolt from his glowing spear that traveled across the courtyard like a starshot and blew the Orbinii off his feet, dead as a doornail.

The place erupted into a mixture of terrified shock and crazed delight. Tawny and Ben made eye contact, shocked. Once everything settled, it was business as usual at Guilder's Mix. It was someone else's mess to clean up.

Mystery guy said, "We must leave," through a helmeted mask, and walked powerfully back through the exit. Tawny and Ben shrugged and followed.

CHAPTER NINE
____

THE TRIO MOVED around the main entertainment complex through the peripheral mall. It was lined with bars and pubs secondary to Guilder's Mix, but no less active. At least here, they could be anonymous.

Ben eyed their new companion. He recognized him from before—the guy at the bar. He was midsized, rangy rather than muscular, and built for quickness. There were three wicked-looking knives sheathed across one thigh, a laser blaster on the other and his collapsed energy spear slung across one shoulder. He was an elusive sort, too, disappearing and reappearing seemingly at will.

His suit was far more than a vacuum bio-suit. With a complex piece of machinery at his back, two main tubes looping into a breather apparatus and a pressure/density activator at his side, this was a complete atmosphere processor. Very compact, highly technological, it allowed for a full range of motion and seemed remarkably light.

This guy wasn't the average cargo runner.

Ben tried to guess his species—perhaps one of the water dwellers of Dionesse. Their planet was a big ball of oxygen and hydrogen combined as liquid. They couldn't exist beyond their endless water vistas. But the temperature regulator on his suit said otherwise. It kept the suit's internal atmosphere at a full three hundred degrees, nearly hot enough to boil the fish-skinned Dionessians.

He wasn't Ionian, either. They breathed semi-solids and required full incubation tanks for travel. Nor was he Tadonian. They breathed toxic fumes and lived in an acidic environment, but not at three hundred degrees.

Ben glanced over his shoulder at Tawny who was clearly trying to determine the same thing. What was this guy?

When he spoke, his voice came from a mechanized sound regulator giving him a sinister, robotic quality. It was buried deep inside a hermetically sealed helm with a full face plate and visor, which was a perfect mirror-black. "They were Orbin bounty squad. From Orbin moon, O'rae. They have been tracking you."

"You're not Orbinii," Tawny said.

"No, I am not."

"Who are you?" Ben said.

A light blinked on his pack. A tiny buzzer sounded. It was a suit reading showing low-limit. The guy checked a control panel on his wrist. "Come. We find a place. Must recharge."

It suddenly made sense. Ben nodded with certainty. The gage was on an atmosphere-to-dioxide conversion unit. This stranger was from Karbatt Krutt, one of the independent planets. It was two planets in one, the western hemisphere flushed in perpetual darkness, its carbon black surface etched with rivers of lava visible from orbit, always raining sulfuric acids. The other half was a lush brown and green world with mountain ranges and forestry. Each hemisphere had evolved uniquely intelligent life, the Krutt and the Karbatt. Ben couldn't remember which was which?

He'd never met one before. He looked at him with interest.

"You're a Karbatt."

The guy half turned as if to face him and said, "No. I am Krutt."

To misidentify one as the other was an insult.

"Ah," Ben said. "Apologies."

"Not necessary. Come."

THEY FOUND a diner bustling with comers and goers. They weaved through a crowd toward the one empty booth in the restaurant and sat, Ben and Tawny to one side, their new companion to the other.

The Krutt placed a wireless energy transfer apparatus to an outlet in the wall and immediately, his suit began collecting power. He was recharging.

"Do you have a name?" Ben asked.

The Krutt said, "No."

"You don't have a name?"

"My name is No."

"Ah," he said amicably. "How did you know they were tracking us?"

"It is what they do. They are... how do you say?"

Tawny and Ben both said simultaneously, "Bounty hunters?"

"Hunt bounty, yes."

"So it's true," Ben said looking daunted. "The Orbin Royal Council has put a bounty on our heads."

"I believe this, yes."

"Why?"

"I do not know." The Krutt leaned forward. "Do you know?"

Tawny and Ben glanced at each other. The answer was clear in their eyes. They had private information about the Menuit-B operation. The Orbinii wanted it back at any cost. Tawny said, "Could be any number of reasons."

Ben said, "How do you know about the bounty?"

"I know the Orbinii bounty squad. Was once among them. No longer."

"Why not?" he asked.

"Friends are, how should I say…"

Tawny and Ben said simultaneously, "Fickle?"

"Yes, this is that. Fickle."

"Is that why you're here?" Ben asked.

The Krutt nodded his head morphing Ben's reflection in the visor. "Yes. I have… things."

"Revenge."

"Yes, this," the Krutt said.

Tawny shook her head curiously, and said, "We haven't seen any Orbinii assignment come through the black market bounty forum contracting for us."

The Krutt nodded. "Orbinii like to be private. Not want anyone know. Not use the forum. Too public. No private."

"Then they must have a private roster of contractors they use directly," Ben said. "A two party structure. No middleman."

"Yes, this is that," the Krutt agreed.

Ben leaned back in the booth drumming his fingers on the table in thought. His eyes went to Tawny. "What do you think?"

She made a cursory face and said, "I think I need another drink."

"Hm. Me too." Ben extended a hand to the Krutt and said sincerely, "Thank you."

The Krutt gave a nuanced reaction, said, "No."

Ben squinted at him, and then said, "Thank you, No."

They shook hands. "Yes."

Ben got up and made his way to the bar. The only open spot was way down at the end through a crowd of drinkers. He rubbed his face and waited for the tender. He agreed with Tawny. He needed a drink. Their earlier drunk was gone. It had been wiped clean, thanks to an Orbinii bounty squad. Already he'd seen more action tonight than he'd bargained for. He rubbed his face. A night out on the town with his wife, some frolicking and play, a little romance... was it too much to ask for?

He sighed.

Thanks to their new friend, all was not lost. He digested the Krutt's words. According to him, the bounty squad had tracked Tawny and Ben all the way from the Orbin moon O'rae. A sudden question occurred to Ben. O'rae was one of three Orbin moons. How did the Krutt know they'd come from O'rae, specifically?

He must've followed the Orbinii bounty squad.

"Whatcha drinking, pal?" the bar tender asked.

Ben looked over to the booth. He could see Tawny's face as she spoke to the Krutt. They seemed to be dialoging comfortably enough. He took a breath, angling in his mind.

The Krutt had also suggested the Royal Council had a private roster of bounty hunters they contracted from. They never went to the Guild data net. But that wasn't true. It made Ben's eyes squint. The Orbin Royal Council had scattered the Heiress contract all across the solar twin system. The last thing they wanted was privacy. They hadn't pulled from some esteemed roster of private contractors. They probably didn't even have one.

"Hey, bub, whatcha drinking?" The bartender threw a towel over his shoulder, waiting.

Ben's eyes widened, still staring across the diner at his wife.

He remembered King Oto offering them a two-party contract for the Menuit-B job. Two party contracts weren't standard practice for the Orbinii. The Krutt had said two-party contracts were the only way they did business.

That was a lie.

Ben's mouth dropped open.

"C'mon, guy, order up!" an impatient drinker called standing behind Ben.

The Krutt hadn't tracked the Orbinii bounty squad from O'rae. He'd been tracking Tawny and Ben. The Krutt was a bounty hunter himself. The Orbin Royal Council wanted them dead or alive. And they were willing to pay big yield.

The Krutt hadn't saved them from the Orbinii bounty squad. He had *stolen* them.

Now Ben gasped, felt the blood flush from his face.

"Hey, pal, is there a problem?" the tender asked.

Yes there was, as a matter of fact. His wife was alone way across the restaurant, sitting with a Krutt headhunter!

TAWNY LOOKED over scanning for her husband. There he was, way over there, through the crowd, across the diner wildly waving at her. The look on his face was horror, panic in his eyes. She squinted at him. What did he know? What had he figured out?

Her eyes went to the Krutt sitting across from her. His

mask showed no life through that opaque visor. No eyes to read. No expression to analyze. But something was wrong. She was in peril. The Krutt was dangerous. She knew it. His head tilted. The Krutt knew she knew it. His secret was out.

Tawny gasped.

Immediately, violently, without warning, the Krutt thrust a knife at her face.

She blocked left.

He missed.

He thrust again.

She blocked right.

He missed a second time.

She bent his arm back.

Twisted his wrist.

The knife dropped.

She snatched it.

Swung at his mask.

He blocked with an elbow.

The knife dropped.

She slapped a hand on it.

He slapped a hand on top of hers.

She was trapped.

She punched his helmet with her free hand.

He recoiled.

The knife slid across the table.

Out of reach.

She reached below, drew her gun.

His boot kicked forward.

Pinned her hand.

She yelped.

The gun dropped to the floor.

The Krutt snatched up the knife.

He swiped at her.

She pivoted her head.

He missed.

He swung again.

She pivoted the other way.

The blade missed again.

It snapped her suspender in half.

Left a stripe of blood on her shoulder.

She lunged, grabbed his knife hand.

He sneered, forced the blade toward her.

She deflected his thrust to the left.

The blade stabbed the booth next to her ear.

He jerked it back.

Stuffing went everywhere.

He thrust for her again.

She deflected it to the right.

It stabbed the booth next to her other ear.

More stuffing flew.

They tangled up, all elbows and limbs, locking against each other.

Then everything froze in combat position. Their eyes went up. The waitress stood at their table looking silently shocked, eyes wide, mouth open. Tawny gave her a wide, innocent smile. "Oh—we're only practicing," she said.

"Combat in close quarter," the Krutt added.

"Oh," the waitress said looking suspect. "Can I... get you two anything?"

"We're about done," Tawny said.

"Yes, about done," the Krutt said.

"Okay." The waitress nodded and turned to leave.

Tawny called, "Oh! Do you serve Raylon vodka with cherry?"

"Yeah," she said.

"How about one of those?"

"Uh, sure," she said, turned her back, and left.

Tawny slammed the Krutt's knife hand to the table with a bang.

His fist opened, released the knife.

She shoved it away.

It hit the floor.

He lunged at her over the table.

She dodged the blow.

She snatched her broken suspender.

Lassoed it around his throat.

Flipped him over.

Bent him over the table backwards.

Whip quick.

He growled, losing breath, clawing at the choker.

She jammed one knee against the edge of the table, teeth clenched angrily, and cinched the noose like reigning a Molosian horse until her tendons became like wire. There was nothing he could do.

And then Ben was there standing over them looking down at the struggle, fire in his eyes. He slid into the booth next to the Krutt. Tawny released and said, "Now play nice, jerk-o." The guy corrected, sat back up rubbing his neck. Ben put the knife blade to his ribs. The guy had lost the struggle. Tawny was too quick. She was like lightning strikes in the atmo storms of Optus. And now he was trapped between the two of them. It showed on his demeanor. He didn't move.

Ben whispered very angrily, "This is what happens when you fight with her. You lose, pal. Trust me." He jabbed the point of the blade against his side. "Why are you here?"

"Contract," the Krutt said.

"The Orbin Royal Council?"

"Possible."

Ben jabbed the knife harder making the guy squirm.

"Yes," the guy said.

"Who else?"

"There are many."

"Who?" Ben insisted.

The Krutt's vacant visor plate turned to him slowly. He said, "Many."

Ben's eyes went to Tawny. "What do you want to do?"

"Is it too late to get that drink?"

He looked at her ridiculously. "Really?"

Tawny sighed. They couldn't let the Krutt go. He'd still follow them, hunt them. At the very least, word would get out that they were soft on killers. They couldn't let that happen. She shrugged. "There's only one thing we can do, babe," she said matter-of-factly. They had to kill him right here in the restaurant, leave his body sitting at the booth as inconspicuously as possible.

Ben nodded, said, "Nothing personal, friend. Looks like you signed the wrong contract, is all."

He jammed the knife forward as if to slide the blade between the guy's second and third ribs right under the armpit, penetrate the lung, sever the trachea...

But the Krutt was gone, vanished in a blink. Just like that. Poof.

Ben jerked back, surprised. The blade was clean. No blood. They looked at each other, shocked. Tawny gasped, "Matter transporter."

He had one on his person. Now he was gone. Very tricky. And there was no telling where he was. He could've been anywhere—a thousand miles away or right around the next corner.

"We gotta go," Ben said.

Tawny grabbed her gun off the floor as they scooted out of the booth and bolted for the door. Back out in the mall, they dashed for the hub exit parting the crowd. They didn't get very far before...

"There!" a voice called.

They both looked over. Another bounty hunter. This one was a Deridiae male from the jungle planet Deridian—jade-colored skin with stark red patterns across his neck and chest, and long marsupial arms. He pointed at them calling to his unseen counterparts with a comm device. "They're headed for the hub exit!" He was strapping a rifle behind his bareback, a blaster at his side.

"Oh, great," Ben said, redirecting.

The sound of a blaster went off joined with the sound of a defiant growl. He knew that blaster. He knew that defiant growl, too. It was his wife. He turned around. Tawny blasted away. The crowd screamed, hit the deck. The Deridian dropped down covering up.

"Go, go!" Ben screamed. They pounded through the exit and out into the main thoroughfare leaving Guilder's Mix in their dust. The passage was wide, well lit, lots of stark white light. People moved in packs and cliques. The mirror planet showed through the viewport to the left, the backdrop of space to the right. They didn't stop, kept running, pealing around station goers.

REX was several hubs away. It would be a very long mad dash. "We should take the zip train," Tawny said from one pace behind.

"No way," Ben said. "We could get trapped on the train. Nowhere to run. We'll have to make it on foot."

No sooner had he said that, he came to an abrupt stop. Tawny bumped him from behind, matching him. They looked way ahead through the crowd. There were four of them. Very suspect. Each one was dressed in bounty gear, light body armor, personal paraphernalia hanging off belts, blasters at their sides. One had twin bandoliers across his chest. They made eye contact. One of them pointed unmistakably at Tawny and Ben.

"Looks like we're already trapped," Ben corrected himself.

"Who *are* these people?" Tawny sneered.

"Don't know, but train. Definitely the train," Ben said redirecting their course.

They flew through the nearest zip train loading station and down a broad stairway where the crowd thickened. A train car waited for passengers. He started swimming through the crowd with Tawny close behind. She threw a glance over her shoulder. The bounty crew appeared at the top of the stairs, each scanning frantically for their bounty.

"Better hurry!" she said.

Ben charged through the train entrance jerking her inside with him. They bumped station goers out of their way, everyone looking disgruntled. Through the long passenger window they saw the bounty crew pursuing, making their way through the crowd. The doors whispered shut as they reached, cutting them off. They were face-to-face through the window, Ben staring into the nearest one's black V-shaped visor and sighing in relief, while Tawny released a loud, triumphant heckle.

"Too slow, you Molosian slugs!" she howled as the train jerked forward. She waved, "Bye bye!"

They flew from the station driven by sudden, mag drive inertia replacing the view of the loading dock with the eternal gut-drop of space.

Ben turned around and rested his back against the viewport rubbing his face. That was close. Too close. He looked around. There was nowhere to sit. Standing room only. Other passengers looked curiously up at them. Blue-skins, gray-skins, green skins. Some with antennae, others with spines and ripples. A thousand different eyes. It made him nervous.

"Come on," he said, taking Tawny's hand. "Let's go to the forward car." He led her through the crowd as people shuffled out of their way. They reached the passenger door, but before he could step across the pass-through, they heard...

"Benjar and Tawny Dash!"

They spun around. A broad figure stood front-and-center wearing a half-helm and large shoulder armor over a bare, muscle-rippling trunk. He pointed a silvery, two-handed wand weapon at them. "You're wanted dead or alive for data theft by the Orbin Royal Council. Come with me... and I won't kill you."

Tawny gave him a flippant show of annoyance and yelled back, "Oh, bi-lords, are you kidding... *mehehehe!*" The man fired a plasma net from his weapon that reached out and engulfed her, locked her up, made her go rigid, surrounding her with plasma energy.

Ben flashed fury, unholstered his wife's blaster from her hip and sneered in rhythm with his blasting: "You" *BLAM!* "Will not" *BLAM!* "Take" *BLAM!* "My" *BLAM!* "Wife" *BLAM!* "You" *BLAM!* "Little" *BLAM!* "Sonuva" *BLAM!* "gitch!" *BLAM!*

Everyone screamed. The guy dropped. His wand clattered to the floor. Ben thrust himself toward it, picked it up and smashed its tip against the floor. It shattered releasing the web. Tawny dropped to her knees shaking her head.

"You okay, sweetie!" Ben yelled going to her.

She stood back up and muttered, "Ouch."

"We gotta get off this station."

"I completely agree."

THREE RAILWAY DOCKS LATER, the train hissed to a stop. A voice called, "Passengers disembarking for hubs one-two-five through one-three-zero may exit now."

Ben and Tawny exploded from the train scanning the crowd. Nothing looked overly suspect, just a bunch of passengers and station goers milling around. They hit the stairs and back out into the main thoroughfare. Fexx Pol's shop was just ahead. They stormed down the reception steps with the view of the huge maintenance bay opening up. Fexx's client vessels were visible—some were fat and bulbous, others were sleek winged-back things. Ben spied their ship. REX had a midsized, nondescript fuselage, but his mag-spires reached way down toward the Speculus void. He was all patched up, looking good. The repair crews had completed the work and moved on.

Ben muttered, "Thank Ae'ahm..."

Tawny muttered, "Thank Wi'ahr..."

Simultaneously.

"There you are!" came a familiar voice from behind. It was deep, almost bottomless. They spun around, prepared for anything. It was Tub'Num holding a *Station Oficium* security blaster down at his side.

Ben's shoulders dropped. There was no running from Tubs, no shooting him. He was station security. That would be against the law. And given his Telosian biology, there wouldn't be any beating him up either. They were trapped.

"What do you want, Tubs?" Ben sneered.

"I hear names Benjar and Tawny Dash wanted by

Orbinii Royal Court. Figured half the station come to your vessel, wait for you. I here to give security. You go now."

Ben and Tawny glanced at each other, both laughing relieved. They had lots of enemies on *Station Oficium*. But they had a few friends, too.

"Thanks, Tubs..." Tawny said, but her face went to horror.

The Krutt bounty hunter blinked into existence behind Tub'Num. Before she could scream, the Krutt stabbed the Telosian with a knife. Tubs's eyes went wide. He made a small, deep groan and dropped to his knees shaking the floor.

Tawny whipped her pistol and blasted away. The Krutt deflected with his force shield, the blasts banking off harmlessly. Ben swept his wife behind him protectively, both stepping backward.

The Krutt approached, that dispassionate visor betraying a heartless objective. "One way or other," he said in his robotic overtone, "you come with me."

"How much are they paying you?" Ben asked.

"More than you have to pay," he said stepping forward.

"Is it worth murder?" Tawny sneered, her eyes glistening over.

The Krutt shook his head pathetically. "I kill Telosian. I kill Orbinii. I kill all in my way," he said. "And now I kill you if you no do what I say."

Ben said to Tawny, "Boy, he sounds angry. I think you really irked him off."

Tawny returned, "It's not my fault he's so slow."

The Krutt snickered away the insult and admitted, "You do good knife work. But now, you have nothing."

"You sure about that?" Ben asked.

The Krutt reacted with a bewildered tilt of the head. "What you have, humanoid?"

Ben smirked wily and satisfied, "Friends, dude."

Two thick arms wrapped the Krutt up from behind pinning his arms to his sides. It was Tubs. He said, "Stupid knives. Stupid Krutt—*hahaha!*" He picked him up, turned him over and body slammed him powerfully down on his head. The helmet flattened shattering the visor. A flush of heat and steam rushed from the Krutt's head as his internal atmosphere evacuated, and he screamed in agony, his natural voice becoming clear. It was shrieky and piercing, an ugly howl. Ben and Tawny flinched back.

The Krutt vanished again—gone.

"Damn that guy," Ben said.

"You must go now. More others will come. Go." Tubs said.

"You okay?" Tawny asked a little horrified.

Tubs looked down at his wound. It was a big bloody mess. He nodded his head. "I have stabs all the time. I get some wound foam. You go now. No time!"

They gave the Telusian a look of gratitude and bolted off.

On their way toward REX, they darted past a waving Fexx Pol who looked a bit surprised at their sudden appearance, and their subsequent disappearance.

"Thanks, Fexx, you're pay has been deposited!" Ben's voice carried away like a Doppler affect as they dashed down the passage.

"Uh, okay..." he said and took a chomp on his sandwich.

They stormed into their ship. "REX, fire up, we're getting..."

"...the hells off this station. I know. I'm so surprised,"

REX said. Systems started winding up. Lights and control panels came to life.

Ben swung down into his seat flipping switches, punching buttons. Tawny took the co-pilot's chair.

"Disconnecting," he called.

"Here we go," REX said dejected, "Another cold burn at top speed?"

"Sorry, pal."

"You always say that—*sorry, REX, so sorry, yadda yadda...*"

The ship dropped from its crane and lowered well clear of the work bay. It turned about, headed toward open space. "Okay, let's go."

The inner-warps wound up, and—*BOOM!* They were gone.

CHAPTER TEN

Controlled Space
Planet Dekorrah'Bha
Moon Chiat
United Confederation Front (Underworld Cabal)

"WE'RE ON APPROACH," REX said.

Ben headed toward the bridge, Tawny coming behind. Dekorrah'Bha grew into view through the wide viewport. It was one of the Cabal's larger civilized planets, over sixteen thousand kilometers in diameter. Yet it also had the lowest population to planet volume in the system with a mere half a billion souls inhabiting. There was only a single contiguous landmass occupying one tenth of the planet. All the rest was hydrogen and oxygen liquid. A water ocean. It was a deep blue planet housing a continent of starkly contrasting emerald green—all swamp.

It was also home to Norg, an ally to the independents roaming the planets, and a member of the Dekkoran, a race of highly intellectual turtle people. Norg was also a close friend. And friends were rare in these parts. This was Underworld space. The Cabal was everywhere.

"Where's the greeting party?" Tawny asked.

"They'll be here soon enough," Ben replied grimly.

REX said, "Yep, in fact here they come."

"Great," he muttered. "What's their position?"

"On approach. Coming around. They'll be in visual range in a few seconds."

Ben took a big breath. "Alright, slowing to comm speed." He and Tawny looked at each other, their nerves edging over into fear. "Here's where we find out if our new identification load-up is any good." But this was no test. This was the real deal.

Tawny tightened her face, nodded, agreed.

The Cabal were notoriously paranoid. The last thing Ben and Tawny needed was an investigation into their identification transmissions. If they discovered them as counterfeit they'd be detained. Then they'd discover Tawny's true identity once their data net displayed her as a war deserter and enemy of the state. The penalty for that was a wiped brain and an entirely new cognitive layover, just before being sent back to the battle front as an automaton to be used as frontline cannon fodder.

Ben couldn't stomach the thought. It made him nauseous. His penalty would be much simpler. An Imperium soldier slipping through Cabal controlled space with faked credentials? That's a quick death penalty. No problem. His wife was the one taking the chance.

They both sighed nervously in unison as a group of Cabal security vessels came up on their bow. One was a gunboat—long and menacing, sectioned wedge design separated into lateral terraces with windows and batteries.

Tawny said, "We're being hailed."

"Here we go. Put them on," Ben said.

A 3-D face holoformed into view over their holopad. As with most Cabal security contingent personnel, there was a no-nonsense look about him. He said, "This is the security patrol vessel *Non Conscientiam*. You have entered United Confederation territory, approaching the planet Dekorrah'Bha, member of the Confederate Planetary Front. You will stop and identify."

Ben nodded, said, "This is the freight hauler RX-one-one-one on approach. I'm Captain Standish, over."

"What's your destination?"

"The moon Chiat," Ben responded, "outer landing. We've been here before."

"Purpose?" the guy said sharply.

"Parts acquisition. We're here to purchase cargo compartments for our freight. Plus we're here to see an old friend." Ben flashed him a characteristic grin, wily but appealing. It didn't work.

The guy said flatly, "Are you on assignment?"

"Yeah, we're aqua haulers headed to the moon Mortus in the outer lanes."

"You're Guilders," the guy assumed with a sour look.

"That's our association. We don't keep ties. We're just contractors."

"Transmit your identification, Guild license and contract data for verification and hold." He cut the transmission. The guy's head disappeared.

Ben punched the transmit sequence and looked at his wife. "These people don't trust anyone, I swear to Ae'ahm."

"I wouldn't mention your god around here, babe." It could blow their cover, fast.

"Hmm," he agreed.

The head came back. "You will hold for detainment and inspection."

A sudden shot of cold ran up his spine, into his cheeks. This was new. "Is there a problem?" he asked.

The holohead said, "Are you refusing to comply?"

"No, not at all. What are my instructions?"

"Hold your position or you will be destroyed," he said quite frankly, no emotion—like player's at a chess board.

"Holding position."

The holohead disappeared. A drop ship lowered from the gunboat and started its approach.

"What's going on?" Tawny asked with an unusually thin voice.

"Our ident got tagged." He smashed a fist into his control deck and yelled, "Damn that Sympto!"

"You think it was Sympto?"

"Who else could it be?"

"Well, if you're right," Tawny sneered angrily, "I'm going to kill him. Do you understand? I'm going to vacuum splat his nasty little carcass!"

REX said, "I'm prepared to make a hot burn, Cap."

"Okay, REX," Ben said jerking the fuel drive toggle all the way open and coming to an immediate decision. They were running ... right this second. "Let's jackrabbit."

"No!" Tawny cried. "We'd never get away. They'd chase us all the way to Proximus. These are Cabal. That's a gunboat."

Ben froze, his hand still on the lever. "If they're coming to arrest us, I'd rather take that chance."

"No," she said, lower, more controlled. "Ease it back before they detect our on-boards."

Ben growled reticently and released the lever back.

There was a thump as their new friends attached to the exterior airlock down in the cargo bay.

He looked at her. His eyes were urgent, severe. "We got about thirty seconds, baby."

She said, "Let them board."

"I don't like it."

"We'll have hostages if we need them."

"The Cabal won't negotiate."

The airlock signaler blipped through the fuselage three times. Someone was knocking.

Tawny said, "We don't have a choice now." She tightened the buckle on her holster belt and said, "So let's go say hi." The grin she gave him both settled his nerves and stretched them taught as wire.

He huffed back. "They'll have to kill me, Tawny."

"Me too," she said. "It'll be fun..."

Ben groaned and strapped on his own holster with twin plasma-drive blasters, one on each hip. He hated wearing them, but under the right circumstances he knew he'd love using them. And he was more than a decent shot. The Imperium had made sure of that. He followed her to the drop lift and went down to the cargo bay.

THE INSPECTION LEADER was a dour sort, sunken face, prim, dark blue officer's uniform, almost black, with buttoned lapel, hawkish eyes locked onto them with accusation. An armed security contingent entered first, eight members each wearing the dark blues and blacks of the Cabal, each displaying security markings on one shoulder, guns in hand. They assumed a ready position with their heavily booted feet coming to a halt.

The leader stepped forward, his face never changing—

not even when he recognized Tawny's vague Raylon markings suggesting she was under the Cabal banner. Not even when he failed to recognize Ben's allegiance.

Ben shuddered just having the Cabal on board his vessel. But he gave them a forced, congenial smile. "I'm Captain Standish of the freight vessel RX-one-one-one, this is my co-pilot, Tannifer. Welcome aboard."

The man's cool eyes went down, then back up, noticing the weapons. He did not look pleased. "I am Consul Troicka, security representative for the United Planetary Confederation Front. You will relinquish your vessel logs immediately for checkpoint analysis."

"No problem," Ben said turning to a secondary control console in the cargo bay. When Sympto's team re-established their identification logs, all of REX's data frames were overlaid with the new information. The Iotian mutt guaranteed there would be no holes. It would appear as if Ben and Tawny had been logging their work in as Standish and Tannifer for years. Or maybe not. In the end, this was where Ben found out how good Sympto's work really was. He entered a final sequence and hit send. He turned around and said, "Transmission complete."

The consul nodded in military style. His eyes narrowed at Ben. "How long have you had this vessel?"

"Five and a half years, universal."

"How long have the two of you been Guild members?"

"The same," he said.

The consul paced over to Tawny who eyed him with a passive glint, and then paced around her and back to Ben. "She's Raylon," he said. "Where are you from?"

"I'm an independent," Ben said. "I don't have any affiliation—not political, military or otherwise."

The consul repeated very slowly, insulted, "Where. Are. You. From?"

Ben took a big breath and said, "I was born in the Golothan lunar front."

The consul stared at him before sucking his teeth slowly, with malice. He finally said, "Imperium."

Ben locked his gaze on him. A stare down. "I'm not Imperium."

The man grunted and turned to Tawny to address her. "How have you fallen in with ..." his gaze went to Ben. "...this?"

She said with a grin so nuanced only Ben could see it, and said, "I forced him."

The consul was not amused. He said, "I could have you arrested."

"If you could have us arrested," she chanced, "you already would have. But that brings up a question. Why *are* we being detained?"

The corner of his lip pulled up. Ben squinted at him. Was that a grin? Tawny knew the game, and she knew how to speak to a Cabal security consul. They loved a challenging dialog. Old habits never died with her. "Protocol," he said.

"I don't believe that," she said.

He stiffened, eying her. "That is irrelevant."

"Not to the law."

"This isn't a court."

"No," Tawny said agreeably. "This is the field."

The consul forced away a grin, made an intrigued grunt. "Are you threatening action?"

"Forcing truth."

Ben looked down, started to sweat.

The consul inhaled slowly. "Go on."

Tawny continued, "The logs will show we've been to Dakorrah'Bha several times. We've never experienced such protocol."

The consul said, "New protocol."

"Random check, then?" she said.

The consul pulled away and took a more open position, facing them both. "Your identification," he said, "fits with our newly implemented scanning procedure."

"Huh," she said. "And the problem is?"

"The Confederation rolled it out very recently. No independent has yet to upgrade to it." He leaned his brow forward deepening the shadows around his eyes and said, "You're the first."

"Since when did efficiency cause a detainment?" Tawny said.

The consul murmured stepping toward Ben, scanning him with his eyes. "It's almost too efficient, isn't it?"

"Meaning what?" Tawny asked.

The consul paced around Ben with slow, decisive steps, racking his nerves. "It's almost as if you had received this identification load from an inside source, perhaps to hide a false transmission."

Ben kept his mouth shut.

Tawny's eyes went to the security team, sliding her hand down to her belt. She could take out half of them. If Benji was quick enough to follow her lead, he could take out the other half.

Maybe...

Of course then it would be a hot burn on the inner-warp engines, lickity split.

A comm device blipped. Consul Troicka stopped pacing and lifted his hand, speaking into the inside of his wrist. "Consul Troicka."

"Sir, we've run the logs transmission. It appears to be clean."

His lips tightened, disappointed. He asked, "Where does it say Captain Standish was born?"

A pause, then, "Golot Major, sir."

"Any strict affiliation?"

"We scanned his known history. Only with the Guild, sir. No mention of the Imperium."

His eyes sharked across Ben looking for one final lie. He said, "How many times have they been to Dekorrah?"

"It says... seven times over four years, universal, sir."

Consul Troicka inhaled a large breath very dissatisfied, yet his hands were tied. They were legitimate freight haulers with business on the moon Chiat, Golothan-born or otherwise.

"I see." He lowered his wrist, looked at them severely. "Proceed to Chiat. Your course has been reviewed. Do not deviate," he said as if to choke on a brick of pride. Giving Tawny one last look, he turned to his security staff and marched them out. Once the airlock shut behind him, Ben and Tawny shared a massive sigh of relief.

"Believe it or not," Ben said, "it looks like maybe Sympto was a little *too good* at his job."

"Well, shoot. No vacuum splatting, then," she said.

A huge sigh came over REX's comm system and he said, "Can we go now, please?"

CHAPTER ELEVEN

THEY BOOSTED into a high orbit around Dekorrah'Bha. Its marble blue horizons turned a brilliant red as the Wi'ahr sunset greeted them. The moon Chiat came into view. Chiat had once suffered an ancient galactic cataclysm that sent chunks of it off into their own orbits around the planet giving Dekorrah'Bha hundreds of tiny satellites. Her night skies were littered with brightly twinkling objects, bigger than stars, smaller than moons.

They also served as places of commerce where tiny outposts conducted their own private business. Norg's was on one of the outermost asteroid-moons—outer landing. It was very secluded, very private. Perfect for a guy like Norg.

"Hailing Norg's Parts Depot," Tawny said. They waited. Nothing came back at first. "Hailing Norg's Parts De—"

The long, slow drawl of Norg's voice cut her off, "Is that who I think it is?" His face holoformed into existence, eyes blinking and searching around. He had a tortoise's beaked skull that always frowned. His bulging yellow eyes blinked from lower eyelids and would have looked severe had they not beamed at them from behind a pair of comically large goggles. The pale yellow spots of his face had all begun to run together with age. They didn't know how old Norg was, but assumed he was somewhere between five and six hundred years. He said in the typically elongated words of his race, "I believe it is who I think it is. Benjar and Tawny? Well, I'll be a Molosian unkie's muncle!"

Another greeting from Norg. It made them both laugh. Ben waved and said, "Hello, Norg."

"Don't you hello me," he snapped back waving a tri-fingered hand at them. "The time for that has long past. You should have relayed ahead. I am ill-prepared for guests of your stature."

"You know that's not necessary."

"Well, it's at your peril. You know my price for business," he warned.

Ben and Tawny nodded mutually. Norg's price was clear. If they ever stopped by his lunar hut he'd give them anything from his yard they wanted. But it meant a visitation. No exceptions.

"Now listen, Norg," Ben said, "we're paying you for parts. We're talking good old yield, this time."

"Oh no you're damn well not!" he declared. "Has my humble abode become off limits? Have you joined the Imperium echelon or standardized me off your docket?"

Tawny said with a smile, "You know we would never do such a thing."

"Then pick what you will from the yard and get your edible humanoid hind ends down here, damn ya!"

No arguments.

They both said, "Yes, Norg."

. . .

THEY SCOOTED through a sector of rotating rock before coming up on Norg's outer landing. His home was a large, misshapen asteroid that housed his hermetic environment, a string of igloo-style quarters attached via a main tunnel. There was a collection of gravimetric towers that controlled the slowly swirling sea of space garbage encompassing the asteroid. Debris stretched for as far as the eye could see—wrecked landers, decaying cargo haulers, pieces of orbiter stations, and a sea of parts, pieces and chunks of stuff—all gracefully spinning around Norg's home. A dilapidating Confederation military vessel pirouetted slowly with its primary and secondary batteries missing. An Omicron passenger shuttle with its innards exposed to space orbited in a gentle end-over-end flip-about. It was sheer tonnage that had been picked clean by visitors to Norg's junkyard.

"There," Tawny said pointing forward.

"Yep—that's what we need."

Ben piloted REX carefully, weaving through the garbage and coming to a mammoth freighter, easily two thousand feet of iron and scraps. Its upper deck had been dismantled and carried off a plank at a time revealing the stacks of cargo carriers within.

"Perfect."

REX glided over the thing's massive hull, settled overhead and began towing the compartments up, locking them down between the mag-spires. There were enough cargo units to gather far more than a full compliment, but they would take only what they needed. Once done, they rotated the mag-spires to an overhead vertical position allowing REX to land on Norg's little asteroid home, and lowered to the surface with a gentle, sandy thud. The umbilicus extended from the nearside igloo, and they exited their ship.

The airlock hissed and rolled out of the way showing

Norg's entrance hub inside. Like his field of space junk, the place was littered with decades, perhaps centuries, of antiquities—machine parts and tidbits the old turtle-man had collected over time.

Norg approached on fat, short legs lending to a full carapace. A narrow, struggling cane supported his weight from one mighty, green hand, and that everpresent frown on his face gave him a discerningly unhappy look. But they knew better. For such an isolated old fart, Norg was as companionable a creature as they'd ever met. And he was always happy to see Tawny and Ben stop by.

"Well, it's been a chelonian year. Thought you two had forgot about me." He stopped and looked closely at Tawny. "Tawny my dear, dear, dearest love. Your beauty grows like muck slime."

Tawny accepted this as its intended compliment. Muck slime was Dekorrah'Bha's primary source of beauty, growing only in the rare mountainous regions. The gelatinous green ooze showed dull and murky during the daylight hours, but glowed a brilliant, lovely color at night. It grew slowly like everything else on Dekorrah'Bha, and more beautifully over time.

"Thank you, Norg," she said giving him an awkward hug. His body was hard, heavy and wide, nearly impossible to embrace.

He turned his old, slow body to Ben and said sourly, "And then there's you. You're still as ugly as a Molosian muggle-wump."

Ben chided, "And you're still as nasty as an old rim husk."

"And slow as a sig echo, I'm afraid. Come here, old friend." They shook hands, embraced. "Of all my clients, you two are my favorite."

"You tell that to all of them, don't you?"

"If I did, you'd never know."

"A man of many secrets," Ben said.

"Ha! I've lived a long time. Secrets tend to pile up. But I'll be dead soon enough, and with me all my secrets."

Ben gave him a curious look. He'd never heard Norg talk about death. Of course, the ancient old geezer could be close to death and still have eighty years left to go. Ben smirked, "A sad day for the system in deed."

"Not for me!" Norg said. "Come on in, you two." He turned and slowly led them through his greeting hut into the adjoining passage.

Ben eyed his old friend. The turtle-man's cane clicked and his feet thumped. He moved very slowly. But that was the nature of the Dekorrans. They were slow, long living creatures, with no need to hurry. Ben said, "You seem to be doing just fine."

"Oh, pah! I should have been dead these two hundred annuals. You're lucky I'm still around. But I accept your flattery. It's obvious though, you're here because you need something, don't you?"

Ben and Tawny shared a look. Ben said, "As we told the Cabal greeting party, we're just here to see an old friend."

Norg waved his cane and cried, "What a bunch of sploof! Nevertheless, you may enter, you clamorous bunch of star kickers. Sit down."

They strolled into his central living area. Parts and junk hung from the ceiling causing them to have to navigate through the room. Slanted shelves on the walls had meticulously placed bits of old machine parts. A stove toward the back housed a collection of steaming pots. The smell of hot spiced tea wafted heavily.

Norg found his spot and sat down with a groan. It was

an old, broad tree stump he'd brought up from his home planet, the one organic thing in his entire abode. He cupped his hands over the cane's nob. "So," he said, "I'm prepared for the good news. Do tell."

Ben and Tawny looked at each other questioningly. "What news?"

"Hatchlings!" Norg declared thumping his cane once. "You're obviously having hatchlings."

Tawny bugged her eyes at him and said, "Uh, no, Norg, no hatchlings."

Ben just laughed nervously trying to evade the topic.

Norg thudded his cane again angrily and said, "Stop wasting time, then! You don't have as much as I, you know. I'll never understand you short-cyclers. Always wasting time you don't have."

They both looked down absorbing his words.

Norg continued, "You have been busy though, haven't you?"

Ben looked at him. "Meaning what?"

"Ha!" Norg grunted. "Modesty. Another waste of time." He said, "The Orbinii heiress job. Well done."

Ben cringed. Their involvement in that case was supposed to have been left anonymous. But he didn't have to wonder how Norg had gotten ahold of it. The old Deko-rran had a way of syphoning information from the stars that the vast majority didn't have—a thousand secret ears, a few underground comm lines, whispers in the vacuum. Even the Solar Twin War couldn't keep secrets from Norg. He had secret access to it all.

"A job well done, you two. I'm sorry it ended as it did. You save their heiress ... now they want your heads on a pole. Doesn't seem right."

"No it doesn't, does it?" Tawny said bitterly.

"Stay away from the Orbinii. They're a lustful and eccentric bunch. They've forgotten the simpler things, the *actual* things. You would think war would fix them. But nope. If you want something from them you have to play their game... and always give them the advantage."

Ben said, "Speaking of the war, have you heard anything?"

"Oh, I've got my fingers where they fit," he said getting slowly to his feet. He turned to his stove and tested the heat of his percolating drink maker.

"What's the latest from the underground?" Ben asked.

"The latest is always old news anymore," he said now rummaging through a steel, overhead cupboard. "New names, same old situation. The Imperium takes the moon ridge of Velinor 10, so the Cabal takes the planet. The Imperium retakes Xyiang'Sut, so the Cabal strikes at Dito. One side declares a victory, the other denies it. Over and over."

He pulled three cups down, started pouring the steaming liquid into each.

Tawny said miserably, "It's been that way for so many centuries. It'll never end."

Norg paused to look up and said, "Ha!" He started pouring again. "A hundred billion souls, each with the technology to visit stars dozens of light years away, yet all trapped in a bubble of space barely a cubed light day in size, able to communicate with each other within minutes of transmission, most of us seeing each other hanging in our skies, and you think nothing's going to come to an end?" He carried Tawny her drink and handed it to her. "Oh, my dear, I'm very afraid you might be mistaken."

She cupped it in her hands feeling the refreshing warmth and asked, "You believe there's an end to it all?"

"I don't believe in beginnings and endings. I only believe in inevitabilities." In his slow, painstaking way, he handed Ben a steaming cup.

"What do you mean, Norg?" he asked.

The turtle-man took his own cup and sat heavily down on his stump with a satisfied look on his face. He sipped, savoring the liquid with a fat black tongue and said, "War is an organism. Like any organism, it must eat. Unfortunately, war has only one food source. Itself. So what does it eat? Well, it eats itself, of course. The more moons that are destroyed, the more planets that fall under siege, the healthier the war. War wants to consume. It wants to rage on and on. It ensures that we are all each other's enemies. It's the perfect formula. If everyone is an enemy, then we must do only one thing. We must fight. We must feed the organism." He sipped again and said, "That's why you two are my favorite clients, my favorite of all."

Ben and Tawny shared a look. She flashed Norg a curious grin and said, "Why is that?"

"To end a war you have to starve it. You two have done that." He took another sip, smacked his big, beaked jowls and looked up, surprised to see them giving him a silent look, both a bit mystified. He said, "You look shocked. It's true, though. It's what you represent to the organism. You two are dangerous. You know what you represent?"

Tawny flushed. She would have reached for her husband's hand if he hadn't been sitting across the hovel. She said, "Love?"

Norg nearly spilled his tea with a hearty, "Ha!" He looked at them both. "Pathetic. No one knows what love is, not really. You vaguely mention the word love and watch how people look at you, watch their reactions. They either look blank, or they act like they know what you're talking about—*oh, yes, love, of course, a beautiful thing, the most beautiful of all*—Ha! They haven't got the slightest clue what you're talking about. How could they? Love occurs to each of us in our own weird ways. Love sees only what it wants and cuts everything else out, makes everything expendable." He said with a giggle, "Love is arse-poo!" and sipped. "No—you two do not represent love. You represent something far greater; the one thing everyone needs and no one wants."

"What?" Ben said almost desperately.

"Character!" and—*WHOCK*—he thrust his cane into the floor making his point. "That's right. Character. It's hard and humble. It requires humility. Character is patient and strong. It pauses from time to time so it can think. It considers more than its own point of view. It's not blind like love. Character goes beyond itself. It learns about the things it does not want to know."

He turned around in a long, slow motion and reached up to tap his cane against the one tiny porthole window in his hovel. "Look out there. What do you see?"

Tawny adjusted to see out the window. There was nothing but Norg's field of junk. She guessed, "Space garbage?"

Norg gave her his version of a dissatisfied grimace, his long mouth arching even more dramatically at its ends. "No. Look beyond my little abode, love. Look out there, further than your eyes. What do you see?"

She pulled back, sat back down. She didn't have to see beyond Norg's junkyard to know what he was referring to. The war, of course. She said, "I see people yelling."

Ben added, "Leaders."

"I see people fighting."

"Armadas."

Norg nodded his big head. "Yes, and they all speak about the things they love, don't they? Love, love, love. But character—no one ever speaks about character. No one ever charges into the fold howling—*for character!* They're too busy trying not to understand the other. They've bent themselves on destroying the other side. And do you know why?"

Ben set his teacup down, folded his hands together. "They do it for power."

Again, Norg blurted a big, "Ha! If only that were so. At least it would be an honest war. No. They destroy each other because it's simpler than understanding them. They kill so they won't have to learn. They even die just to avoid a conversation." He chuckled pathetically and got to his feet carrying his cup back to the stove. "Looking the other in the eye is far too much to ask. And all that's left for them is doctrine—the doctrine of nations, the doctrine of gods." He poured again and turned to face them.

"And that brings me to the two of you. A Wi'ahr assassin..." he lifted his cane and tapped Tawny on the shoulder, "and an Ae'ahm warrior..." now he tapped Ben and continued, "... putting down their arms and coming together. Tisk tisk. How can such a thing be?" He sat back down. "You two have broken the bonds of war, broken the shackles of ideology. You've starved the organism, you see?" He swished a thick wrist at them. "You can speak to me of love all you want, and perhaps that is what you feel for each other. But how do you feel about yourselves? Hehe—oh, I know the truth. It's written all over you, both of you. You feel responsible. You're aware of consequence. That's character. Period." He punctuated his point with a big, fat finger. "It has outweighed the hatred you were taught to possess for each other. It's even outweighed the love you were taught to have for yourself. Nation. World. System.

Even god. All wonderful things, but they belong at home. You step out your door with them and they become perfectly good reasons to kill. But no, not for Benjar and Tawny, eh? You've adopted character. And through your character, you've shown that peace among people is possible. You've shown that the war machine can be put to rest, once and for all. You've even shown that love can exist between foes."

He took a big, weary breath and said, "But you must be warned. In a galaxy so determined to destroy its other half, it will view the two of you as its greatest enemy. You present a model of peace and preservation. You protect one another, even in spite of who you are and where you come from—in spite of your own ideals. You are the solution in a machine that wants to be broken. Character. It's a despicable thing to worlds at war. And because of that, this galaxy will try to rip you two apart from each other. It will tear you down and destroy what you have built up. That's its mission. Remember, the organism must eat. And it's a very hungry organism. Don't let it." He leaned dramatically forward and said, "Do. Not. Let. It."

CHAPTER TWELVE

Outer Commerce Routes
Planet Hydras
Non-partisan space region

IT WAS VERY cold in this region of space. Both suns shown distantly no larger than grape-sized discs pulsing with light—Ae'ahm flickering a hot white to the starboard, Wi'ahr showing a bloody red to the port. Independents operated out here always under the watchful eye of a patrolling Cabal battle group, or an Imperium gun runner sliding through. They usually took what they wanted without payment, simply allowing them to continue operating.

Hydras was one of the more resourced planets. It was completely lifeless having an atmosphere comprised almost entirely of methane and hydrogen. She was a proud, white gas giant tinted a deep blue toward its center as methane populated her lower skies giving it a dizzying sense of depth. Huge tankers collected entire lakes of hydrogen from the upper atmosphere, transporting it to their orbiting fusion centers and splicing the gas with oxygen. At the end of a complicated filtration process, the crews turned the natural skies of Hydras into enormous tankers full of clean, drinkable water. It was irony that tagged such a lifeless mass as the 'life-giver.'

As they neared, the planet took up the entire viewport. It was so large it seemed they would go tumbling down into it, and yet tiny in the distance they could see one of the process centers hovering over the atmosphere. It was a massive steel latticework with multi-levels and operation quarters lending to a series of pressure engines. A central drive chain spit out whole mega tons of new water in great big tanks—each one big enough to pressure pump water into their dozen cargo haulers.

"Hailing," Tawny said. "*Filtration Station River*, this is the private cargo freighter REX on approach."

"REX, we're receiving. What's your business?" a voice returned.

"We have a purchase slot for a hundred thousand units of H_2O, appointment one-zero-one-one-two."

"Commercial or private?"

"Private."

"Okay, yeah, gotcha. Come to oh-ten planet side, dock up at seventeen for filling. We'll have the invoice transmitted upon receipt of payment."

"Copy," she said and input the money transmit.

A few seconds later they heard, "Received. You may proceed."

Ben huffed. "What, no surprises?"

"Yeah, that's kind of a surprise itself," she said. "Okay, *River*. Seventeen it is."

REX slid up under the superstructure as outbound vessels, their steel bellies full of new water, moved overhead. He came to the planet side where the view of Hydras was unobstructed, performed a graceful about face and lifted toward pump station seventeen. They connected. A service drone under *Station River's* command began working diligently to move from one cargo hauler to the next, attaching a tremendous feed hose to the couplers and pumping water into the haulers. The process would take an hour, maybe less. It gave Ben and Tawny some downtime. While she disappeared into the main hold, Ben found himself looking down at Hydras. A sensation of relief took him. This was not like staring woefully into Speculus, the mirror planet. This was wholly different. In fact, Hydras was full of energy as great billowing bands of cloud churned and boiled giving the planet a moving, breathing quality.

Life giver.

Before long, one final thump let them know the last cargo unit had been filled with water, the coupler disconnected and the drone's work completed. A voice said, "REX at seventeen. You're full, clear to disembark."

Ben replied, "Thanks *River*," as Tawny rejoined him in the cockpit.

"Happy flying."

"Yep. See you again."

They scooted out from the traffic, beyond superorbit and out into open space. Hydras began falling away.

"REX," Ben said. "Plot laid in?"

REX's mechanical mind analyzed their drive plot, said, "Yeah, Cap. Next stop, Mortus."

"Okay. We're set and met and the systems are go. Let's burn."

BOOM—gone.

CHAPTER THIRTEEN

Outer Commerce Routes
Planet Tantalus
Moon Mortus
Non-partisan space region

THEY CAME in like a blink from the ether, halting over the moon. Ben and Tawny stared down at it as they settled into orbit. Tantalus sat below the moon with its rapid rotation visible as gray, black and white bands of toxic atmosphere moved across its face in a slow rhythm. There were no other space vehicles here, no cargo runners, no tourists with roaming eyes, no military vessels.

It was a lonely moon, fairly large by lunar standards at four thousand kilometers in diameter lending itself to one full gravity. Mortus was surrounded in mystery. There was no primary source of life on Mortus, yet the moon radiated methane from deep pools of organic waste that had spent millions of years seeping up from its core. Some thought

Mortus had once been a living organism that died and was slowly decaying. Others figured it had colonies of microbial life growing in its deep subterranean caverns that ultimately released methane as they decomposed. Nevertheless, as Ben and Tawny looked down at the moon, they could see the millions of hair-thin, deep blue veins of methane that consumed the planet's upper atmosphere like ivy. The in-between spaces were gray and black surface rock crafting a mountainous lunar body, broken by endless canyons, plateaus and high peaks, all suffused in a lower atmosphere consisting almost completely of helium. It was breathable at the surface, but not for long. They'd have to wear bio-suits.

"Okay," Ben said, "let's get them on the horn."

"Hailing," Tawny said. "Mining operation *Zephrim Colony,* this is private cargo freighter REX on approach, over."

After a moment a 3-D head grew over their holopad wearing a bulbous headset over disheveled hair. A pair of workman's goggles were slung down under the chin and the guy looked around at them with a grin. This was definitely an ore miner roughneck. He said, "Hey guys, welcome to Mortus. This is *Zephrim Colony.* Are you the aqua runners?"

"That's us," Tawny said.

"Great, we've been waiting. How you guys doing?"

They looked at each other. Tawny said, "Happy to be here. What are our instructions?"

"I'm feeding the drop off zone coordinates to you now. Come around to quadrant four, far side hemisphere. It's our usual drop-off and pick-up zone."

"Okay, *Zephrim Colony,* hold."

Ben entered the coordinates. A projected 3-D map of Mortus formed over the holopad breaking the moon's surface down topographically. It auto-zoomed into the proper coordinates showing a sector several square miles large. Overlaid with the surface detail was a twinkling, real-life rendering of methane bands. The *Zephrim* crew had chosen a large, flat lunar plain surrounded by a mountainous region for the drop-off area where the methane had released its hold on the moon lending to a vacuous sky.

"We got it," Tawny informed. "ETA, one hour."

"That's perfect," the guy said. "We'll send out our welcoming crew. Looking forward to meeting you."

"Affirmative, out," she said. The head holo-zipped away. She gave Ben a look that oozed with skepticism.

"What?" he said.

"They seemed awfully happy to see us."

"They're rough-neckers stuck way out here in the middle of cosmic nowhere, sweetie. Of course they're happy to see us."

"No," she said. "They acted like we were a Molta-Danoran bikini squad. They were *too* happy."

Ben inhaled big showing he was ready to accept her doubt, and said, "Okay, what's on your mind?"

"I just don't buy it," she said.

"You think something's up?"

She shook her head. "I mean, why would I think that? But still..."

"I tell you what," Ben said, "let's study their drop-off coordinates. Maybe it'll tell us something."

She nodded, agreed.

"REX," Ben said, "move the map image to the passenger hold."

"Boss is right, you know," REX said. "Rough-neckers—they always cuss and spit and scratch themselves. Most of them have missing teeth and bad breath with bad hair and bad manners. They all stink like some kind of—"

"What's your point, REX?"

"That guy seemed awfully sweet, Cap."

"Just send the map, please."

They moved down the main corridor into the passenger hold where REX emitted the moon surface image over the main holotable. It glimmered and pulsed. Every detail showed with vivid clarity.

The drop-off zone was a large moon plain miles across, all hardpan and flat rock. Any atmospheric methane that might have been present had been removed, probably by automated vortex creators. The plain was surrounded on all sides by jagged, mountainous peaks, some a thousand feet tall, where the methane had collected in and through its crags, valleys and low spots. Deep mountain shafts pierced the tortured landscape in perfectly vertical wells, like planetary veins plunging through the mountain peaks all the way to the planet's core. They were similar to volcanic shafts which Mortus had used for eons to breath its deep methane product out into the sky.

A scrolling window showed specs on the moon's composition and makeup. Ben read it, intrigued. "There are water pools in the mountains. Hydrogen and oxygen. Almost drinkable. Full gravity."

"Where's *Zephrim Colony?*" Tawny said.

"Zoom out twenty percent."

The map pulled out opening more of the moon's surface area. There was a facility highlighted. It was tucked away in the mountains to the northeast.

"Rotate ten degrees, zoom back in," Ben said.

The map rolled over, zoomed in. "Here," he said, pointing to an operation complex built into a steep mountainside—a series of terraced operation huts connected by passage corridors, all weaved in and out of jagged rock formations.

A mountain pass snaked through ridges and valleys, opening into the flat drop-off zone. "This passage is how they shuttle equipment to and from their station."

"Look at all the methane," Tawny said. "Why would they place a miners outpost smack dab in the middle of a methane cloud? That's just asking for trouble."

"The whole moon is a methane cloud. They gotta go where the nickel ore is. I'm sure their safety protocols are as long as my arm."

"Or maybe..." she started to say.

"Or maybe what?"

"Maybe they're not mining nickel at all."

Ben laughed. "Tawny, come on. You're not being paranoid, are you?"

"Well, what do we know about these people?" she asked.

"We know they sent a contract through the Guild service. We know Sympto vetted them."

"And how well does Sympto vet his customers, especially if there's money involved?"

"Tawny, we've dealt with outliers before. This situation isn't unique."

She bit her lip dripping with doubt. Borderline concern. "I don't like it."

Ben rubbed his face. He was the tactician, the one that spent his career pouring over combat coordinates, studying maps, improvising enemy troop movements. She was the combat specialist. She knew weaponry, how to fight, the proper way to break a bone. Maybe that gave her a sixth sense about such things. He capitulated and said, "Do you want to treat this like a hostile situation?"

"I think we should," she said.

"She's right, Cap," REX chimed in.

He looked up, annoyance showing, and said, "Thank you, REX." To Tawny, "Okay, given the nature of the terrain, I say we go with drop-off protocol number two. I'll be front and center, you set up shop at long range."

She nodded, pursing her lips in thought and leaning toward the map. "This looks good, here." She pointed to a mountain face off to the west. It was a rock ledge at three hundred feet elevation, open to the lunar flat but collared by high mountain walls behind and to the sides—a perfect cubbyhole for a long range sniper scout to set up.

Ben said, "Okay—you leave ahead of time. Take the drop pod, set up. I leave REX in orbit, take the mag-mule, land in the center of the drop-off zone and wait for company. Stay on our covert channel for comm."

"Yeah, that sounds smart," she quipped.

"Still say it's overkill. All they want is water."

"Blah blah blah," she said.

He chuckled, leaned in and kissed her. "Okay, let's go."

TAWNY GEARED UP. Her-bio suit was a United Confederation Corps-X body-forming bio sustainment vacuum combat suit, tight to the skin constructed from a vacuum weave—very light weight, very flexible—with a rigid upper body harness, breathing apparatus, maglev-motion boots and seal joints.

She opted against applying the Titan-Y1 dura-armor blast-protectant, pierce-proof, battle-mech exoskeleton. The armored suit was too bulky with its alloy plated body pieces, and though it had been known to save her life against direct projectile and light laser blast impacts on countless occasions during her time in the war, she preferred the more streamlined effect of leaving it aboard REX.

Her swivel frame for the M-209 strapped on at the waste with its arms collapsed, tucking the body-length cannon closely to her side and ready to unleash in a split second, its power charger on her upper back. Her slick, visored helmet coupled onto her breastplate with a hermetic hiss. She checked her optical overlay system—sniper cannon targeting, visual map feeds from REX's upload/download systems and bio-suit readouts, all painted into her visor micro optics web. Everything was operating perfectly.

The drop ship was next. She fed the map and its coordinates into its REX-sub-A.I.-mind, which was hot-spliced wirelessly into REX-prime's control function, and received an *all readouts* signal. The light was green. She gave Ben a look through her visor, which showed all but those deep, gold-brown eyes of hers and said, "See you after, baby."

He nodded touching her visor as if laying a hand on her face and said in a tender, demanding way, "You be safe, you hear me?"

She huffed, giving him a ridiculous smirk, and said, "Such a man. Watch your fingers." The airlock slid shut. His heart sank, as it did every time feeling Tawny's drop pod undock from REX's underbelly and whisk off toward the moon. With that, Tawny was on her way quick as a bullet, ripped, equipped and ready to blow some stuff up. Ben shook his head. Bi-gods, he hoped it wouldn't come to that.

He went to the cockpit. The countdown had wound down to fifteen minutes. Likewise, the rendezvous was coming up through the viewport. REX had dropped to very low orbit making the mountaintops seem nearly touchable. Up ahead, the endless ocean of rocky jags and sharp, unlivable peaks broke suddenly away and the open plains of the moon spread out before him. From orbit, it looked massive. He could only imagine how endless those gray, drab flatlands were from surface level. It didn't matter. If there was trouble, Tawny's M-209 had plenty of range. And she was a deadeye hot shot.

"Okay, REX, prep the mag-mule. I'm taking her down."

"Okay, Cap."

Outside the ship, the mag-spires rotated on their turnstile to the straight-up position with the mag-mule's tiny bubble cockpit tucked between, putting the REX fuselage at the bottom of a tower of cargo units. Ben crawled through the starboard mag-spire's newly repaired control hub and up into the flight control. Pulling himself into the pilot's chair and gripping the dual directional levers, he said, "Okay, REX, all systems go. Disconnecting."

A jet of release gas huffed out and the entire mag spire attachment separated. It scooted away until it was clear of the main fuselage and cargo bay, and Ben lowered it down toward the moon.

"Good luck, dummy," REX said.

"Okay, stupid," he responded drifting down and down until REX was a dot falling away in the distance.

From inside his bubble, Ben looked up. His space bubble showed only the tonnage of the cargo units right overhead, while below, the moon came up. He glided over the towering mountaintops and toward the moon plain, dropping in altitude.

He flipped his bio-suit comm control to their private frequency and said, "You in position, hot shot?"

"Copy," her voice came back. "I'm four clicks westerly. I see you."

"Perfect. I'm coming in for a landing."

TAWNY STOOD at her mountain ledge surveying the drop-zone. The mountain ranges standing as tall as the sky around her shadowed her hideout in a deep blue. Below her was a sheer three hundred foot drop off showing a rocky, jagged terrain that leveled out into the expansive flatlands, a distinctive gray, almost white. The distant mountains far to the east broke up the horizon pasted against the backdrop of space.

This was where she belonged; at altitude, everything distant, yet within a moment's reach of her M-209. She was tiny in this space, but her vision was far and wide. The whole moon was hers on a whim.

She watched the pin straight wake of Ben's mag-mule as it churned the thin atmosphere, falling in from outer space. It lowered to the surface leaving an immense ground-born cloud as it settled. He was four clicks away making the huge mag-spires look tiny as they stood perfectly vertical. But he was clear as day.

She reached behind and thumbed on the optical feed to her weapon. The digital overlay illuminated inside her visor. It showed distances, planetary curvature, atmospheric motion—a host of calculations that would automate upon her data input. The zoom capacity was a circular reticle that she could highlight with an eye command, and a window would appear to the lower portion showing her target. Currently, she had Ben exposed. She watched him slide out of the mag-mule's command bubble and step outside.

A secondary overlay integrated itself with the targeting suite that showed potential activity in the surrounding area. Bringing it up, she saw highlighted blips several clicks beyond his position worming their way through the far mountain range. They were too far to get a full read on—no way to know exactly how many there were—but they were definitely moon vehicles of some type. Somebody was approaching.

Here they came.

This was where her theory would be proven wrong, hopefully. Or right. Were they lonely rough-necking ore miners looking forward to an aqua drop, or was this something else? She tightened her lips as they began fanning out over the lunar flat way to the east.

It was time.

She checked her plasma cannon charge. One hundred percent. Perfect. Unfolding the tri-pod at the end of its long, steel barrel, she lowered down into the prone position, her weapon jutting out over the edge of the mountain face. Her targeting paradigm narrowed in on the incoming, searching for succinct bull's eyes. They would need to come a little closer before she could make a solid read. It would only be minutes. She pasted her targeting painter on them and waited.

"Okay, boys..." she muttered, "this is where the fun begin..."

Something zipped toward her very fast, whistling through the sky. She heard it before she saw it. It was small, quick. It made her gasp.

A bullet?

She made a tiny noise as something clicked onto the exterior of her visor. She pulled focus on it, expecting anything. It was round, the size of a coin. Then she heard chuckling. It was low, menacing, and she knew immediately...

It was an audio coin.

And she knew that chuckle.

A voice dripping with malice said, "Hello, Tawny."

She breathed out long and angry, and muttered, "Rogan." She looked around with her eyes. There was no telling where he was. His audio coin had probably flown for miles searching her out. And now here she was, hearing his ugly voice.

"Yeah, baby," he said. "If I were you, I wouldn't move. Not even a finger."

She knew immediately, she was in someone's sights. There was a sniper out there scoping her right now. She'd been beaten at her own game. Everything just changed in a real bad way. It made her heart sink, made her fume with anger. She said through clenched teeth, "Well, that's too bad, because I got your finger right here."

More chuckling filtered through. "Oooh, baby. I like it when you talk dirty."

BEN STEPPED AWAY from the mag-mule with its two hundred foot spires standing directly vertical like a tower reaching for the low skies above. The cargo containers, each carrying twenty thousand gallons of water, were tucked in between, held in place by the super-magnetic conductors of the spires. He looked out across the plains. The mountains shimmered distantly.

At first, he couldn't see their approach but his opticals began tracking them several minutes before they appeared. Eventually, he saw their rover lights like mirages against a deep black wall of rock. They grew toward him distantly, very slowly at first. He watched them using the naked eye. After a minute, one rover became two. Two rovers became three.

Three rovers became four.

It made him squint.

This was one big greeting party.

And then there was something else. Not a rover. It was big.

"What the heck is that?" he whispered.

There was sudden recognition. He'd seen this before. A stitch of concern crawled up his back.

A lunar tank.

He took an instinctive step back toward the mule and said, "Uh, Tawny, you reading this?"

She didn't respond.

He tapped his visor, said, "Tawny, you copy?"

She still didn't respond. His nerves spiked, made him nervous.

Now they were close enough to see clearly. The rovers fanned out. There were eight of them. The tank was front and center, the whole convoy stirring up a cloud that stretched across the horizon. They kept coming, not slowing down.

This was no greeting party. His hands went down to his weapons, one to each hip. The vehicles reached him skidding to a stop in a half circle, flanking him to the right, to the left. The tank rumbled up on four axels, big tires, armored, hulking body. A spinner turret jutted toward him. A gunner was perched at the top gleaming at him through a red helmet and black visor.

Ben's blood chilled under his bio-suit. The insignia on the tank's forward armor became clear. He recognized it.

A square.

Three dots.

Non-linear.

The Hominus IV job. The Heiress Orona captors.

He knew these narse-holes.

He slid his twin laser blasters from their holsters and held them low at his hips, prepared for a confrontation.

One of the rovers moved forward. It had an open design like a moon jeep with a driver up front, a gunner at back manning a twin barrel cannon. It rolled to a stop twenty feet from Ben's position and the passenger stood up in his seat.

Ben's shoulders slumped. He recognized this guy, too. He wore a bounty hunter's light-armor over a bio-suit, a green/black helmet with opaque visor. Yep, another narse-hole.

Ben growled as the guy hopped down and strutted toward him in slow, swollen strides, over-confident and gloating, loosely holding a laser blaster in his hand. He flipped an audio patch-in coin and it zipped across the space thudding against Ben's mask. He heard, "Well, well, well. Looky who we have here."

Ben nodded his head, said, "Rogan."

"Ben..." he scoffed back.

Ben said, "Tawny, you reading this?"

"Oh, she's reading alright. She can see everything," Rogan said through a voice bloated with glee. "And guess what, buddy boy. We can see her, too. Oh yeah, loud and clear. We even cut her comm. She says anything, and zap! She makes a move, and zap!" Then, in a tiny notion made huge with its condescension, he said, "Oops."

Ben glanced across the entire entourage. The last time he'd seen Rogan, these two parties were shooting it out on an asteroid. How had it come to this? He said, "Rogan, what have you done?"

Rogan strutted toward him and said, "Don't look at me. You're the one said I should get a sniper. They're awesome, right? Well, shoot," he laughed, "I gotta tell ya, that was a good call. You got me there. I mean, yeah, that's some good advice."

Sniper. He had Tawny locked down. He yelled, "You Molosian leach!"

"Oh shut up, Ben!" he yelled back showing real animus. "This is your fault. You caused all this. Soon as you kidnapped their heiress you kick started the whole thing."

"I didn't kidnap the heiress. *They* kidnapped the heiress! I just took her back."

"You have no idea who these people are. You don't have the slightest clue, chump. But I do. Yeah—they told me all about what they're doing, what they have in store. And they're bigger than the Guild. They make the Guild look like a bunch of amateurs. Well," he thrust a thumb at himself and bawled out, "I want to be a part of it."

Ben shook his head pathetically and said, "Is that why you're here, to join with these criminals?"

"Yeah. And guess what. That's why you're here, too. Whether you like it or not."

"You're insane," Ben said.

Rogan made an insulted, snickery laugh.

Ben looked out at the far mountains to the west. "Tawny, what's your situation?"

"Yeah, go ahead, Tawny *girrrl!*" Rogan heckled. "Say something. Get zapped. Oh, they're on their way right now. They know where she is. Yeah—" he said very proudly, "I told them."

"What do they want with us?" Ben demanded.

"I don't know. Maybe your head on the wall. Or on a

pole. Or on a plate. I don't know," Rogan said, still snickering.

Ben eyeballed the tank. It sat quietly as if observing the exchange. He gazed across the rovers. Their crews sat quietly, watching. Ben shook his head, and said, "No. If they wanted us dead, we'd be dead. They want us alive. Why?"

Rogan focused on him and said, "Who cares? This time ... I get what's mine."

TAWNY still lay prone at the edge of her mountain ledge overhearing the entire exchange. One word was all it would take, they told her. And she'd get sniped by some phantom operator hiding somewhere out there in the near-facing mountain range. She had no reason to believe Rogan. He was a backwater hillbilly. He wouldn't kill Tawny. He didn't have the sack.

But his new sniper was an X-factor. For all Tawny knew it was an android following orders as pragmatically as any machine would. And she was in its crosshairs right now. She couldn't take any chances.

But it's what her husband had said that gave her reason to act. His mind simply worked in a deeply tactical way. It was a beautiful mind, a strategist's mind. He was communicating with her. He wasn't talking to them. He was talking to her, directly. He'd said, "... they want us alive."

They weren't going to kill her. Not unless they absolutely had to. It made her grin, come up with a plan.

Taking a breath and holding it, she folded to her knees, got to her feet, stood upright folding her gun to its neutral position against her flank. Nothing happened. No plasma grenade. No laser bolt. No gas projectile. She was still alive.

What next?

She said into her bio-suit's user comm, "What's our altitude?"

"To the planet's surface, two hundred and seventy three feet."

It was an extreme drop, but it would give her jump engine time to fire off before she hit bottom. She said, "What's my jump capacity?"

"Uh, what're you thinking, Tawny?"

"Jump capacity."

"The jump feature's charged. You're at one hundred percent, easy."

She closed her eyes, swallowed hard. Her throat was dry. She said, "Prepare for a boost."

"Tawny, no," the bio-suit rebuked. "Not in gravity. It'll kill you."

Tawny knew her bio-suit was right. Boosting in a gravity environment freefall had been known to snap spines, blow out pelvises, crack vertebrae, pop ball joints out of their sockets—like hips—or hyperextend knees, splinter bone, whatever. The feature was designed strictly for outer space. But she had to try. Benji's hands were tied. Breaking this situation was up to her. She whispered, "No it won't."

Without warning she stepped off the ledge and out into an ocean of negative space. In the moment before full freefall, she knew whoever was tracking her, wherever they were, would fire. She put her eyes up searching fast and hard. Sure enough...

Here it came.

A condensed light beam fired laser-straight from the dark mountain across a deep ravine, up higher than her perch, on the next peak over. She couldn't see the shooter, just a powerful kill shot demarking his location. Then her fall began.

Tawny screamed as she dropped below the ledge and the shot came down erupting into a huge shower of rock. The blast impact knocked her further out showering rubble all around her, pelting her with rocky debris. She cried out feeling the hands of gravity pull her down faster, faster, and for one tiny second, her vengeful mind hoped the narse-hole up their shooting a sniper round at her would follow her down with their own jumpsuit, meet her at the mountain base below. Oh, she'd love that—meet this jackwad at the bottom, then bend him inside out, bounce his head off the rock like a gaga ball.

But no way. No one would be that stupid. Not even with a jumpsuit. It was a good way to crush a humanoid body into a wad of dough. But for her, it was too late. This was going to hurt like Wi'ahr hell!

She locked out her joints like mad. Locked her knees, locked her hips, her back, arms, neck, even her fingers, preparing for a mid-air jump boost.

"Bio-suit!" she screamed. "Jump boost, now-now-now!"

The igniter mechanism wound up in its harmonic tone as the mountain face slid away. The ground approached— that pitch black mass of rock and stone rising up to meet her at the speed of terminal velocity.

"Now!" she screeched in full panic.

BOOM—her jets ignited only feet over the surface. The power of the kick passed through her body with a jolt like a cannon shot. Everything rattled—muscle, bone, flesh, even her eyeballs. It stopped her plummet, broke her fall, suspended her perfectly still in mid air, but left her body limp under the pressure.

Then her fall resumed.

She hit the rocky mountain base as though she'd fallen from a dozen feet, bounced off one rock formation, crashed into another and settled on the dusty lunar floor. The jumpsuit tactic was the only way to minimize the impact of a three hundred foot fall. But the price had been dearly paid as her body absorbed the full energy of a sudden, jolting boost. As she settled on the ground and everything came to a stop, she closed her eyes wondering if the darkness consuming her was sleep, or death.

BEN'S VISOR reflected the sniper beam. It was a thousand feet of light blinking through the dark sky at four clicks distance. But it was enough to snap his attention and spin him around. He looked way across the flatland and toward that mountain ledge. The explosion it caused was tiny—just a blink of fire sending rock out from the mountain at multiple angles. But he knew better. Up close, that blast was an enormous show of power pulverizing a whole section of frozen, solid rock. His eyes went wide, he gasped out loud. That was his wife.

"*Tawneee!*" he screamed. On pure impulse, he unholstered his twin blasters, spun back around and began blasting away. Strike points blossomed across the nearest rover, then the one next to it, sending bio-suited figures scurrying for cover. Even Rogan bit some sand.

Return fire from the spinner cannon atop that tank struck at Ben in a long jagged beam of light sending him diving to the lunar ground and rolling over. It was a lightning bolt, slicing overhead. It struck distantly lifting a curtain of topsoil. His suit's power blinked and ebbed just from the laser bolt's proximity. That was an electromagnetic zap.

He was outnumbered. Now he was outgunned. Time to go.

He scurried to his feet and ran for the mag-mule shouting into his headset, "Mule, fire up!" Its power indicators lit up, the bubble turret dropping open. And then...

Something pounded him in the back, picked him up and threw him powerfully across the land. His bio-suit coughed sparks and went dead. They hit him square, and they were going to hit his mag-mule next.

He landed hard and screamed one last command before his comm function died, "Starboard booster, fire. Fire now!"

And everything went heavy as he settled to the sand.

The mag-mule's starboard booster boomed against the ground. Lunar sand exploded underneath and the entire two hundred feet of mag-spire tilted—a tower swinging over, losing its balance and breaking into a fall.

If he couldn't destroy these bucketheads, he'd let his machine do it.

They all looked up as the shadow of the tumbling tower consumed them, eyes huge. Those standing in its path scattered like bugs, a few of them firing up rover engines, kicking gear transmissions into reverse. The tank lurched backward, started swinging around, but that shadow grew and grew, faster and faster.

Ben growled through a tight, desperate face and threw himself into a roll.

Rogan stumbled to his feet tripping and bumbling out of its way.

There was a final scream as the few doomed members of the party realized they were doomed, and the entire thing came down with a moon shattering crash, sheer tonnage banging down. The tank crushed like a beer can sending pieces of it squirting out. Water exploded like a geyser and came raining down. The cloud that lifted was thick and immediate. It offered Ben some cover. He pulled himself up to his knees shaking his head. Without power, his breather was down, his visuals were dead. Nothing worked.

Bio-suit lights pierced the dust screen. His enemy came near, and they were angry. He was pinned down, couldn't move. As they surrounded him all guns drawn and pointing at him, he chuckled at the calamity he'd caused. One of them moved front and center pointing a rifle at him, and fired without hesitation. The bolt spread across his body in a web-work of electricity arching his back and locking his joints stiff. Through it all, he couldn't stop thinking to himself through a sea of infuriated regret—*Tawny was right. Bi-gods, she was right. These aren't roughneckers. These are bad guys...*

And then he blacked out.

CHAPTER FOURTEEN

BEN JOLTED AWAKE AND SCREAMED, "TAWNY!"
His outburst pounded off metal walls and everything went
silent. He lay supine on a tabletop inclined at a forty-five
degree angle, wrists and ankles cuffed hard. He shook his
head, looked around. This was a large stainless steel room, a
hundred feet long with a full viewport toward the front. His
table was only one in a long row. They each had cuff
devices. He laid his head down miserably. This was a prisoner bay. Worse, it was an interrogation room. A torture
room.

The stun shot he'd taken earlier left his body wracked
and sore. He wondered how much earlier that had been.
How long had he been here?

A voice chuckled from the shadowed corner. It said in a
quirky, irritating, singsong fashion, "Tawn-ee. Oh Tawn-ee.
Ta-ta-Tawny, bay-bee..." Rogan stepped forward.

Ben thrust his head up, looked hard. Rogan had traded
his bio-suit for his civilian attire—a stolen utility jacket
studded with ammo pockets, space pants and boots. He still
had his characteristic lamb chop beard with greasy hair

hanging in his face, most of it swept back behind his ears. He had a patch over one eye. That was new. Ben assumed he'd met one too many people at some out-of-the-way guilder's pub. Good way to lose an eye, apparently. Ben sneered, *"Rogan."*

Rogan's voice dripped with narcissistic glee, "Uh-huh, yep, that's me." He laughed.

Ben squinted his eyes, cocked his head over giving him an angry look. He demanded, "Where's Tawny?"

"Wouldn't you like to know?"

Ben flexed against his restraints, hard. *"Where is she?"*

He pranced around the table making a condescending face, lips puckered, eyes wide. *"Woo-hoo-hoo.* Look at you, all yelling and hollering and screaming and such. Look, I don't know where she is. I'm not the one to talk to about all that. I mean, I like the girl. She's a banging little piece, ain't she? Hotter than Ae'ahm and Wi'ahr on a colliding course. I hope she's okay, I truly, truly do. In the mean time, you and me get to go around and around the ransom hole."

"What?" Ben said, ludicrously.

"You don't know what a ransom hole is?"

"No."

Rogan stopped on his feet, gave him a dumb look. "It's like a ransom."

"Rogan, what're you talking about?"

"C'mon, man! It's a ransom. It's like a ransom, you know?"

"Maybe it would help if you gave me some context."

Rogan said, "Huh?"

Ben groaned, rolled his eyes and said, "You said ransom hole. What does any of this have to do with a ransom, or a hole?"

"You're trying to confuse me."

"I'm not trying to confuse you, Rogan. You're just confused."

Rogan smacked the table making a metal *whop!* And yelled, "Stop trying to confuse me!"

Ben yelled back, "I'm *going* to try to *kill* you."

"Hey!" Rogan rebuked hotly, started pacing around again, "you're the one that left me down there fighting it out with these wart scums." He started reliving the moment comically as if watching Ben blast off in his jumpsuit—"*Oh yeah—look, there goes Ben in his jumpsuit with my cargo, my yield. And what about me? How about some help, eh? But no! Instead it was, bye bye, Rogan. Have a nice fight, Rogan. Thanks a lot—BEN!*" He looked back at Ben, suddenly grinning, "But surprise, surprise. Things didn't turn out the way you thought they did, did they?"

Ben laid his head back and said with a sigh, "I don't know, Rogan. I hadn't really given it much thought."

"Oh, very funny. Well let me tell you. I guess you could say me and the Faction came to a happy sort of ending. But only sort of. Look what they did to me." He flipped up the eye patch and pointed at the wound wildly. It was just a hole with a flappy eyelid covering it. "You think this tickled? Hells no. This hurt like a Molosian wasp, only worser. Now I'm going to have to grow me a new eyeball, soon as I get the yield. *A new eyeball!*" he exploded flipping the patch back down. "You think I like doing business with these mac wads?"

"What did you call them?"

"Mac wads."

"No. Before that."

"Wart scums?"

"No, not that, you moron." He thought a second. "You said—Faction?"

"Oh yeah—Faction. That's what they call themselves."

"Are they your new friends now?"

"Well, they like me a lot more than they like you, pal. And thank Ae'ahm for that. I'd be dead otherwise. Yeah—maybe I don't have any friends, but damn, your enemies are some surefire flip tards."

Ben scrunched his face absorbing his testimony and said, "Flip tard?"

"Yeah!" Rogan yelled. "As in flip. Tard. Got it?" He paced again, "You'll see. They're going to do this to you too, only worser. And I'm going to sit and watch, knowing every groan and every scream is because of me. Oh, I'm going to embellish in it."

"Relish," he corrected.

"What?"

"Relish in it! Gods..."

"Oh, you're so smart," Rogan chided him. "The real smart one. Look who's got the brains. Yeah, only look who's also strapped to a dimpler table. Man, they're going to dimple you all over. Dimple dimple dimple." He poked him with a finger. Ben found it particularly infuriating.

A thought snapped Ben back. He said, *"Your* doing."

"Huh?"

"You said this was *your* doing."

"Yeah," Rogan said, "and it is."

"No it's not," Ben argued. "You didn't do this. You didn't bring me here. This was a job, a contract. I was contracted to deliver water. The only other person who knew I was coming was ..." his expression melted, eyes went wide. He said, "Sympto."

"Sympto!" Rogan cried, flapping his lips. "Sympto didn't have anything to do with this."

"How did you know I was going to be here, then?" Ben asked.

"Huh?"

"How. Did you know. I. Was going. To be here?"

"Oh, uh—I just figured it out."

"You figured it out."

"Yeah, simple as that."

"You can't even figure out insults, Rogan."

"Yeah, I can."

"No, you really can't, actually."

"Yeah, I can!" he barked, feelings hurt.

"Did Sympto put you up to this?"

"No."

"He had to have."

"Well, he didn't. And I'm a fine insulter."

Ben took a breath, laid his head back. He didn't have time for Rogan's antics. He angled in his head, thought about the situation, seeing it from all sides. He said, "These people—this Faction—didn't kill you back on Hominus Four. They captured you, didn't they?"

Rogan crooked his lips, looked at him, kept quiet.

Ben continued, "They tortured you. Took an eyeball. You cut a deal with them, didn't you? You agreed to bring me to them. I'm the one they wanted, not you. You got Sympto to help." He shot his gaze back and forth as if following his thought. "*He* didn't contract *you*. *You* contracted *him*." He speared an angry look into Rogan. "You set a trap."

Rogan laughed in fury, loud and over-played, "*Hahaha! Like a Molta-Danoran whore in a virgin house.*"

Ben clicked his teeth. He corrected, "Virgin in a Molta-Danoran whorehouse, you idiot! And your context is still all wrong."

Rogan looked at him confused. "Huh?"

Ben said, "What was the payoff?"

"What payoff?"

"What. Did you offer. Sympto?"

"Oh, ha—that's the whole best part. Do you really want to know?"

"Color me curious," Ben said.

"Do what?"

"*Yeah! I want to know!* Gods, how do you even breathe?"

"A million yield bits split in half. Fifty, fifty. His half, my half."

Ben blinked, thought. A million yield bits? He looked up angry, and said, "The Heiress Orona bounty."

"That's right," Rogan said like a big reveal and started dancing around. "I'm going to get what's mine. I'm going to get what's mine."

Ben dropped his head back to the table, infuriated, insulted, beaten.

Rogan continued, "That's right, old buddy. And guess what you're going to do. You're going to give them to me. All of them. All million of them."

"You must be out of your mind."

"Oh no. In fact, look whose got the brains now. See, I told you I'm not stupid, at least not more stupider than you. Now, where is it?" he roared unsheathing a portable computer upload/download device from his jacket pocket and began scanning it over Ben's hand. "Where's your finance mol? Is it in your hand?" The device showed nothing. Rogan sneered and jumped over the table straddling Ben painfully. "Your arm, is it in your arm?" He scanned the device across his arm.

"Get off me!" Ben growled.

"Where is it!" He showed Ben a fist. "If you don't show me, they'll use a worm bug on you. You think Molosian wasps hurt?"

The door whisked open and a man entered wearing a long, official-looking greatcoat that flowed down to his ankles slimming his narrow frame and giving him a patient, sinister appeal. Rogan dismounted the table looking suddenly nervous at the man's presence. The man said in a toneless voice, "Leave."

Rogan swallowed and said, "I was just—"

The man said, "Get," and swiveled his head to Rogan, "out."

Rogan looked down and ushered himself quickly from the room.

Ben followed his new company with his eyes. The man went to the full viewport and stared out, his hands placed behind his back. It was a magnificent view of the lunar night at altitude. This room was at the top of a mountain set into the mountainside on enormous pylons. Far below was the expansive lunar flatland reaching out toward the horizon.

Several long seconds passed in silence before the man took a breath and said in his smooth even tone, cold and icy, "Benjar Dash. Born eight-one-two-sixty-two of the universal calendar, Solar Twin War era, thirty-seven years old, universal. Citizen number nine-nine-three-six-nine-eight-four-six-four, Golothan system, Golot Major, sector seven-one-seven. Member of the Golothan service, Red Guard, assigned to regiment three, battalion eight, five-oh-first high altitude assault squad, Imperium. Later assigned to combat intel, then promoted to full combat officer and collapse-wing drop pilot."

He turned away from the night moon vista and paced

around Ben's captor table, continuing his long, droning diatribe, "You were a combatant in the Primus sub-Wars. Survivor of fourteen drop missions, in all. Impressive. It was a dirty action. Some say the most reckless campaign of the Solar Twin Wars, second only to the Denubis campaign." He stopped, turned, started pacing again. "It did offer you some commendation though, didn't it? The Red Guard valor award and the leadership nomination clover. You're a hero."

Ben turned his head away insulted by the word.

The man stopped, took a sigh and continued, "Of course then it was off to the lunar front of Sarcon, one of the Imperium's more futile attempts to strike at a Cabal home-front. Big mistake, yes? It cost you a leg and ended your time at Sarcon. But then, only then, you were given the most fateful assignment of your military tenure."

He turned his long, angular face toward Ben with the lunar shadows cutting across the deep crags of his features and said with a wild grin, "Malum ... A true military disaster. For both sides, I might add. A logistical nightmare. An exercise in tactical futility. A waste of resources—and the bloodiest universal year of any lunar campaign yet launched. Entire regiments scattered, leaders abandoned their men, entire columns registered as casualties of war, everyone driven mad with the *Dark* found there." He said, lowly, "Monoxide toxins seeping up from surface pores in the rock. Unexpected, that." He continued, "Compatriots turning on each other, brothers in arms at each other's throats, the enemy always a whisper away." He kneeled down by the head of Ben's table and ran his fingers through Ben's hair, whispering the words, "Pure insanity." Ben jerked away.

The man stood back up and said, "And that is where the hero lost far more than a leg, isn't it? In fact, he was never seen again, not by an Imperium outpost, an Imperium officer, not so much as an Imperium trooper. The hero lost his thirst for war, as it appeared." He stood back at the far viewport just looking out, but turned his head slightly, revealing the angular slopes of his face and asked very curiously, "Or is it possible that you found a greater cause to fight for amidst the *Dark* of Malum?"

Ben oozed disdain. He knew what this man with the flatulent words was referring to, and it wasn't his experiences on Malum. He'd never wanted to hear that word again. Malum. The only good thing that ever came from his time on that place of human carnage was...

"Tawny Dash," the man said, low and mean. "No previous surname, only *Group Zero,* as was given to all her kind—" he looked back and said, "orphans of war." He turned his head back to the moon vista and continued, "No known age. Homeworld Raylon. Brought up a ward of the state where she was found to have an early aptitude for certain combat skills, namely..." he made a noise, almost like a chuckle, and said, "all of them, but particularly hand-to-hand. Served in the Underworld's Raylon Destroyer Apiary, stratum four-four-one, sector nine-zero-subset-B. The assassin group. Raylons make excellent assassins. An interesting story, that one."

He pulled himself away from the window and began his pacing. "Her services were used to great effect on many fronts, namely the orbiter skirmishes of Digitus and Malitus; the Cabal victory at Tericron where her campaign repelled the Imperium's direct frontal assault on Omicron Prime, capitol world of the Cabal. Then came Gorba, Tremus, Jingut and a number of others—all before her time spent on the moon Juto of Dionesse." He kneeled down next to Ben, seemed to take a great deal of joy in his next words. "You're aware of her time at Juto. They tortured her, didn't they, made her do things she dare not relive." A long silence passed. The only sound was Ben's breath being drawn tight and angry through his nostrils. In. out.

The man stood suddenly as if to break the moment, and said, "Thank whatever god she chooses, rescue came shortly when the moon Juto was taken, at least for a short while, by an Underworld offensive, and the Cabal reclaimed their prisoners of war. But doubting her resolve, the Cabal sent her to her most fateful campaign just as the Imperium did you. Malum. Where, coincidentally, she was never seen nor heard from ever again either, lost by the Cabal. And now, here you both are. Curious, wouldn't you say?" He whispered to him, "You're both deserters."

Ben turned his head and sneered, "Where is she?"

The man went back to the window, looked out. "Somewhere out there. Captured. Fighting. Who knows? Perhaps, she's dead."

Ben jerked on his restraints, then settled. She wasn't dead. Ben believed that. He looked up. This man knew her past, somehow. He'd found her records scattered amongst the Cabal data nets, pieced together their relationship. Ben knew, even this man wasn't convinced she was dead. Ben assumed, "You're hunting her."

The man turned his head and looked at him with emotionless eyes. He said nothing, but the answer was clear. They *were* hunting her.

Ben grinned bitterly. "You'll never find her. She'll hide in places your men will never know to look. If there's a nook, she'll find it, a cranny, she'll use it. And shadows? Heh —shadows are a weapon to Tawny. And if that doesn't work, she'll hide in plain sight. It's what she does, pal. Let your men search. With any luck, she's already off planet. Oh, and one other thing. Tell your men not to pursue her. If they have her cornered, tell them to surrender. Cornering Tawny is the last thing they'll want to do. Trust me."

CHAPTER FIFTEEN

———————

TAWNY'S EYES opened and she came to consciousness swimming in a sea of agony. She was on her side, her back propped up on a rock. Everything hurt. She couldn't tell where her injuries were. It seemed she'd broken everything.

First, she checked her hands. Going to need her hands. She flexed the fingers of her right hand. Still worked. Then the left. They were okay.

Feet—could she feel her feet?

A broken back would spell certain doom.

Yes, she could feel them. The right, then the left. But somewhere between her foot and her brain was a pain so perfect it dizzied her. Left knee. It was a goner. As this registered, it made her wince in terrible pain. She'd blown it out. There were probably pieces of it scattered all over the inside of her bio-suit pant leg. She inspected. A large plug of floxa-foam had been secreted by her suit to plug the breach. It had also dampened the pain, but its effect was obviously wearing off.

She dug her right foot in and tried to sit up. More needles and pins of pain articulated throughout her body.

Something felt funny in her back. Bone was probably pressing into her spine.

Wonderful...

And for the first time, she realized how painful it was to pull breath. Every rib in her body was probably bruised, some of them cracked.

"Ugg," she groaned, her own voice bringing her fully back to reality. "This sucks..."

"Would you like a bio scan of your injuries and..."

"Shut up."

"Sorry," the suit said. "Congratulations are in order, though."

"Huh?"

"I've never heard of anybody surviving a fall of that distance using only a boost apparatus. Of course, no bio-suit has ever been successful in preserving its pilot from that kind of..."

"Please be quiet," she said between labored breaths.

"Of course. Would you like a systems check, at least?"

"I need deadener."

"I've had to patch three primary suit breaches. The floxa-foam is down to fifteen percent."

"Good, I'll take it," she wheezed. "My back."

The floxa-foam had a double use. Her bio-suit released it at the point of a breach to seal the hole, but also as a pain dampener. The bio-suit manufacturers deemed it logical that a suit breach also meant bodily injury at the point of puncture. They were generally right. Tawny felt the cool, lubricous foam secrete from its woven fibers and plume across her lower back, at the point of the most pain. Its deep numbing affect began working immediately. She figured her knee would have to wait. She had two knees. One back. She groaned in relief and muttered, "Okay, give me that systems check."

"Aside from the overall suit breaches, we also have a puncture in the two-oh-nine charge pack. You have what charge is left, then we're out."

She glanced over. The cannon lay next to her, undamaged, save the charge pack strapped to her back. It had probably cushioned her fall from some injury. She said, "How many shots do I have?"

"At full strength, one."

"Can we conserve?"

"Mmm—I can recalibrate with the gun itself through the suit interface. That might conserve power."

"Do it."

"What percent?"

"Twenty."

"Done." The idea was to decrease the payload of each shot to give her additional barrages.

"Oxygen?" she asked.

"We have only seventy-one minutes left at your current rate of consumption. Not bad. Not good. You have three reserve canisters, I notice. They were not punctured."

She felt for the small canisters of compressed O strapped to her thigh. Had one been punctured, the resulting explosion would have blown a leg off. She was lucky. Nevertheless, there they were.

With her back numbing, she was able to prop herself up against the rock and look around. She was in a lonely place, swallowed by the girth of the sheer stone face directly above, and the impassable terrain all around her. Getting out of this mess would be a trick. She wondered about her comm system. She needed to talk to REX-sub, have him come pick her up. She knew the suit's infrastructure was in workable condition. What about the electronics?

"Give me a full digital and electronic optical layover diagnostic."

"Systems are operable. That includes comm and weapon targeting. But the integration processor has been damaged. You'll have to use them one at a time."

She winced forcing herself into an upright position leaning all her weight onto her right foot. The integration processor was the least of her worries. If she had to lose a system, that would be a fine one to go.

"What about our visor connection with REX-prime. Is he still feeding?"

"No, but my hard drive memory can recall the map. Want to see?"

"Yeah, give me local," she said, still trying to choke down a body-full of pain. The visor emitted a map of the surrounding area. Rock formations showed in 3-D topographical display—a confusing mess of ovals, circles and wavy lines. She immediately gasped. There were red blip indicators. Over a dozen of them. People advancing, the closest were closing to within fifty meters.

"Uh oh," her suit said. "Are you seeing this?"

"Yeah," she said, alarmed.

"Who are they?"

"Narse-holes. Give me targeting overlay."

"No integration," her suit said.

"Wipe the map," Tawny said frantically. "Give me targeting!"

The gun swung into her grasp as her targeting optics zipped in. They were very close, a hundred feet. Hadn't seen her yet. Too many stone outcroppings. Too many shadowed hiding spots in the jags. But they knew she was there. And now she knew they were coming.

Sneering from the pain, she stepped around the nearest cleft in the rocky terrain and looked over. They spotted each other at the same time—three bio-suited figures, each with blipping suit lights, armed to the teeth. Her reticle circled in, gave her a tri-beep. She pulled the trigger. The gun in her hands spit a twenty percent fusillade. The plasma grenade streamed through the air and erupted against one of their chest. What would have been an explosion of molten stone at a hundred percent merely blew one of them off their feet, a huge flame-rimmed hole burned through him.

Her visor showed one of the approaching life forms blink out. Got one. There would be no multiple kills with one shot, but it was enough to halt the others on their feet, make them duck way down.

"We have to move," her bio-suit said. The words were like a nightmare in her ears.

Move? Easy for you to say!

She started picking her way around the base of the mountain, clawing with her hands, hopping on her foot, hissing and sneering at the pain of locomotion. Her targeting screen showed another target to the west, a few hundred feet. She peeked over the rock, desperate to see. It was a moon vehicle buzzing toward the mountain over the nearby flatland, coming directly toward her.

"Target," she said still fighting agony. The reticle honed in, the gun poised in her hand. "Firing."

Another plasma ball zoomed out, yellow, hot and bright as a tiny sun, skimming the planet surface with only one intention. The moon vehicle braked in a panic. Too late! The plasma ball struck the forward compartment, burned through the metal and sank into its engineering, all in the blink of an eye. The following explosion tumbled it over into a barrel roll, one guy flipping out one way, another flipping out the other, lunar sand being kicked into a cloud.

She leaned back, sank into a shadow.

"Tawny," her suit said, "I'm worried about your bio signs."

She shook her head. "Shut up and give me the map."

Her visor optics rotated her targeting display away, switched to the map layover of the general vicinity. "Zoom in," she said. The area expanded up illuminating terrain details. She stood on a surface cap of distinctive phytokarst-formed rock towers, most of them ending in tiny peaks of their own, others forming into stone flutes, all of them with ripper-capable razor-sharp edges. The field spanned across the entire foot of the mountain range and out into the flats by several acres. Passage was impossible. She needed to find another way.

There!

A tunnel.

The map showed these mountains were veritable networks of underground passages. Most of them were large enough to pass through. One opened up into the stone face several paces ahead. She could lose them in there, at least buy herself some time.

There was more motion coming from directly ahead. It was indistinct. She couldn't tell exactly who or what. But she had a feeling.

"Switch to targeting," she groaned leaning against the mountain, absorbing the agony. There was no time to hurt. Her screen displayed. They moved in threes. They looked to be on foot, picking their way slowly across the base of the mountain, headed toward her.

Take the shot, or don't take the shot? She wondered. *Preserve my final two or three pulses, or kill while I got the chance?*

"Screw it," she snarled and joined her targeting device with her weapon. "Firing!"

Another plasma ball lit up like a bubble of light streaking through the dark until it struck its target. An explosion blinked across the distance. They halted.

She tucked the cannon away and picked her way up the incline hissing painfully as her weight shifted from right...

... *Then screaming and trying not to faint...*

... as it shifted to the left.

She could feel tears hot and moist on her cheeks, feel the fatigue wracking her body. She pulled herself the final pace toward the tunnel and looked in. It was small, dark and long. Perfect. She reached in, pulled herself up, pivoted her body, clenched her teeth, squirmed forward, made it with a groan. Once she was inside, she went limp and laid there, heaving deep and hard, each breath like a kick to her ribs. Eventually she'd have to get out of this, get back to Benji.

She would have to get to REX-sub first.

She said, "Please tell me I can still comm with REX."

"Your communication system is operable. Lots of interference from the terrain. Might be difficult getting a signal out."

Hope. There was hope. If only.

She'd take it.

She turned over, looked ahead. The tunnel wound away to the right. Only darkness met her. "Map," she said, hauling herself a pace forward.

The map illuminated. She could see her position—a flickering blip broken by the surrounding rock. Her pursuers still approached, now alerted to her location. They were getting closer with each passing minute.

The map showed the tunnel jigging and winding through the mountain, joining with others, all creating a hive under the tonnage. "Scroll north," she said, pain clear in her words. The map scrolled north showing a main thoroughfare stabbing deeper and deeper through stone... straight to a mountain shaft. Oh, thank Wi'ahr. If she could get to that shaft she'd have open sky to get a signal through. She'd have to move. It was a hundred meters ahead.

She picked herself up, moving forward on her right knee, dragging that mangled left leg behind, one lurch at a time. Yet she scrambled, haste growing inside her. She wound around the bend in the tunnel having to squeeze through in some areas, others broadening in the tunnel making passage easier.

She sat down taking a breath, checked the map. They were still coming. Getting closer. A thought struck her. "What's the air composition?"

"Mostly methane. Maybe a few trace elements of ethane, heptane and..."

"Fine," she gasped. Methane. She'd take methane.

She reached down and palmed one of her oxygen cylinders from her hip. All she needed was a crag or a hole to hide it.

"Tawny," her bio-suit said.

"I know," she groaned and forced herself forward. Her good knee was beginning to throb with each motion. It sent fiery hot stitches of pain up her thigh, into her hip, yet it hardly dampened the agony of her other leg. The deadener was beginning to fade. Nerves were exposed to injury. Her brain kept telling her to faint. Her mind said—*no, bi-gods!*

She needed a place to conceal her canister. A gap, a

hole—anything! Frustration building, she had to wonder how a tunnel in such a jagged, tortuous landscape could be so even-textured. There were ripples and cracks throughout, but no gaps, no holes.

"We're about to have company, Tawny," her bio-suit said. She shot a look back, squinted her eyes. The curvature was way back in the tunnel. Then darkness.

And then there were lights. They were bio-suits getting closer.

"Power down," she whispered.

"Tawny..." her suit rebuked.

"Power down!"

Everything in her suit shut down. Her external operation lights blinked away. The automated breather unit feeding oxygen to her mask wound into silence, the tiny hum falling silent. She still had breathable air in her helmet, left in her feed tubes. It would be enough, she hoped. Her M-209 whirred down, went to sleep, its lights blinking off. She couldn't let them see her in the tunnel. Without her lights, if they looked ahead they'd see only darkness. Of course, so would she. But she had the head start. And she knew where she was going.

She looked forward again. The exit to the tunnel was visible ahead, but only barely. It was a nighttime-dim hole surrounded by the pitch-blackness of the tunnel. And it was still way up ahead. She could make it, if her body held out.

She reached forward and felt something that shot a ray of hope into her. A divot in the stone, deep enough to grab hold. She thrust her hand into it.

Yes!

It was elbow deep; deep enough for one of her oxygen canisters.

She slid it from its thigh harness and finger-felt for the

nozzle at its top. She twisted and felt the tiny rush of oxygen flow against her gloved hand. There were several cubic feet pressurized inside, enough to burn this whole tunnel. This place was a methane lung. Mix it with pure O and light it up—*kaboom.*

She looked back at her pursuers one more time. They were still a good distance behind, but yep—just as she suspected. They were coming. They knew she was in the tunnel. Perfect.

Must keep going...

Growling into her helmet she heaved herself forward. Her breath was coming deep and fast. She had to conserve her oxygen mix, make it last. She shook her head. This was a survival situation. Fight or flight. Forget conservation. This was reckless-time.

Thrusting herself forward on her one good leg and dragging the other behind, ignoring the sheer agony of each bump, each draw, each little motion, she came to the end of the tunnel. She looked back. They were still coming. It was hard to tell how many. They were single file, crawling toward her, still a hundred feet back. She hoped there was a dozen. A *hundred.* With what she had in store for them, the more the merrier.

She pulled her head out from the cave exit and inspected. Just as she thought. Her little tunnel opened into a mountain shaft—a huge, round cavern, like a well carved out by Wi'ahr himself, perfectly vertical, two hundred feet in circumference. Looking up, she could see a star-speckled night sky way overhead as the well opened up at the top of the mountain. That was her chance to get a signal out to REX-sub.

Then she looked down and sank back. The fall would be a hundred feet, easy, into a pool of shimmering hydrogen and oxygen. Liquid water. Methane gas escaped through the surface in bubbles giving it a boiling affect and filling the whole mountain with fart-smelling explosive gas.

She groaned. This was probably where she would die, in this cavernous, lonely, back-vac hellhole in space where no one knew her.

Oh well. Had to happen somewhere.

All she knew was that she was going to take some of these jackwads with her.

She looked back into the tunnel. They were still coming, only eighty feet behind her now, getting closer. Without injury, they'd made far better progress than she had. But now she was exposed.

Be patient, girl. Wait. Wait a few seconds longer.

The guy in front hesitated. He looked down, curious. She perked. That was it.

There!

That guy had just discovered the oxygen canister pumping fuel for her fire into the tunnel. He picked it up in his hand, was probably inspecting it thinking something like —*what is this, oxygen?*

She said, "Power up!"

What has that little Guilder wormdog got in store now?

Her suit lights blinked on. The M-209 hummed, its power indicator light booting up, iridescent green in a pitch-black tunnel. Their attention was caught. She could see them jerk, looking toward her suddenly.

Oh, holy bi-gods, she's going to...

"That's right, scumbags," she said, and pulled the trigger. "You're dead."

... blow us back to Wi'ahr!

The cannon kicked in her hands sending a lightning fast plasma ball, blindingly bright, straight back at them through the tunnel. A few superheated particles of flaming death met with a few stagnant particles of methane, which met with a few bouncy particles of oxygen, which became a tunnel full of combustible gas, and the chain reaction began with a...

BOOM!

A very big

BOOM!

The fireball blew toward her in a blinding, hot rage.

Tawny rolled backwards out of the tunnel and began her plummet toward the pool below. Gravity took her and down she went, falling, falling, falling.

Above her, the tunnel spit a rush of flame out into the cavern and, much to her surprise, everything turned to fire. The explosion never stopped expanding. It began engulfing the whole mountain shaft above her. Golden red fire rolled and boiled in huge plumes, one after the other, bloating toward her in her plummet, expanding closer and closer as she fell.

The boom shook her insides. It rocked her very guts.

Methane wasn't the only gas seeping up from the pool of water. Apparently, oxygen had too, turning the whole mountain into a sitting bomb, waiting eons for some arse-poo to come along and shoot off a fiery plasma ball from a sniper cannon. The following explosion threatened the very mountain itself.

Tumbling further down, picking up speed in her fall and staring up at the sun-like eruption she'd caused, she grinned and thought—*Wow. It's stunning. It's gorgeous. It's absolutely beauti...*

SPLASH!

The landing kicked the air out of her as she plunged into the pool. The fire above her rippled through the water's surface, licking the lake and withdrawing back up through the shaft. The entire fireball dissipated. Darkness enfolded her and the water seemed remarkably depthless. She sank down into a bottomless void unsure when it would stop, unsure if she wouldn't reach the lunar core.

"REX," she groaned fading in and out of consciousness, "can you see me?"

Nothing came back. No voice. No response. The fear of never being found struck her hard and cold.

"REX," she said.

A voice filtered through her mask's comm. It was broken, fighting for a signal. "I hear you, Boss. Oh dear, is that you blowing up a mountain?"

"Yes. Help."

Out in the eternal night, the drop ship's RX-111 sub-A.I.-personality blinked on as the control board fired up. Its scanners spotted her immediately. She was across a deep valley where a column of flame rose up and up into the sky igniting the planetary band of methane. The whole sector of atmosphere was crawling with fire. It looked alive, eating the sky in great vesicles of searing flame. It was brilliant.

No time to sit in awe. The drop ship boosted up from its mountain perch, nosed down and jetted off. In only seconds it reached the mountain shaft where the flames had usurped the entire area of atmo, and raced down into the well. It hovered over the pool of water and fired its underside tow cables powerfully. They splashed beneath the surface and began inspecting the murk for their pilot.

She'd sunk a hundred feet below the surface, maybe more. But she could see the blipping cable sensors come snaking toward her through the dark. She reached for them as they came. They connected to her bio-suit's mag couplers and she stopped sinking. She felt her direction reverse as they began reeling her back up.

As she broke back up through the surface limp as a doll, the drop ship was already ascending the shaft. Its belly doors folded open, pulled her inside and closed, laying her onto the floor. A rush of atmosphere enfolded her and the interior airlock thudded open.

The helmet unfolded and she breathed in the refreshing, cool, filtrated and re-processed air of her drop ship. Thank Wi'ahr.

She was home.

It was then that the pain of her busted body occurred to her. Everything hurt. Her back had been compressed. Knee ripped apart. Tendons stretched gossamer thin. Bone shattered. Ribs bruised. She couldn't stand, couldn't crawl. Couldn't hardly breathe.

"Awe gee, Boss, what went wrong?" REX-sub asked.

"Everything," she groaned through gritted teeth. "They got Benji. We have to go back."

"I don't think that would be very smart, Boss."

"REX!"

"I'm not armed. You can't even stand."

"They have Benji!" she croaked.

"We have time, Tawny. They want both of you. Going back now would be suicide ... for both of us."

He was right. She couldn't even pull herself to the pilot's seat. How was she going to argue? She had to cool her jets, think. "Okay—get us back to the ship."

"Uh, yeah that's another situation."

"What do you mean?"

REX-sub's recall sensor bleeped in rapid succession as it searched out REX-prime's location. It came up with nothing.

"He's out of range," REX-sub suggested. "But I know where he is."

Tawny made an irritated face. Something smelled like another betrayal. Not REX too. No bi-gods, not REX.

Pushed by anger, she clawed her way to the pilot's chair and hoisted herself into it, growling and fuming with agony. They were rocketing skyward, leaving the moon below. "Why did he break orbit?"

"Well," REX-sub said, "there was a problem."

"What?" she demanded.

"It looks like we may be running a blockade."

"What do you—" Her eyes expanded as the space-drop greeted them above. "Oh no..."

Those twittering objects way out there weren't stars. They were too big, too close. And they were in convoy column. Those were warships.

She squinted, studying them with the sudden, quick clarity of a warrior. She couldn't recognize them.

"Those aren't Cabal. Are they Imperium?"

"That's a fat negative, Boss."

"Who are they?"

"Whoever owns this moon."

They raced toward them watching them grow through the viewport. A thousand questions darted through her mind. What were their capabilities? What kind of armaments did they have? Could they be outrun? But only one question mattered. She cried, "Can we make it?"

"Without inner-warp chances are slim, and that's only if they *don't* have single-craft fighters," he said.

"Maximum speed, REX, maximum boost, maximum everything. We have to try."

"You got it, Boss. Hang on."

The accelerator control screen buzzed into life. It

showed thrust, booster control, fuel feed. Everything maxed out, little upload bars glowing red. They rocketed forward picking up speed, fast.

The blockade approached with the warships coming into clearer view—big, garishly designed cruisers, each tool-crafted in some private hangar, not stamped and assembled like the massive armada factories of the Solar Twin War. This was definitely from some outlier group.

An alarm sounded.

"Did they spot us?"

"Yeah," REX-sub gasped. "I was hoping to close our proximity first."

Defensive targeting screens buzzed.

"They're tracking," REX-sub said. "Uh... *They're firing!*"

A trail of laser blasts came at them from the distance. Tawny yelped, ducked in the seat. They streaked over the bow.

"I think it was a warning shot," REX-sub said.

"Don't stop. Don't slow down."

"Ohhh—this might hurt."

The ships zoomed up coming closer at speed, each vessel painted with a broad center stripe—some red, some green—denoting their vessel class. More buzzers sounded.

"We're being tracked. They got us locked."

Tawny held her breath. She needed her husband. This was his wheelhouse. He'd know what to do. Without him, there wouldn't be any spinning the monkey this time. She looked up. The squadron approached. The lead battle cruiser came into view. It was the biggest one. It had a blue stripe. Her eyes widened. An idea hit her straight from Benji's brain.

Tickle the snake, sweetheart!

She giggled lightly. She didn't mean to, but she did.

"That one, the big one!" she screamed pointing it out.

"Yeah?"

"Get in close. As close as you can."

"Closer?" REX-sub cried.

"Skim them. Skim the surface. It'll screw their tracking. Now, now!"

More laser blasts came at them. REX-sub bucked over, slid right up next to the mother ship. The blasts zipped by, exploded against the bigger vessel. Pieces of her outer decking blew into shards and flame. REX-sub could feel the heat.

"Oh, nice!" he yelled.

"Go over, go over!" Tawny barked.

REX-sub rolled up over the cruiser's upper deck, viewports and terraced cannonades zipping by, more blasts raining at them, more strikes exploding against the ship. It was blinding, made Tawny wince, turn her head. They were hitting their own lead vessel. Morons!

REX-sub slipped quickly away and back into open space leaving the blockade behind.

"Give it all you got, REX, go go!"

REX-sub emitted a snarl pushing his engines. An overload klaxon wailed out.

"We're gonna—"

"Forget it!" she cried. "Keep pushing!"

In seconds they had all but faded away.

"Are they pursuing?" she said.

"Doesn't look like it. I think they knocked out their own tracking systems—*Hahaha!*" he laughed. "Nice move, Boss. I bet the squadron commander's really irked off about that one."

Tawny exhaled feeling the agony of her body return,

and sank into the chair. "Well, don't slow down, REX. The further away ... we can get ... the better off ... we'll ..." Her eyes fluttered, rolled up into her head, closed. She went out like a light.

"Agreed," he said and continued beating a path for the stars.

CHAPTER SIXTEEN

THE MAN SHOWED PATIENCE, standing rigid at the window. He turned around to face Ben. As he did, out in that black, starlit distance, a tiny tower of flame went up from a mountain peak and began crawling in fingers across the far sky, silent and brilliant. Even horrifying. The man never saw, his attention attuned to his captor.

But Ben saw it. It drew his attention, made his eyes widen, made him grin. That was his wife out there. Bi-gods, she was giving them both hells. That girl would eat the whole moon before letting them get to her.

Yeah—that's my girl. Please, stay safe...

The man smiled, switching the previous mood. "You've mistaken my intentions, here. So, let me be clear. You are not my prisoner. You see, I once fought for the Imperium as you did, a nameless number sent into futility many times. But I have found a much greater mission here at this facility. We are the Faction. My name is Zelit, administrator of this station, and you, Benjar Dash, are my guest." He lifted his left hand showing a control bracelet with a single button, and pressed it. Ben's cuffs clicked open freeing him.

Ben looked at his hands with surprise etching tiny across his face. He sat up rubbing his wrists, bringing blood back into them. He said dryly, "Thanks for the hospitality. What about my wife?"

"She, too, is invited," the man said, "if she chooses."

Ben laughed at him. "You think she'll accept your invitation to this little dinner party?"

He said, "I hope she does."

"You should have just RSVP'd."

The faraway sky suffused momentarily in flame, blinked out as the cosmic background choked it. The man turned back around to face Ben, the viewport showing only a night sky now. "She'll come."

Ben gave him a pathetic look, said, "You're funny. You talk and talk like you know who she is, like you've studied her character, analyzed her personality. You don't have a clue, though, do you? You read some scattered bits of data and then send your men out there looking for a mark in the dark, searching for something they'll never find. Your men just walked into a storm, buddy."

"And what about you? Did you not walk into the same storm?" he returned coolly. "Yet, she *married* you."

"I didn't try to kill her."

"Oh no? A Golothan soldier and a Raylon assassin meeting on the bloodiest battlefield known to the Solar Twin Wars, and there was no walking into a storm?" He sniggered, "You underestimate your wife's judgment."

Ben returned the snigger. "The only underestimation going on here, is yours, bub."

"We will see. But to answer your question, yes. I want her to come to the dinner party."

Ben gave him a questioning look. "Why?"

"Because I value—we value—what you and your wife have."

"Don't tell me," Ben said. "Character?"

The man looked at him curiously. "Character is a funny thing. What some consider to be of great character, others might consider to be immoral."

Ben responded, "Depends on your standards, I guess."

The man studied him for a few seconds and said, "It's possible that you are the one that doesn't yet understand me. So, let me show you. Come."

Ben pondered his new company for a second before swinging his legs off the table and standing. He followed this man, Zelit, out into the passage. As they strolled, Zelit said, "This is our Mortus headquarter. As a faction, we're small in comparison, but growing."

A pace behind, Ben said, "Comparison to what?"

"The other factions."

"Other factions?" Ben eyed him. Surely he didn't mean—"The Imperium, the Cabal?"

"Precisely."

Ben laughed, said, "Small in comparison? Buddy, you're microscopic."

"It is the germ that kills, Benjar."

They turned a corner. Ben said, "Depends on the cure, but if you say so."

"We have outposts just like this one scattered throughout uncontended space. We function as a fully militarized body, autonomous, capable and with a mission."

"What mission?"

Zelit dripped with pomp and said, "Let me show you."

Uncontested Space.

Outer Commerce Routes.

Unmapped.

REX HAD BEEN EXPERIENCING the strangest feeling, one he was not entirely familiar with. His cognitive neural net had been asking questions he couldn't answer.

Where was Cap?

Where was Boss?

Why can't I communicate with them?

What if they met with danger?

What should I do?

In the end of all his digital swooning, he discovered he was worried. Actually worried.

And then his proximity sensors fired off. He scanned nearby space and discovered his sub-personality moving toward him. The drop pod approached. He sighed very much out loud.

It swam toward him through the greasy black and came about under the fuselage, both pieces of the net-mind coordinating perfectly, until the lower umbilicus connected. A swish of atmo made them one. The entire dialog in which all of REX's questions were answered occurred over a microsecond as their experiential data banks connected and their vessel logs shared.

It seemed the drop-off had gone wrong. There was an unforeseen event. Tawny suit-jumped off a mountain. Blew up a bunch of bad guys. Ended up at the bottom of a mountain shaft. Now, she was hurt. The indications were multiple injuries. REX would have to analyze her.

But how?

He wasn't a medical bot or ambulatory vessel. He didn't have so much as a med bay, surgical bots or physician tools, much less the necessary diagnostic machinery.

But he did have two auto-assist utility bots with crane arms down in the cargo bay, a bevvy of engineering tools and an assortment of civilian gear. Not to mention some general hospital drugs that Ben and Tawny kept in reserve, just in case.

REX intimated a thoughtful head scratch searching into his hypothetical scenario capacity.

Ah—a possible solution.

The dual utility bots powered up down in the cargo bay, both turning to the airlock, communicating through a series of blips and bleeps, and headed over. With their hover engines humming, they descended into the drop pod, went to the sleeping Tawny and, commanded to use their highest tactility setting for meticulous engineering work, they picked her up, one at the feet, the other at the shoulders hardly jostling her, and escorted her back up through the air lock, very carefully maintaining her position. There, they laid her across the flat bed of the All-Terrestrial-Vehicle, now doubling as an operation table, took her over-garments off very quickly, yet very gently, and left her to REX's devices.

He used his onboard security detection sensors to scan her body. It would only be a surface render, but using his vague understanding of bio-humanoid-infrastructure, he quickly spotted the broken knee, a deeply bruised lower back, the discoloration of her torso section and the multiple abrasions. From there, he commanded the crane bots to assemble a splint using some cargo netting and one of Ben's shirts as a dressing. They did so with meticulous proficiency.

Afterwards, they were given a series of commands, each of a medical nature that they went about performing as though they were assembling a bomb, and with one final command to inject her with a bio-stimulant, they slid away.

She gasped tremendously as her eyes fluttered open and she screamed, "Benji!" She shook her head, looked around. At first, she didn't recognize her surroundings, then she squinted, scanned the area left to right. The cargo bay. This was REX.

"Hey, Boss, how do you feel?" he asked.

"REX?" she said through a parched mouth, dry throat.

"Yep, it's me."

"How'd I get here?"

"I was able to rendezvous with the drop pod. I brought you here with my utility cranes."

"The cargo bay?" she said still coming fully back.

"Well, technically I guess. For now it's more like the medical bay."

She looked up at the invisible A.I. She only remembered bits and pieces before she passed out. There were spaceships. A full armada. "How did you get away?"

"Uh, well, it wasn't easy. When I spotted them moving in I had to make a decision. I just turned around and ran. Nothing I could do, Boss. Figured I'd be more good to you out here than scrapped."

That sea of agony still had her in its undertow. She laid her head back down. "You did the right thing. How long have I been out?"

"A few hours, ship time. I had to stimulate you. You looked like you would have slept another half a day or so."

She gazed across her body. She was in her cotton fatigue undergarments which consisted of thigh-length body shorts and a combat halter top. Her leg had a full splint constructed from cargo equipment—two flat-sided leverage rods, some tightly woven cargo netting, one of Ben's shirts.

She recognized this style of medical treatment from her time spent in combat. Back then, they'd sutured, closed or splinted injuries in the field any way they could. It made her grin, amused. She said, "A field dressing?"

"Does it look right? I had to look into Cap's med logs to find the right practice. I'm not much of a doctor."

"It looks real good."

"Heh—should have been an auto med-kit. Sister model, maybe. How's the pain?"

She groaned heavily. "All over."

"Really?" REX said disappointed. One of the utility cranes shuttered, ready to go back into corpsman mode. "Maybe I got the dosage wrong. It said fifty milligrams of Floxa-codone. I gave you eighty."

"No it's fine," she said, and the crane bot folded back into its sleep position.

She forced herself into a sitting position wincing in pain.

"You shouldn't get up," REX said, very doctorly.

"I have to."

"Boss, that leg won't hold you. The dressing will keep it stabilized, but you put weight on it and you'll drop like a Molosian dino dump."

"Well, I can't just lay here. We got problems, REX."

"What do you want to do?" he asked.

She looked around, thinking. REX was right. She couldn't put weight on this leg, couldn't walk or so much as stand on it. Her lips pursed. She needed something to lean on, something to support her weight. A thought occurred. She said, "My exo-suit. Get it."

BEN and his new host went through a set of double sliding

doors and entered an enormous space. It was octagonal in design with terraced rows, each housing busy workstations. Operators with headsets and overlay computers worked diligently at their posts. Compu-bots shuttled back and forth. The place was a show of organized chaos, an operation center.

The room's central periphery was an enormous window revealing a dual-sided radar dish sitting outside. It was massive, a hundred feet in diameter spinning at a slow revolution, constantly extrapolating an ocean of long distance data from the solar system.

"This is our command octagon," Zelit said. "Only very few have seen this."

"I'm so lucky," Ben said half blithely, half-impressed.

"From here, we've crafted a network of data collection second to none in the galaxy. We are integrated into every piece of political infrastructure from Omicron to Solaptra, from Golotha to Pendulos. Our eyes are everywhere, our ears are on the inside, dwelling within every hall, every chamber, every conceivable office of policy in the civilized front—all integrated into the very fabric of operation for both the Imperium as well as the Cabal."

"Sounds complicated," Ben said.

"It is, actually," Zelit said before leading him around the upper periphery of the command center. "We've spent a generation developing our network, a complete labyrinth of perfectly arranged personnel and alternative mech that funnels information here, to us. From these cubes we keep intimate track of every piece of legislation, every sanction, every maneuver made by each side—from the congressional cathedral of Golotha to the halls of the Omicron capitol. Departments of defense, military cabinets, councils of war—our influence reaches all of them."

He grinned pacing slowly, and said, "Yet ... we are secret."

Ben showed dry acknowledgment. "You work on the inside, from behind their back."

"In a matter of speaking. It's more a case of infiltration. We sit among their leaders, we move within their ranks. We *are* them, securing our ulterior objectives in silence and with covertness."

"A network of spies," Ben assumed.

Zelit put a finger up to make his next point. "They're far more than spies, Benjar. Through them, we report on or even coordinate the direction of every politic body."

"You conduct the war."

Zelit stopped, turned to him. "No, not the war. The ensuing peace."

Ben tilted his head a little surprised at the word *peace*. "Well, pardon me for saying so, but you guys don't seem like the most peaceful lot."

Zelit flashed him a knowing smile, turned and continued walking the perimeter. "We're not interested in each side vying for power against the other. We work to topple governments." He stopped again, turned, said, "From within. Our targets are culture, tradition, the normative underpinnings of each society. Our weapon is entrenchment, deception ..." he said with a gleeful snarl, "change."

Ben chuckled piecing this place together. "So the theory is, get each side to blow itself up, and they won't blow each other up."

"Put very simply, yes. It is, after all, more realistic than believing each side will simply put down their arms." He started walking again and said, "This is where we work each day to orchestrate the downfall of the Imperium, as well as the Underworld Cabal."

"Civil war. Civil uprising. Heh. That doesn't seem very peaceful to me."

"Peace will only be had through other means. A world at war is more likely to come to an amicable end than *worlds* at war, wouldn't you say?"

"Uh-huh," Ben said casting his gaze across the entire panorama, and then beyond, to the radar dish blipping and turning. "And how do you people pay for all this? It can't be cheap."

"I'll show you that, too," Zelit said and led him through another set of doors. The next room was very different, but equally as technological. It was a long room with enormous screens reading interplanetary stock reports. Financial sectors were broken down by graph and hologram charts. Industrial news reports blasted across the screens with real-time occurrence. Meanwhile, more operators sat at their high-tech workstations buzzing about.

Zelit leaned on the railing overlooking the entire operation floor and said, "The interplanetary banking system."

Ben scanned the place, fascinated. "The IBS, huh? How much of it do you touch?"

"Oh no, Benjar," Zelit laughed. "That is the wrong question."

"What's the right question?"

"The one in which you ask how much of it we *own?*"

"Oh boy," Ben said. "And?"

"We *are* the IBS."

Ben hid his sudden trepidation well. This place was bigger than he could have possibly imagined. Its slimy tentacles were endless, and the influence reaching across the solar system from this very room had been known to ruin entire planetary markets, leave industries in ruin. These people were scurrilous. This was pure evil. Glimpsing this place was a death sentence. Ben sighed, forcing himself to play along.

"You're the Currency Reserve," Ben said.

Zelit chuckled. "The Currency Reserve is a front, of course, to direct attention toward misnomer and lies, and away from us."

Without making eye contact but rather looking across the work floor, Ben said with a pragmatic tone, "But you *are* misnomer and lies."

"No," he said putting his hand on Ben's shoulder. He looked at him. "We are conspiracy."

Ben forced an uncomfortable grin and said, "Tell me about it. So, what does all this have to do with Tawny and me?"

TAWNY MOVED THROUGH THE VESSEL. She had REX disassemble her battle-tech exo-suit, taking its left leg apart and applying the alloy plating to her injured leg, electro-hydraulic mechanism and all. She also wore the right boot to balance her height along with the lower back support harness. The piecemeal tech suit whirred with each step, basically doing her walking for her while completely supporting her weight. It allowed full mobility, even heightened her physical capability.

She stepped toward the holotable in the passenger hold where REX had emitted an assortment of 3-D images he'd collected during his split-second run from the Mortus armada. The warships flickered in digital brilliance, their detail clear. They had rounded features with parapets, and operation quarters bulging sleek and long along their flanks. The upper decking was all radar dishes and turret housings. Tawny tightened her face looking at them. It was odd. They didn't have the angular, wedge design of Underworld craft or the garish, imposing look of the Imperium.

The lead craft did, however, bear the logo of their people detailed across its large, forward command structure—square, three dots. She pointed it out. "These marks—they're the same as before."

"Yeah," REX said.

"Back on Hominus Four."

"Yeah."

"This is the same party that kidnapped the Orbin heiress."

"That's what I figured, too. Seems logical enough."

She scanned her eyes from one warship holo-image to the next taking in their detail, wondering about them. She said, "So who are they?"

REX said, "I've been running reference probes on the data net ever since I left Mortus. I have a pretty good processor, Boss, but I can't find anything."

"Nothing at all?"

"Nope. Their marking is unregistered. I don't get any construction project on Mortus. There's no way to know what their affiliation is, or if they even have one."

Tawny shook her head, doubt dripping off her. "They have battle cruisers. I saw them. You saw them. How can they have battle cruisers and no one know they exist?"

"Mmm—I have a theory, but it's stupid," REX said. He sounded reticent.

"What is it?"

"It's so stupid, Boss, I'm kind of embarrassed to say."

"Just say it, REX," she demanded.

He groaned, "Okay. I'm assuming that wasn't an ore mining facility, right?"

"Yeah."

"It was probably something else."

"Okay."

"It was probably a headquarter of some kind, maybe an outpost or something."

She crossed her arms. "I'm following."

"They're way out here in uncontested space. This isn't even non-partisan. This is where people go to hide."

She nodded agreement. "Yeah."

"Only these aren't criminals and pirates and cutthroats, you know, like the Guild. They're very organized, very powerful. And they're big."

"So what are you thinking?"

"Okay, this is where it gets stupid. Geez, I'm so embarrassed."

She stamped her foot at the end of her patience, the battle-mech making an unintended echoic bang. "Just say it!"

"Okay, here goes." There was a pause as if REX were gathering his courage, and he spit out, "They're a conspiracy group!"

Tawny blinked, thinking. It actually made sense. She said, "Conspiracy group..."

"Like a secret society or something, like an underground party."

"Yeah, go on."

"Well, what if they've been with us forever, in fact they run large corporate or economic entities like the IBS or the Currency Reserve." His voice grew as he went on, "And what if we've known about them all along in, like, myth and lore and wives' tails—you know, the boogey man and Saint Dread and things like that." He grew louder, more feverish. "And, get this, what if their plan is to operate in secret for the purpose of creating corrupt, internalized power structures to topple governments internally. Maybe they have sleeper agents inside every planetary government, even right there at Orbin. And—here's the kicker—" Now he was out of control, barely clinging to rationality. "What if they're in league with the Mythic Ones from another star system who are using them as pawns for their ultimate goal of taking over the universe and stripping all known planets of their..."

"Okay, REX!" she cut him off. "I get it."

"See. Stupid. I told you," REX cried.

"No, it's a good theory. It's, uh—yeah, it's a good theory."

"So what do we do?" he said, settling down.

She leaned on the table with both hands staring daggers into the rotating, flickering images. "All I know is that they have my husband and I want him back. I left him down there."

"You didn't leave him, Boss. You didn't have any options."

Now she punched the table, said, "But he's down there all alone."

"And you would be too if you hadn't gotten the heck out of there. It was the right thing to do."

"Fine," she snapped. "But how do we get him back?"

"We'd have to get through their armada."

"Can we do it?"

"Odds aren't good, Boss," REX said this like delivering a terminal prognosis. "They nearly snagged me once already, and I wasn't even approaching. I was running like a scolded monkey."

"We have to try."

"It's risky."

"They're going to kill him!" she yelled.

"We don't know that."

"Yes, we do." Her words were angry, resolute. "I know these people. I know their type. They'll use him to get to me. As soon as Ben lets them know he won't give me up, they'll kill him—my husband."

REX didn't respond at first. He allowed the silence to settle between them, cool things off. He finally said in an even tone, "Okay, then, let's think. What do we need?"

She paced through the passenger hold cringing and fuming. She hated this. She needed a strategy. She needed her husband to help her free ... her husband. What would Benji do, how would Benji think?

Very basically. Very fundamentally.

She turned around and addressed the A.I., "We need an armada."

"Okay, great. How do we get one?"

She thought. They couldn't build one. They couldn't buy one. They couldn't steal one. But...

Her eyes widened. A thought. She said, "We enlist one."

"How?"

Who has an armada? Another thought. It was desperate, made her close her eyes and say, "The Cabal."

"What?" REX said.

"We go to the Cabal. Yeah—I turn myself in. I'm a war criminal. They arrest me, bring me before their local war consulate. We tell them about Mortus. We have them launch an attack."

REX paused, thinking. Then said, "That's a great idea, Tawny. In fact, that's so good it might be the *STUPIDEST thing I've ever heard!* And I thought I was bad..."

Her desperate anger flared like a gas torch. "Well, do you have any better ideas?"

"I'm just saying—you're a criminal, Boss. You said it yourself. They wouldn't bargain with you. They'd just incarcerate you. Can you say, hello mindwipe? *Oh, yay!*"

Something caught her by the brain stem. That word. *Bargain.* She repeated it. "Bargain. That's what we need. We need a bargaining chip, something to bring to the table. Something with leverage." She stood perfectly still for several seconds as something else caught her by the brain stem. Another thought. Something hopeful. Her face broke into a clever grin. Then she started chuckling. Then laughing. Laughing out loud.

Then REX offered a few huffs of curious laughter himself. He said, "What? What is it? Tawny!"

She said, "Bargaining chip! We've got the biggest bargaining chip in the system. Oh, REXY, baby, you're brilliant!"

"I am?" he said.

"Yes you are!"

"I am!"

Tawny bolted from the passenger hold, down the main corridor and into the cockpit. She said, "Set a new course, REX, top speed."

"Okay. Where we going?"

She swung down into the pilot's chair and declared, "We're going back to Orbin!"

REX suddenly groaned. The mood broke. It shattered. He grumbled, "Oh, shit."

"HEIRESS ORONA," Zelit said slipping a forkful of steak into his mouth. After leaving the command center he'd brought Ben to the leadership dining area. It had a nice atmosphere, plush for an out-of-the-way moon stuffed in the backwaters of uncontended space, with a full view of the facility across a lunar mountain valley—large windowed terraces jutting from rock face and built into the mountainside. Escalator passages zigzagged through the jagged formations. Zelit continued, "She was a very small part in a much greater plan." He grinned with contempt. "And you foiled it, Benjar."

"That was your attempt at conspiracy, huh?" Ben hadn't eaten much. His appetite was understandably gone. He was worried about his wife. Worried about himself. Admittedly, what food he did eat was delicious—bovine steak cuts from Molos with steamed sweet vegetables and an odd, thick but tasty carbohydrate that held its shape quite nicely.

Zelit said, "When one strikes from within they have to accept that their role may include the unsavory." For a gaunt character, he ate like a Molosian land slug, all mouth and throat.

"You mean like kidnapping certain royal members of certain royal families, things like that," Ben said matter-of-factly.

"In deed it does. But in all things there will be unforeseen contingencies. You and your wife were that contingency. Let's just say, you were brought to our attention."

"And now I'm here."

"Yes. As will be your wife, very soon."

Ben looked at him across the table. He glared a red-hot spear into him momentarily. He melted back into his seat. "Where does Rogan fit into all this?"

Zelit smiled sardonically and wiped the corners of his mouth, a sign he'd completed his meal. "Rogan—a tiny cog in a greater machine. We needed him to serve a purpose." He sipped from a glass of green wine.

"You used him."

"As he used you, yes."

"He still hasn't gotten what he wants, though."

Zelit cocked his head to the side, assumed, "The million yield."

"That's right."

"He'll be reimbursed. Or you will."

Ben nodded. That's right. They were the Interplanetary Banking System. The Monetary Reserve. Print the money. Spit it out. Make the payment.

"Would you prefer him to receive it or no?" Zelit asked.

"You can do what you want, but no, I would prefer him not to get my million yield."

"Then, he will be a problem."

"What're you going to do with him?"

"Perhaps he can be used as leverage, yet." He picked a last piece of food from his dish, plopped it in his mouth and pushed his dish aside. Leaning forward with his fingers locked, he gave Ben a serious look, and said, "Honestly, we haven't gotten what we want, either."

Oh boy, here it comes. "I'm afraid to ask," Ben said.

Zelit stared at him for a long time, an uncomfortably long time, and finally said, "Join us, Benjar."

Ben gave him a sympathetic look. An escape plan began screaming through his brain. Nothing yet.

Zelit continued, "You can play a much larger part in bringing about an end to the war than you ever thought possible. If you despise this war as I believe you do, this is your chance to help end it. Put a stop to it—you and Tawny, both."

And here it was, right in front of him. It was almost laughable. One contract. One war. One moral dilemma.

Ben nodded his head, hoping to look amicable. "So, this whole thing is a recruitment effort."

"Yes," Zelit said. "We have very particular standards in those we invite into the Faction. I'd like to think it says something about..." he looked up reading Ben, and said, "*our* character." A pause. He continued, "Compare, Benjar. As a Golothan youth, you yourself were drafted into the war. Your wife—she was raised for the single purpose of fighting. Never given an option. Never offered any real path or purpose. You were lambs to the wolves and nothing more."

Ben put his hand up stopping him politely and asked, "Why us?"

Zelit rolled his tongue against the inside of his cheek, sucked his teeth studying him. "We see in you and your wife precisely what we're looking for. You've already abandoned the war. What's even better, you joined forces. You represent both sides and yet you've found togetherness and unity. You share our mission. Plus, you're resourceful, capable. Who better to help us lead our people into a better future, one without death and misery?"

A decent sales pitch, Ben had to admit. But—no.

Ben said, "You mean by committing espionage, intrigue, kidnapping, conspiracy, that kind of thing."

"A means to an end."

Ben shook his head with a huge breath and got up from the table. He moved to the viewport and stared out. All he could think about was Tawny. Where was she? When would he see her again? How could he serve her now? He shook his head no, and said, "It breaks every rule we live by, every code we share." He turned back around. "It's sacrosanct."

"Would you rather have war?" Zelit asked, his words lined with the vaguest silhouette of anger.

"This war was never mine to end," Ben said. "It was

only mine to fight. My wife and I—we've chosen a different path."

Zelit cleared his throat, gathered his words. "The war will go on and on. Moons will disappear. Planets will turn to rubble. One day, our solar system will collapse. There will be nothing left."

"I've destroyed enough of it," Ben said trying not to sound defensive. He failed. "Not anymore."

Zelit got to his feet. "Benjar, you must reconsider." Now moving around the table. "This is your purpose. This is why you're here."

"No," he said quickly, cutting him off. "I was just here to deliver water."

"Then you must see with greater vision."

"Than delivering water to the thirsty?"

"Yes!"

Ben couldn't tell if the man was demanding or pleading. Maybe both.

Ben looked at him curiously and said, "You thought I'd come in here and you'd show me all this cool, sparkly stuff and I'd just go along with it, didn't you?"

"We're talking about putting an end to this war, Benjar."

Yep—now the guy was insulted.

"But you never will," Ben snapped back. "You know why? Because no one knows how this war even started. Was it them, was it us? Was it a thousand years ago, two thousand? Three? Does it even matter? No one cares! They don't fight for sides. They just fight to ... to avoid a conversation. It's ideology. There's no logic to it. You can't reason with it; you can't change it. It just goes on and on."

"Then someone must act. It must be our mission!"

"And to what end? When you've succeeded and both

sides are in shambles, squabbling for whatever's left over, what then?"

Zelit smacked the table hard—*WHOCK!* "There will be only us, and then we can orchestrate a new peace!"

The following silence was resounding. Ben let it cool the room. He said, "Ah—and there it is. It's all about control."

"It's about bringing peace!" Zelit roared.

Ben roared back, "Then stop! Just stop!"

Zelit heaved at him. He'd abandoned his composure completely, hunched over the table, one hand planted onto its surface, heaving like a hunchback. He finally whispered, "There is no stopping it. The machine is in motion. The future will come. It's too late. There is no turning back now."

Ben gave him a sad look, full of pity, full of hopelessness. "Then, you're just feeding the organism," he muttered.

Zelit stood taught, straightened his collar. He gave Ben a deep, hard, cold look, void of warmth, no understanding, no compassion. Pure pragmatism. "No more words, Benjar. Join us."

Or what, he wanted to ask. But he didn't have to. He already knew the answer. This wasn't a choice. This was no different than Golotha drafting him into the war, or Raylon forcing his wife to fight. It was all the same. This place was just another battlefield waiting to happen. He meant—*join us, or die.*

Ben shook his head almost imperceptibly, and said, "No."

Zelit closed his eyes, took a huge breath, and said, "Ben."

He repeated, this time with definitive certainty, "No."

CHAPTER SEVENTEEN

REX ZIPPED in from inner-warp like the blink of an eye—*VWAP!*

Orbin was still a hundred thousand miles distant, yet it was big and citrine with its deep blond glow. Tawny looked on nervously. She was here to arbitrate a deal with the Orbin king. She needed their war machine. She needed it badly. But cutting deals and bargaining with hostile party members was not her forte—unless it included beating folk into pulp. This was Benji's arena. It made her nervous.

They'd been detected. The Orbinii knew her vessel well even without the great mag-spires, and they'd obviously entered it into their criminal mainframe as suspect. Once their planetary defense systems spotted an RX-111 entering their space, they perked up. Security cruisers slid toward them.

"Here they come," REX bemoaned.

A hail alert flashed. She took a breath, put them on. The Orbinii head that looked at them was unfriendly.

Tawny cleared her throat and said, "This is the privateer freighter REX on approach."

"You have been detected by the Orbin planetary security vessel *Ordan-o'ant*. You will come to all stop and prepare to be towed."

"Cutting engines," she said and killed the drive systems. The *Ordan* emerged getting bigger and bigger until it swallowed the entire viewport. They felt the internal grav systems adjust once they fell under its tractor beam. They began sliding back toward the planet.

They were tugged back to the *Orbiter 1* space frame that pulsed with life. Personnel craft moved around, lights twittering. Everything parted as the mammoth *Ordan* pulled overhead and a reticulating umbilical reached up to greet them. It thumped against REX's undercarriage.

"We're going to have visitors," he said.

"Here we go." Tawny got up and moved toward the rear lift with her battle-mech parts thumping heavily along the main passage.

REX said, "Hey, Boss?"

She stopped, turned. "Yeah?"

"Do me a favor when you're down there."

"What?"

"Think like Cap."

She gave him a grunt and went down to the cargo bay. When the airlock slid open the security force that looked in at her were serious and armed. She put her hands forward together at the wrists and said, "You got your man."

CUFFED, Tawny was led gruffly through the station and into the processing wing with two tall Orbin security officers shoving her along from behind. Her battle-mech kept pace better than the rest of her body. She didn't like enemy combatants putting their hands on her, pushing her around.

She'd broken plenty of arms in the past, but she had to think like Cap. Think like Benji. He was the one with the patience. She was the one with the fuse.

They brought her to the front processing desk where a low ranking administrations officer watched them enter. At first sight of her Raylon red hair, he made a disgruntled face. "Is this the criminal?"

The lead security guard said, "Yes, sir. She is the one."

A flat-headed, pentagonal floor bot to the left skittered its displeasure and scooted back. Tawny frowned at it and said to the admin officer, "I'm here to talk to the king."

He scrunched his face. "What king?"

"The king, the king. The Orbin king. *Your* king," Tawny insisted.

He eyed her with skepticism, his thoughts clear on his face—*who does this little Raylon witch think she is?*

And then his cheeks puffed out attempting to withhold laughter, but failed, and he went into a hilarious guffaw. The others followed suit, each Orbin laughing uproariously —*Hahaha! Hehehe! Hohoho!*

She eyed them bitterly until they cooled. She said, "I'm a prisoner of the royal court."

The admin officer wiped the remnants of laughter off his face and said, "You are a prisoner of whatever we say you are."

"Then let me talk to the general. He'll want to see me."

"What general?"

She clicked her lips impatiently and said, "The general, you know, the general! What's-his-name. The king's guy."

He flinched, said, "Ona'Oona?"

"Yeah, that one."

This time, the laughter was immediate, painful, gut-busting. All of them laughed holding their bellies, slapping each other on the back. Even the bot vibrated and shimmied with the electro-giggles.

Feeling the blood in her veins begin to simmer, she told herself—*don't do it. Think like Benji. What would Benji do? He'd look over his shoulder at me. Yeah—and then I'd do this:*

She spun around, mech-knee up, and kicked the nearest guard across the room. He smashed into the wall. Before the others could react, she went up into the air and came down on top of the floor bot with a crushing mech-boot that splattered its cogs across the floor. The other guards snapped to, each of them poised.

At least she was thinking like Benji. It was almost like he was in the room.

With her cuffed hands up in a defensive posture she sneered, "It's important."

The admin officer looked at her wide-eyed. He wasn't laughing anymore. "Why should we trust a Raylon scum like you?"

She looked at him preposterously and said, "Because I'm a Raylon scum, dummy!" She relaxed, everyone taking a breath. "Look, there are plans to destroy your planet. I mean, destroy it. Blow it up. As in no more Orbin. The general needs to know."

The officer glanced over at his yeoman and nodded. The guy put pen to paper, ready. The officer said, "What message would you have us send?"

Tawny licked her lips, thought and said, "Tell the general Tawny Dash calls him a green-skin."

The officer's face showed perfect insult. He snarled, "Disgusting!"

"Look, I'm telling you, if he doesn't get this message, you won't have many tomorrows. The Cabal will come, and there won't be any stopping them. I think it's worth one stupid message."

The officer nodded for his man to continue scribing. Tawny grinned in a tiny show of triumph and said, "That's G-R-E-E—" They looked up at her. She said, "Yeah, you got it."

SHE WAS STUFFED AWAY in a holding cell. She shared space with a dozen other supposed criminals, each waiting for their next stop on the way to a planet side prison container. Most were Orbinii, others were from off world and had been caught in Orbin territory breaking citizenry laws—a Stathosian over there, a Pendulosi over here, there was even a Tremusian in the corner looking silently enraged.

For Tawny, whatever patience she had was gone and she sat against the wall going silently out of her mind. Was her husband dead? Were they torturing him at this very moment? She didn't have time to sit and wait, hoping that the general paid her a visit. She was ready to tear the whole roof off this place. Then, there was a voice, low and cutting...

"I had to come see for myself. I would not have believed the reports otherwise."

She looked up. General Ona'Oona stood looking down at her with severe disgust written all over him. "The coward returns. The coward from Raylon."

Everyone in the cell acknowledged his presence and sank away. But not Tawny. She stood to greet him at the barred gateway and said, "Go on, get it out of your system."

He said with a frown, "You are a monger of the Cabal. You have no decency. You are bereft of essence. You are the intolerable one from a world of the intolerable many. It disgusts me to lay eyes on you, for it stabs my very guts even to see you rot in an Orbin cell."

"Are you done?"

"Your filthy kind is a blight to the entire system, you callus, filth-stinking wretch."

"Guess not," she supposed.

"Your hive of disgust should be wiped from the planets. It should be rent away like the scum that it is, and you along with it."

"Now you're getting personal."

He snuffled at her, sneered, "When the only thing sharing the banner pole of my great people is your head perched atop it I will know my mission is complete."

She said dryly, "That's very poetic. You're a very poetic man."

He shook his head articulating his lips, and for a moment she thought he might spit on her. He said, "I would ask why you are here but it would do me no good. You are a traitor to your own people, you have betrayed our confidence, and now you would do it again. You do not deserve the trial you will be given. But I will be there when you stand, and I will ensure you a trip to the moggot pits of Ontral."

He turned away, his low cape swishing at his feet and strode to the door. She blurted out, "I'm here to destroy the gun platform on Menuit-B." He stopped in his tracks, turned his head slightly. She continued, "I'm here to wipe out the Cabal presence from the Stathos moon rim forever." Now he turned around to face her. The look on his face was of utter deflation. The Menuit-B job. He had to know more. It was his duty. She grinned with a shrug and said, "What can I say, I've reconsidered the contract."

. . .

CALLING the Royal Council to immediate congress wasn't rare, but certainly unusual. It occurred when ushering a topic through the usual, legal circuits of the senate took more time than they had. A planet at war sometimes required such measures, and would then lean on the world's wisest minds to decide for all. As General Ona'Oona had determined, this was one such time. The king agreed.

Now, Tawny stood in the High Chamber of the palace facing those "wisest minds." There were nine of them, with the king sitting front and center. They all bore administrator titles—Administer of Internal Defense, Administer of Interplanetary Commerce, Administer of War Communications, and on and on. Their platform was raised like a dais, the panel surrounding her in a horseshoe. She had to gawk up at them from her position on the stone floor. The ceiling was vaulted, the entrance doors massive. Four bailiff guards stood behind dressed in their regal uniforms, each holding long staffs.

With Benji on her mind she had navigated her impromptu opening remarks as diplomatically as she could. The deal she laid at their feet was enticing. In short: Help me free my husband from the Mortus complex and we'll agree to the Menuit-B job, no charge. She even added, much to her own surprise, "We'll eradicate the threat of the Cabal from the entire Stathos moon rim and ensure the safety of the Orbin people from the interplanetary pounder they're constructing."

Eyes switched back and forth. Conversations whispered across the panel. Tawny looked to the council member sitting at the far end. A woman—the Administer of Peace

Affairs. She conversed with her associate sitting next to her. They all snuffled a final sentiment and looked down at her.

The king said in his congenial manner, "You yourself are a member of the Cabal, are you not?"

She gulped, maintaining her composure and said, "I was. I was a soldier. I was an assassin."

A round of gruffy snuffles.

"But no more. I left the war a long time ago. I'm through fighting it," she said.

"Why should we trust you?" This was General Ona'Oona. He sat to the left. "You are Cabal. How do we know this is not a ploy? This smacks of a scheme."

She chanced a step forward. "I don't care about the Cabal. I don't give a damn about your war. They have my husband. That man *is* my war. He *is* why I'm here."

The female at the end raised her eyebrows.

King Oto said, evenly, "You want us to deploy an armored wing and engage in combat against an unknown enemy."

The general added viciously, "To save the life of your husband, a known miscreant, data thief and criminal to the state!"

"No!" Tawny rebuked. "I want you to deploy the—*thing* —and do the—*whatever*—as your price for having Menuit-B wiped out. How many different ways do I need to say it?"

General Ona'Oona gave her a gnarled look.

The Administer of Internal Security said in a robotic, foreboding way, "And that is why we should trust you? Because of merely what you say?" He looked to the other panelists before concluding, "I am sorry, but your words fail to carry such weight in these palace halls."

Tawny narrowed in on him. She recognized this Orbin. He'd been the one to interview her and Ben when they first arrived on *Orbiter 1*. Supreme Viceroy Olan, Administer of Inernal Security. She remembered his words, and grinned. "Eviscerate them like Molosian shark bait," she said. Olan's eyes widened. He perked. Tawny pointed at him. "I think you once said that."

He nodded, coolly. "I recall."

"This enemy that you'll engage is not unknown. You know them." She paused scanning her gaze across the entire panel, then returning to Supreme Viceroy Olan. She said, "They're the ones that kidnapped Heiress Orona. They took her away from you, waited for your own security to drop its guard and stole her right off the planet."

The panel gasped and snuffled. Some of them cursed in the smooth-syllabled Orbinii tongue.

"That's right!" Tawny said keeping their attention. "They have already moved against you once. They'll plot again. You need to destroy them."

Supreme Viceroy Olan bawled out, "Another ruse. Have you no shame? What is next, or should I ask?" He chuckled ridiculously. "Perhaps you have the key to the Omicron war consulate building, too. What would be your price for that?"

"They bore the same markings. It *is* them."

King Oto raised a hand, silenced the room. He said, "Who is this group you speak of?"

Tawny blinked. She didn't know what to call them. She said, "They are a conspiracy group."

"Ha!" Supreme Viceroy Olan blurted. "Her preposterousness grows!"

She closed her eyes. What had REX said? Her ship had described the group better than she ever could. Her eyes opened and she yelled, "They operate in secret for the purpose of creating corrupt, internalized power structures to topple governments internally. They have sleeper agents inside every planetary government, maybe even right here at Orbin."

"Impossible lies!" the supreme viceroy sneered, pounding a fist into the dais.

General Ona'Oona turned his head slowly, gave the viceroy a curious look.

Tawny argued, "There's reason to believe the heiress kidnapping was an inside job. Someone right here in the palace helped coordinate it."

Viceroy Olan, screamed, "That is blasphemy!"

"Is it?" Tawny challenged him. "How are you so certain? you're the Administer of—what was it? Interior Defense, or something like that?"

"I am," he sneered.

"How can you be so sure? Have you investigated this?"

Her words dripped with accusation.

General Ona'Oona's stare narrowed on the viceroy.

Viceroy Olan's eyes went into severe slits and he whispered to Tawny dripping with anger, "Excuse me?"

"Why would you not pursue this? What are you hiding? Could it be that *you* are a traitor to the royal Orbin family!"

"You hold your tongue you vixen wench!" the viceroy barked, angry beyond measure.

"Or what?" she screamed back, and then repeated. *"Or what?"*

General Ona'Oona's glare switched between them. The Raylon had a good point. He couldn't refute that. Supreme Viceroy Olan was hiding something.

"You are a Raylon traitor, a war deserter, combatant against the Imperium and an enemy of the state," Olan yelled at her a hundred miles an hour. "We should have you executed, eviscerated and dismembered such that your pieces would be spread across our society as an emblematic showing of how we deal with your kind."

"Then come down here and do it, Viceroy!" Tawny cried. And with that, any shred of Benji's diplomacy went right out the window. It was her way or the highway, now. This was a dogfight.

"Perhaps I will," his words came slow, full of intent.

"You're a coward—*and*—a traitor."

"Guards, imprison this little gitch!" Olan demanded pounding the dais.

Ona'Oona watched with mighty fascination. Who could they trust? Which one of these was the traitor?

The four bailiff guards encroached from behind, but true to her impulses, Tawny met them first. The first guard dropped with a leg swipe from her exo-suit that sent his staff clattering to the floor. She grabbed it—it was heavy to hold, very pleasing—and caught the next in the jaw before he could react. He went down hard. Tawny dropped straight down as the next one's staff whizzed just overhead. She came back up with a rib-crunching jab to the mid-section putting him out of the contest, and spun around to face the final guard. He hardly hesitated; just came in with a spinning flurry. She blocked high to the left, high to the right, swung her staff. The guard doubled over with a shot to the flank. She finished him with an upward crusher to the head and he dropped down.

... four guards either moaning and writhing, or unconscious altogether.

Ona'Oona was impressed, much to his own chagrin.

Tawny threw the staff violently to the floor facing the dais and hissed, "Who else do I need to fight? You—" she pointed out one of the council members. "Do I need to fight you?" The member's eyes became like moons. She looked to the next, said, "You?"

"She is a crazy woman!" one of them cried.

Tawny pointed to the next member. "You—do you want to fight me?"

He shook his head, sank down.

Tawny opened her arms in an invitation. "General, perhaps you?"

Ona'Oona gave her a dazzled grin.

The king said, calmly, "I would not suggest that."

"Then who do I need to fight?"

"We do not understand your request."

She said clearly, succinctly, "Who. Do I need. To fight?"

The king gave her a confused face. "What do you mean?"

She roared, her words banging off the walls and reverberating through the chamber—"*YOU WILL NOT TAKE ME FROM MY HUSBAND!*"

The panel members leaned back from her blast, each going rigid, looking on. The room quieted.

She asked again, "So who do I need to fight?"

The Orbinii looked at each other as if trying to conjure a response. King Oto finally said in his calming, clear way, "You come to us with a proposition, and yet leave us with no choice."

She stepped forward collecting her breath. "You do have a choice, your Highness. Do you want my husband and me to deliver the payload to Menuit-B, or not? Do you want to obliterate the ones who kidnapped your heiress, or not? These are choices. They're *your* choices."

He said with open hands, "And you are willing to fight the entire palace to prove your integrity."

She said, "Yes," with a head nod.

"You would only fight us all," he said.

"Then you first. You and me. Let's go." She licked her thumbs, put her dukes up, ready.

He blinked surprised.

One of the council members said, "He is the king! That is ridiculous!"

"Why?" Tawny asked. "Why is that so ridiculous? He is the king of a world at war. Let him fight in his own chamber."

"We have palace guards," the council member said.

"Where are they? I'll fight them, then," she said.

"We have royal guards!"

"I'll fight them, too."

The guy twitched and asked in surprise, "Common guard?"

"And them."

They all looked at each other more intrigued than offended. One of them murmured, "Congress and senate?"

Tawny said, still with her dukes up, poised on her feet, "Them too. Bring them on."

King Oto put his hands up. No more words from the panel. He took a breath and asked, "What do you want us to do?"

Tawny's shoulders relaxed, she stepped forward, made a fist of determination and snarled, "I want you to fight *WITH* me." A moment shuddered through them.

Ona'Oona said nothing. He only looked at her with burning eyes. Far be it from him to admit anything ... he was starting to like this putrid Raylon. She'd uncovered a potential conspiracy within the very palace—one that could soon see Olan executed if proven right—now she wanted to fight everybody. How impressive.

Tawny said, "I'm offering you exactly what you said you

wanted. Take down the crew that kidnapped the heiress. Deliver the payload to Menuit-B. Done! Why are you waiting? Grab a column and follow me to Mortus. Seven hours at top speed. Easy as that."

"And then you deliver the payload to the moon Menuit-B?" the king clarified.

Tawny slapped herself in the forehead—*what about my proposition don't they understand?*

She said loudly, *"Yesss!"* Then, "It'll be a piece of cake."

"A what?"

"An easy job. By this time tomorrow, it's done."

After a long pause in which each council member stared at Tawny, some of them curious, others with scrutiny, the king said, "Council!" They got up and shuffled off into a rear antechamber. Tawny was left in the room alone with four guards laying around like rugs, one of them slowly getting to his feet, keeping his distance.

THEY EACH STOOD before the king in their respective positions. One said, "Our words, our protocol, our very laws mean nothing to her."

Another, "She is impetuous."

"She is insulting."

"How dare she!"

"I like her."

All eyes went to Madam Administer O'ah demanding more. She said, "The woman has purpose."

Another member taking her side, said, "We have leverage. She needs us."

Another said, "For Menuit-B, she makes a solid bargain."

The king took a breath, his eyes hawking across his council members. "Suggestions?"

"Play it out."

"Yes, let us see."

"She is Cabal!" Viceroy Olan sneered.

Madam O'ah said, "She is a married woman. And she is in love."

Her words sank in. A moment of silence flittered by. King Oto shared a glance with General Ona'Oona who hadn't said a word. He finally nodded his head in the affirmative and said, "Time is of the essence. If her husband is killed at their hands, she will not comply."

King Oto gave him an affected look. He asked, "How soon can we deploy?"

Ona'Oona said, "We have three armada wings at the ready, each in orbit."

"Within the hour," the king assumed.

Ona'Oona nodded.

King Oto gave his council one last look, each in the eye. "Final word?" he said.

"Let us see."

"Let us see."

"Agreed."

King Oto looked at his general, firmly. "Then give the word. And we will see."

The council turned back toward the entrance to the dais, but Ona'Oona grabbed Olan by the arm, turned him around privately. He gave him an untrusting stare and said, "Not you."

Olan's stare went to the floor.

Ona'Oona snuffled with disgust and went to face this new Raylon ally with the rest of the council. It was time to prepare for battle ... on multiple fronts.

. . .

WORD WAS GIVEN. REX's surveillance data of the armada was shared among the Orbinii. The plan was simple. Approach the moon, kick some narse.

The war machine was already preparing for inner-warp by the time Tawny got to the ship. She couldn't suppress her glee. Her plan, against all odds and with very poor diplomacy, had worked. They were headed into combat ... right now.

She exploded into the cockpit.

"Congratulations, Boss," REX said, "I think."

"You ready, REXY?"

"We're set, all parameters met."

She plopped down excitedly and declared, "Burn, baby, burn!"

Everything stretched out—stars, space, time. And they were off with Tawny pumping her fist and hollering for joy. She wanted to be first. She wanted to see the looks on their faces when she dropped out of inner-warp with the Orbinii 1st Home Fleet behind her. And then...

Even at top speed, the surrounding Orbinii battle cruisers looked like star shots stretching out into the distance and then disappearing altogether. Within seconds, the entire Orbinii war machine was gone, one at a time —*boom boom boom boom*—heading toward Mortus, leaving them in their space wake. Tawny was left looking a bit mystified, her fist frozen in the air.

REX grumbled, "Uh, they're a little faster than we are."

CHAPTER EIGHTEEN

———————

BEN WAS on his knees hunched over counting each breath. His hands were cuffed behind his back at agonizing angles. He couldn't move. All he could do was sit and think about the pain that was sure to come his way. They'd torture him, just as they had Rogan. They'd beat him, remove parts, pull eyeballs, until he agreed to the disagreeable, or he died. This was horrible.

He put his face up to the ceiling.

Where was Tawny? He needed to see her. Not to be saved, not to be freed. But simply to know she was okay, to know he wasn't alone.

The door to his cell whisked open. Zelit strode in looking grim. He didn't seem happy to have his captor, but rather operated with a morose sense of duty. He stood over Ben looking down. He finally said, "I have something you should see."

"I bet you do," Ben muttered.

Zelit laid an emitter cube on the floor. It opened an image cone. It was surveillance. The torture room. The long viewport. The row of stainless steel tables. Ben dropped his head.

There was Rogan laid out on the central table. A trio of physicians stood over him, two holding him down, the other working at him. Rogan's feet kicked defiantly, despite their ankle cuffs. He struggled like a trapped animal.

Zelit murmured, "Volume."

The screaming blasted through the image cube filling Ben's cell. That was Rogan, all right. He recognized the screaming. It was high-pitched, full of neurotic mindless wailing. Ben shut his eyes hard, wishing he could cup his ears.

"Turn it off!" He yelled.

Zelit flipped a wrist at the cube and the image cone zipped away.

Ben cried out, "Why are you doing this?"

He started his pacing, back and forth, around and around. "Rogan doesn't suit our needs."

"He brought me to you, didn't he?"

Zelit tilted his head. "Well, he doesn't fit our standards, either."

Ben huffed, "He's not good enough for you, huh?"

"The answer—no. He's not," Zelit declared almost proudly. He stared into Ben, said, "Do you feel differently? Does he fit your standards, Benjar?"

Ben looked away, angrily. He suddenly didn't like the answer. No, Rogan was a moron, a disreputable space insect, dim as a broken bulb, always getting in the way. Shoot, he was always getting in his *own* way. Ben drew a big breath as if in admittance. Despite the fact that he and Tawny were in this mess specifically *because* of Rogan, he felt the tinniest stab of pity for the man.

Zelit read him with those black eyes, showing fascination, and asked, "Aren't you beginning to see where you fit into the great scheme? There are a million Rogans in the system, but very few of you and Tawny. Have your eyes opened at all?"

Ben shot a look up at him, stabbed him with sudden fury. He blurted in one powerful breath, "What I see is a sick, delusional nutjob who suffers from bi-gods complexia and who would rather watch the world burn around him so he can stand among the ash heap proclaiming authority to the few humanoids that might be left, rather than step the hells out of the way of true peace and true liberty!" Out of breath, he inhaled large.

Zelit laughed at him. "That's pretty good. You are an impressive character, even in the face of execution. You're truly a disappointment, Benjar."

Still heaving he growled, "That's never bothered me."

They shared a moment in silence before Zelit said, "Come. I'll allow you to share a final conversation with a member of your chosen ilk."

THE FLAGSHIP *LEAGUE* sat above the Mortus lunar division of the Faction proudly bearing the broad blue stripe of its designation as armada leader. Her secondary crafts, each enormous in their own right, hovered around her, some sliding through the vacuum from several miles below giving the distant Mortus surface a grand dimensional reference.

League's forward command hangar was perched at its uppermost point overlooking the long, swooping design of her upper deck. On terraces, a set of radar dishes wheeled about constantly probing for lurkers in the deep—vessels on approach, or other star cruisers that might move to intercept.

Its captain stood with the armada leader, both tall, both bearing the prototypical stoicism of their affiliation, proudly at the upper catwalk with the viewport open to space on all sides. They observed the other vessels of their armada as they moved in a graceful column formation.

The communication center for the entire armada was set in a row along the starboard wall, technicians constantly relaying message points to designated craft. Voices hummed lowly over the soft, organized commotion.

One of the technicians listened to the alpha-wave hum of space, waiting to detect the slightest glitch in an otherwise perfect etherium. And there it was. She squinted, leaned closer to her instrumentation. Yes ... a voice from the deep. Her indication light lit up overhead showing a positive find. This signal was not errant. It was real time, displaying a potential threat. She flagged the signal and sent it on down the line.

The shift manager sitting in his lead cubicle received the finding. He tapped into the tech's particular radar stream, listened. There it was, a frequency. He referenced it to any known vessel motion within the sector and quickly discovered it was alien. Likewise, he sent the finding off to the upper platform where a windowed command center housed the operation officers.

The comm officer, a tall, chiseled woman with platinum hair in a bun was notified. She sent the data through her identification program and waited momentarily. The computer's type and brand suggestion came back. The information made her eyes go wide.

Vessel. Attack craft. Cruiser class. On approach.

Bearing twelve-twelve-point-three, one degree on vertical plain. Inner-warp speed. Likely match: Orbin.

She strode from the command center and to the forward bridge where the captain and armada leader stood with their hands behind their backs gawking out at the depths of space. "Sir," she said on approach getting the captain's attention. He turned to her as she showed a holo-display of her findings.

He made a concerned face. "Orbin. How many?"

"Not certain."

"This is an errant signal. Notify me when there's more."

"Yes, Captain," she said and turned around, but froze. The communications deck to the starboard was alight with indication blips. More signals were flooding in. Her techs were beginning to scurry around. This wasn't errant. These were multiple signals. She turned and said, "Captain?"

He noticed the commotion across the comm deck and shot a look out the viewport at twelve-twelve-point-three, one degree on the vertical plain. The first Orbin battle cruiser zipped in from inner-warp. It was enormous with large, rounded decks and wraparound viewports, gun bays forward and cannon platforms at the rear. Then another. And another. They were landing in perfect combat formation—a central battle unit, flankers to the left and right, wings of fast attack corvettes above and below.

Their intentions were clear.

The armada leader grinned, dawning a wild fiery look and said, "Our trial begins today."

The captain turned to his inner-ship comm officer and yelled, "General hail! Battle stations!"

BEN ENTERED the stainless steel torture bay with his

hands cuffed at his front, Zelit paced behind. Rogan reacted when he heard the door whisk open. His head raised from the table where he was bound, and he looked around. Ben noticed immediately ...

Rogan wore a medical swath across his face. He had zero eyes. They were gone. Both of them.

Ben sighed sadly and moved to Rogan coming to a stop at his table. Rogan muttered frightened little noises and turned his head side to side as if to see. But he couldn't.

"Ae'ahm, Rogan," Ben said. "Look at you."

"Benji?" he whimpered.

"They took your *other* eyeball?"

He laid his head down. "I can't see nothing. Now I need *two* eyeballs," he said in a small, frightened way. "I'm never going to get that kind of yield. Can't get no yield if I can't even see." He sputtered for a moment and said, "It don't matter. They're going to kill me anyway. I'm a goner. I'm so wasted."

Ben was torn. He hated seeing him like that. But deep down, he knew better than to show sympathy. Rogan was a villain. He'd cornered Tawny, and he'd trapped Ben. This whole situation was his doing. Ben's anger flared in a miserable, self-loathing way and he said, "Well, that's kind of what you get, Rogan. Why are you even here, huh?"

Rogan said, "They said I'd be impotent."

Ben shook his head, said, "They probably said important."

"Yeah, that."

He kneeled down and said, "No, Rogan, you came here to take something that wasn't yours, and you trusted the wrong people to help you do it. These people used you because you're a fool, Rogan. You've always been a fool, and now it's going to cost you your life." Ben stood back up and walked to the window. He looked out sullenly. He should have listened to his wife. She had known the score. He hadn't. Looking out the viewport he said in a low, even voice, "But don't worry, Rogan. In the end, you're not alone." He turned around. "I'm a fool, too. And I'm going to die right next to you."

"Benji?" he said.

The name curdled his blood. Only Tawny called him Benji. It forced patience. He groaned, "What, Rogan?"

"Why don't you just give them what they want?"

There were rules he couldn't break. But more importantly, there were ethics. This place flew in the face of his very code. He had his wife to thank for that, and gods willing, he'd get that chance. He shook his head and said, "No, I won't do that."

"How's come?"

"I guess it comes down to," he took a big breath and said, "character."

Rogan flapped his lips in a show of hopelessness. "Then you're more fooler than me. I don't know nothing about no character. I don't know nothing about no love, neither. Maybe I don't got neither one. Guess I'm just lucky. You and me—we're just like two birds in a bush."

Ben scrunched his face. More bad context from Rogan. He said, "That doesn't even make sense, Rogan."

Rogan said so low Ben had to bend over to hear, "Makes all the sense in the world to me."

And that was the difference. One was stupid, the other not. One had no ethos, the other did. But they were both going to die. And neither of them deserved it.

Ben got close to Rogan and said, "I don't know how yet, but I'm going to get us out of here, Rogan."

Rogan twitched. A spark of hope.

From behind, Zelit said, "It's very touching. See, enemies can be friends."

Ben turned to face him. "I know what you want."

"I want peace."

"Peace, huh? Then why don't you, oh I don't know, deliver water. Transpo med supplies. Shoes for the orphans. Toys for the tots. Maybe even rescue the occasional heiress, that kind of thing."

Zelit grinned. Hubris painted across his gaunt face and deep, dark eyes. "You and I have very different views on peace, Benjar."

"I'm not the one with the armada."

"No—you just carry plasma pistols on your belt."

Ben shrugged with humility. He wished those plasma pistols were still there. They'd taken them, stored them away. "Hey—there's a lot of people out there want to kill me."

"Mmm, yes," Zelit said, still dripping with that superior look. "And before we execute you as an enemy of the Faction, there's someone who'd like to get reacquainted with you."

Ben's eyes went into slits, curious. *Who could he...*

The far door whisked open.

possibly be...

And there stood a tremendous, angry-looking fellow, armor plating over a scaly torso, and thick, spiny limbs.

talking about?

Ben's face fell, shoulders went droopy. He knew that man-thing's scythe weapon strapped long and ready behind its back, that sinister visor and those powerful arms. There was perfect recognition. He gulped, "Oh yeah, I remember you. You're what's-his-name."

The man-thing stepped inside with heavy, menacing

footsteps and said through a deep, snaky voice, "I am Ravekk. I want you to know my name before..."

"...you kill me. Yeah, I remember that part," Ben said. "Aren't you dead?"

He said again, "I am Ravekk. I want you to know my name before..."

"Oh, bi-gods," Ben said. "You're a dim one." Ben looked over at Zelit expectantly.

The man said, "I am sorry it comes to this, Benjar. I had such high hopes." With that, he pushed the cuff release button on his wrist device, and Ben's cuffs shed to the floor.

Ben shook blood back into his fingers looking at Ravekk. He inhaled a large breath and took on a boxer's stance, light on his feet, dukes poised. "Okay, one-called-Ravekk, let's party."

ONCE ALL THE Orbin vessels had completed their jump, all of them assuming combat positions and slipping toward the Faction, hells hit the fan. The Orbinii fired first. It started with long distance compressed light beams slicing the black of space, turning the vacuum iridescent.

Hangar vessels among the Faction lowered tremendous bay doors feeding their auto drones out on turnstile tracks at a rapid-fire pace. They flooded into the space between armadas, entire swarms of them.

The Orbin laser strikes seared into their numbers, and they began blinking out in tiny bursts of energy taking the initial volley with them. Everything went still.

It was a Faction defense mechanism. No damage had been done at all.

Now all breath held on the Orbin side as a thousand cannon turrets turned on them and started unleashing a return volley. Strikes stitched the space erupting against the Orbin vessels. Shields held, repelling the initial blasts, flickers of flame depleting into space.

But shields could only hold for so long, and the strikes began to cut through. One of the Orbin corvettes shuddered from internal damage breaking apart and turning into a sun. Debris littered the field.

Communications began streaming back and forth:

"We have lost the *Oron*."

"Gunships, impulse five. Close flank."

"All units, take up positions."

"Targeting, engage enemy ships!"

"Bay vessels, release craft, release craft!"

"Wave one, released."

"Wave two... wave three..." and so forth.

Single-manned fighters—long, sleek fuselages and big booster engines at the rear—came zipping forward in waves leaving their larger brethren behind and entering no man's land between armadas. The Faction fighter wings moved in kind—small, forward pilot designs—streaking at them, turbines burning hot. Zippers of blaster fire arced across the distance, and blew into each element's numbers until they met in the middle. Both sides collided together and created a spiraling, flipping, spinning vortex of combat.

The cruisers lurched forward, slower and more majestic, each side encroaching on the other. Swiveling gun minarets unleashed guided Orbin rocketry. The Faction got pounded. Explosions shredded through upper decks in big starbursts, incinerating battle panels and bulkheads. One destroyer class vessel began tumbling vertically before an eruption split it apart at its seems in glorious red and gold flame.

The Faction returned fire desperately until the big

boats split through the scattering fighter combat and engaged at point blank range. Cannon turrets and gun decks slid past one another. Light beams and plasma bombs fired their charged payloads. Explosions ripped through hulls scattering plumes of debris and wreckage into space. The smaller craft zipped back and forth in loops and maneuvers, each pocket of combat playing out its own life-and-death drama at the speed of a heartbeat, everything culminating into a confusing, reckless frenzy of pulsing and ebbing war; a huge, shapeless creature slowly rumbling over the Mortus moon eating everything it touched—like an organism.

BEN FLEW like a shot across the room, an easy fifteen feet, and smashed against the wall. He slouched, groaning, "Oh-oww, that hurt." That was like no gut shot he'd ever experienced. He shook his head asking himself if he were bleeding internally. He just might be. No time to ponder.

Ravekk stormed toward him, wrenched him up by the collar cursing, "You Guilder wormdog!" and spun him around releasing him at the zenith of his power—and his power was, unfortunately, a magnanimous thing. Ben smashed into a nearby work desk that didn't budge. He bounced off it. It rattled his kidneys and he groaned, "Aye-aye-aye, that smarts like a mother." He would probably have to retrieve said kidneys off the floor later.

Ravekk approached again. Ben was a rag doll in his clutches. He'd shot the man-thing with several blasts at Hominus IV, and it barely put him unconscious. Without his plasma pistols, he was a goner. Ravekk leaned down, picked him up by the neck. Ben's teeth clenched, face went purple. The man-thing growled, "Guilder wormdog."

"I—heard you—the—first time!" Ben choked, and kicked him sharply between the legs. It had no affect. Ben's hope fell away. A man who couldn't even be kicked in the balls was no man at all. This was something else. Maybe a bio-mech halfsie. Maybe a Minotaur-bot. Or maybe the man-thing just had tough, flubbin' junk.

"HOW FAR OUT ARE WE!" Tawny cried, eager to get into the fray. The inner-warp tourbillion swirled beyond the viewport like a kaleidoscope, all reds, blues and blacks.

REX said, "Not far. In fact we should be arriving in three, two ... *one!*"

They felt the lurch of an inner-warp dropout, and the view switched to the Mortus moon zooming up at them, going from a gray speck to a big, bloated planetoid. The battle was a speckling of twinkles one second, the next they were amidst it, zipping in between two huge cruisers locked in combat, explosions bucking them around. This was the valley of death.

"Evasive drive!" Tawny called.

"Yeah—" REX said as if through clenched teeth. They hurled through a web work of zipping laser blasts bull-nosing bits of space debris off their bow.

"Hold on!" REX called.

He sidled up against the portside Orbin cruiser dodging structural outcroppings. Everything zipped by in a speedy blur. An explosion rattled them violently. Tawny banged around in the cockpit seat. This wasn't exactly like tickling the snake.

"Sorry, Boss."

A flurry of fighters streaked by them from behind at break neck speed, enemies pursuing enemies, some zipping by just overhead, others coming from below. They carried off between the cruisers until opposing cannon decks unleashed a gauntlet of laser fire. The fighter craft evaporated into swirling chunks. All of them.

REX screamed, "We gotta get out of this mess!"

He dipped down and pulled a sharp veer maneuver shifting their position under the cruiser's fuselage. Belly cannons roared out at a lower target. And below, that lower target sent streams of firepower back up.

Laser blasts pelted at them from above and below. This was no better than the valley of death. It was an endless crossfire. And they were right in the middle of it.

REX navigated a field of evacuating columns of atmosphere from rupture points in the overhead cruiser. Everything bucked and jarred as the artigrav struggled to adjust. Something erupted up ahead. A huge blast of fire emitted. Tawny's eyes went wide, mouth dropped. It was too late to juke around. They burst through the wall of flame, both screaming. Ahead, the battle only thickened.

"Awe gee—where's Cap when you need him?" REX cried.

"Just get us to the moon," Tawny groaned.

"Point A to Point B," he said and nosedived at a ninety-degree angle. "Uh oh," he groaned. A Faction gunboat below zoomed up at them. A field of zipper fire burst toward them, red blinding streamers. They split through it and darted past the gunboat, but the parapet swiveled around keeping them in its sights.

"We're being targeted!" REX screamed. He felt his own bubble turret ignite a stream of laser blasts from its spinner gun. He threw a quick glance behind using his three-sixty optical sensors and watched the parapet burst apart. He laughed, said, "Oh, I get it. Nice shot, Boss."

Tawny had slipped below and manned the bubble gun. She laid down a stream of laser fire pivoting the gun back and forth wildly, clearing away anything that might be behind.

They approached the moon descending through the combat zone.

An alarm sounded. Tawny saw the problem before REX did.

There were two of them flying in tandem, coming right at them.

REX said, "Boss, we got a—"

"I know!" she screamed. "Push it, REX!"

A Faction battle cruiser had spotted them on a course for the lunar surface and deployed a pair of seeker missiles.

Seeker missiles.

They were known to lock onto a target and never let go. It had been reported on many occasions that a seeker missile would pursue for hours through open space at long distance. Rarely, they'd even caught up to targets that had escaped through inner-warp days later and destroyed them. They were patient things. Deadly.

Tawny put the near one in her sights and fired. It was a good shot. Pure talent. The blasts bounced away harmlessly.

Yep—she was afraid of that. They had shields.

"Rex," she said. "We're in trouble."

"Hang on, Boss," REX said. "It's about to get real bumpy."

They sank into the moon's thin atmosphere. Everything quaked and rattled around her. She never took her eyes off those missiles. They were big, relatively slow moving, but persistent. She murmured, "Those missiles get much closer, and we're going to find out what bumpy really is."

. . .

RAVEKK HURLED Ben across the room again. He smashed into a tray full of operation tools. med canisters and suture kits and bandaging fell down around him. So did a steel scalpel. Ben picked it up pinched between thumb and finger, looking at it miserably. The thing was puny. But he'd take what he could get.

Ignoring his pain, he launched himself at Ravekk leading with the tiny knife. It sank into the man-thing's neck making him growl and thrust Ben away. He pounded into a bracket of steel rods that clattered down around him. He threw the scalpel away, grabbed a rod—three feet of deadly leverage.

Again, he'd take what he could get.

He charged at Ravekk poised for a shot. He swung like a madman. Ravekk absorbed the shot with his head and sent Ben far away, yet again. He smashed into a tall locker crashing it open. Debris fell down around him, namely his plasma blasters. He laughed in a serendipitous way and discarded the pole for a blaster. Much better.

Ravekk reacted quickly, unsheathing his scythe weapon from his back and flipping it around, going into an attack posture. Ben pointed the blaster and unleashed a volley. The blasts sluiced off his armor in a shower of sparks. It did nothing.

Armor upgrades.

Ben looked at the gun in his hand, aghast.

Ravekk lunged forward, his scythe held up in a death strike. Ben fired a final, desperate shot. If he couldn't kill his attacker, maybe he could disarm him.

He was right.

The shot pinged off Ravekk's hand in a blossom of

sparks, loosing the scythe from his grip and sending it flying through the air. Even Zelit had to duck from it, flinging his arms defensively. It hit the ground and slid to a stop at the far end of the room.

Ravekk hesitated, supremely angry. His eyes slid over to Ben, mean and bloodthirsty. Ben shrank back. This was going to hurt. Ravekk charged. The man-thing was on Ben before he could fend him off, picking him up and throwing him across the room. As Ben sailed through the air, the strangest thought passed through his mind, full of odd tranquility—*Well, here I am again... airborn.*

REX SCISSORED BACK and forth through the black mountaintops. The rockets pealed after him. They looped and spiraled, veering apart, avoiding the natural landscape, then closing formation, always blasting forward.

The ship dropped in altitude entering a deep, broken valley, weaving and bucking. The rockets followed, pinned in, constantly approaching, then falling back, avoiding obstacles, always resetting and continuing their pursuit.

REX heaved his way around a huge mountain formation following its curvature in a tight, looping path. One rocket followed, the other split away taking the opposite approach. REX read his sensors well, saw the second rocket taking on a collision course. It startled him, gave him the most scurrilous and intriguing sensation.

It ticked him off.

"Trying to outsmart me, eh?" he said, and jerked into a ninety-degree climb. There wasn't a second to spare. The first rocket read him, followed. The other sensed REX evading, extrapolated a second object approaching—its counterpart rocket.

It juked trying to avoid and went spinning away, out of control and tumbling through the night.

REX exploded up above the mountains, leveled off and came back down. The rocket tracked him well and followed tightly.

REX said, "I think we shook one of them."

Tawny, who was still down in the bubble turret, looked hard. She couldn't see the second one, but the first was still hot on their trail. "It's better than nothing, REX, but we still got..." Something stole her attention away, made her scream.

A hot-white, laser-straight blast of light came at them from the pitch-black mountain face. It struck the fuselage and exploded. Tawny winced. REX bellowed in pain. He started vibrating, lights blinking off and on. Sparks Shot up from Tawny's gun panel making her yelp and jerk back. She looked out the bubble window, saw where that blast had come from. She knew that weapon. She'd seen it before.

Rogan's sniper.

He or she, or it, or whatever it was, was still operating out there in the night. Probably a robot with one thing on its mind: kill Tawny Dash. And now she knew where it had come from.

"Boss!" REX hollered. "We're losing power." His engines sputtered.

Tawny looked out fraught with desperation. That rocket. It was gaining now. Gaining fast.

She scurried up the turret ladder and into the cockpit, throwing herself into the pilot's seat.

Gods, Benji baby, I need you now! Take my hand!

She snagged the two-handed control stick and screamed, "REX, give me control!"

"Take it, take it!"

She slammed the thruster control forward. She could

feel the catch and go of a sputtering engine. It was better than nothing. She pealed into the tightest, fastest arc she could muster, U-turning toward that mountain peak, and straightened out. The rocket followed suit, constantly gaining. It moved closer—a hundred feet. Seventy feet.

That mountain neared, grew through the viewport, a big black world of death approaching fast.

The rocket speeding ups from behind was at fifty feet. Thirty.

REX screamed in a panic, *"Boss, we're gonna die!"*

Twenty feet.

"Ahhhh!"

Ten feet.

Tawny wrenched the vessel to the port like a mad woman. The rocket attempted to adjust. Too late. It struck the mountain.

REX boosted off leaving an exploding mountaintop lighting up the whole area with a blinding, dazzling show of fire. His engines kicked back on and they sailed away.

Tawny sighed huge and sank back into the seat. A moment of satisfaction enveloped her. She got that little narse-headed jackwad. No one could survive that. Not even an android. That whole mountain started coming down, avalanche style. She heard herself laugh...

Then the proximity alarm rang.

She sat back up, looked down through swollen, panicked eyes. The other rocket had reacquired. Distance: a hundred and fifty meters.

They pealed over the flatland at low level, leaving a twin rooster tail of sand in their wake a hundred feet tall. The rocket followed.

"REX," she cried, "show me the complex!"

His digital map holo-zipped into view. She read it. Eighteen degrees west. She veered toward it watching the far mountain range approach. She pulled back on the thruster control.

"Boss, what're you doing?"

"I'm going to let it get closer."

"Closer! You're always getting closer!" he wailed.

"It throws off their timing," she said.

"Oh—*then* we explode?"

"There!" she cried pointing through the viewport. The flatland sped by beneath. The mountains approached. The lights of the complex were visible tucked away in areas of utter dark, miles away. "We're going to hit it."

"Cap's in that place," REX said.

"We're not doing him any good out here," she rebuked.

"Are we going to do him much better blowing the place up?"

"If my baby needs our help, this is the only way he's going to get it."

BEN CLENCHED HIS TEETH, eyes like slits, face turning purple. Ravekk had him pinned against the viewport with both hands around his throat squeezing. The man-thing was unstoppable. A machine. A force of nature. And it seemed it deeply enjoyed inflicting pain.

Ben wondered how much more a throat could take? This was it. He was going to die. He knew it.

He looked defiantly into Ravekk's basilisk eyes. The man-thing returned a look that was both mad and gleeful. Suddenly, those yellow lizard eyes looked away, saw something through the window, something way out across the lunar landscape. The creature gulped, eyes went wide.

Ben gave the thing a curious look—*Uh oh, something bad is coming...*

Ravekk threw him down. Ben landed, choking and rasping at his neck. A roar came from the distance, growing into thunder. Something big was coming, fast. Ben shot a glance up through the viewport. REX screamed by hardly twenty feet over the complex making the entire prisoner bay quake. Ben gave a triumphant howl, fist in the air, "Yeah, Tawny!" Following closely—way too closely—the seeker rocket streaked after REX in hot pursuit, missing the viewport by only feet, and Ben froze looking a bit horrified. "Oh hells ..."

The rocket skimmed over the upper command deck. REX banked straight up at break neck speed. The rocket slammed into the mountain with an earthquake explosion. The mountain shattered into huge streams of rubble throwing tonnage into the sky like geysers.

The whole complex shook with enough violence that Ben came up off the floor. Even Ravekk lost his footing. And then the whole superstructure began splitting away from its rocky foundation.

Ben looked up through the enormous viewport. The whole building began to tilt underneath him. Iron moaned. Steel wreaked in agony. Huge pylons began twisting, snapping. The floor took on an increasing decline. The lower mountain rose up to meet them.

Ben's eyes went huge, his face spilling terror. They were about to go tumbling down the mountainside—prisoner bay, upper command terrace, east wing, west wing, everything.

He grunted, spun around and assessed his shifting surroundings. Everything began sliding across the tilted floor—equipment lockers, chairs, big pieces of furniture. He found himself dodging them as they tumbled passed.

Rogan, still strapped to his execution table, opened his mouth and wailed a high-pitched scream of terror. He couldn't see a thing. But he didn't have to. He knew what was happening. He could feel gravity begin pulling him into an unnatural decline.

Ben's tumble began as the floor dropped away beneath him. He grabbed for the nearest stationary object. A table. He held firm feeling his weight begin to pull him down. Ravekk went by, wind-milling his hands at him trying to grab him. He missed and plummeted through the room. The man-thing crashed down on his back against the view-port. Free falling debris pelted down around him.

A tremendous jerk ripped Ben's grip free. He fell, landed hard on the forward viewport next to Ravekk. The entire building jolted to a stop. The right side viewport showed the leeward command center had slammed into a mountainous outcropping, jerking the whole operation to a halt. But only momentarily. The superstructure out there began peeling away in tremendous heaps of rending tonnage—superstructure being reeved apart by the mountain.

Ben's jaw dropped as he spied the destruction taking place. Those people were getting their narse cheeks kicked over there.

The prisoner bay began swinging over. Gravity shifted. Inertia switched. Now everything began sliding to the left. Ben floundered for something to grab.

Rogan's scream took on a whole new pitch, still trapped on his table as junk and garbage rained down on him.

Ben went into a headfirst belly slide, completely out of control. He found himself slipping across the slick floor underneath the torture tables, passing beneath them faster and faster, trying to avoid smashing headlong into their leg supports. Somewhere in his split-second periphery, he saw one of his plasma blasters go sliding by. He grabbed at it, missed. "No no no..." he moaned.

Then, Ravekk's scythe weapon caught up to him sliding across the floor, about to pass right by. He reached for it, grabbed it.

Yes! I got a weapon!

He streaked past Rogan's table. The man's screaming came and went, fading away as he slew by. The scythe weapon caught one of the table legs, ripped from Ben's grip.

Gah! There goes my weapon!

He went into full plummet and landed hard against the far wall at the bottom of the room trying to catch his breath.

Ravekk ended up in the corner growling defiantly as stuff pounded down on top of him. Everything crashed to a stop as the building hard-landed at the mountain base and came to a rest.

Everything went sill, breathless.

Ben opened his eyes. What would have been like looking across the lengthwise direction of the prisoner bay was now like looking straight up. At the very top of the room, Zelit clung desperately to a pipe. He hung perfectly vertical, his arms extended over his head, his greatcoat waving around him. His face was tight under duress, the fear of falling painted all over him. It would be a hundred foot fall straight down.

Rogan, still cuffed to his torture table, lay supine, upside down with gravity trying to pull him into a free fall, save the cuffs that held him in place. He sniffled and snuffled, every-thing desperately hanging on to the moment.

Then, with the sound of bending metal and crunching steel, everything started tilting. Ben reached for a bulkhead —something to hold on to—as his body weight began swinging back toward negative space. The entire room teetered at the edge of collapse and settled, just sitting in position like a big leaning tower, balancing at its zenith.

Everything fell silent, tense.

One of the suspension rods overhead shivered under extreme tension, the cable being stretched to its fullest capacity. And then—*SNAP!* The cable broke, sprung back like a whip and slew the table in half next to Rogan's. He flinched. The tension rod shot across the full length of the room faster than a bullet, its kinetic energy fully released. Zelit gasped, still dangling. It was going to guillotine him. He saw it coming. No time to react. Nothing he could do.

The rod jammed against the wall severing his arms. Without his hands, he began his fall, screaming as he did. His body bounced off the first stationary torture bed, flipped into the nearside wall, banged back toward the center, cartwheeled over Rogan, ping-ponged off several other structures. He screamed like—*ook-aak-eek-gak*—and thundered down like a big bag of guts next to Ben who covered himself defensively, then lowered his arms and looked over. Zelit's eyes stared at him half open. Everything else was blank. Dude was dead.

Flump!

Something fell in Ben's lap. He glanced down. It was Zelit's arm from the elbow down. Ben yelled, "Yeesh!" and batted it away.

Then, the zenith broke. Everything tipped over, started falling again. This wasn't over yet. Ben held his breath as the entire structure went crashing down to the lunar surface on its top, everything inside suspended upside down. Ben fell to the floor, which was technically the ceiling, and came to rest.

·   ·   ·

REX RETURNED to the site of the complex. Everything was dark under the cosmic, lunar sky.

"Flood lights, REX," Tawny said, anxious of what she might find. Light beams kicked on flooding the area with visibility. It made her frown.

The complex had sheered away from the mountain and tumbled several hundred feet downhill breaking apart along the way. A huge trail of twisted debris littered the mountainside. Pieces steamed and sparked. Superstructure had been strewn everywhere. The place was a wreck.

A big piece of it rested way below at the foot of the mountain. It looked to be intact, for the most part.

"Get down there, REX."

REX lowered under his gentle maglev pivoting around to keep the mountainside through his viewport. They descended until they reached the base where the flatlands began. What was left of the complex appeared to be laying butt-end up with broken spires and steel embankments all jagged and ripped apart. One part had a long viewport that had miraculously remained intact. It was too dim to see inside. If Benji was here, and if he was alive, that's where he'd be.

"REX," she said, "soft land and fire up the ATV. I'm going out there."

"You got it, Boss. There's one thing."

"Yeah?"

"I'm getting some activity. Check it out."

His sensor readings displayed on the 3-D pad. The battle overhead was thinning out. Faction battle cruisers were zipping away in retreat. Part of the Orbin fleet was left up there mopping it up. But a group of bomber cruisers were moving into position over the complex. She knew exactly what that meant. They were going to strike bomb the whole area from above.

"We don't have much time," she said.

"Nope," REX agreed.

"Okay, stay ready."

____

CHAPTER NINETEEN

BEN SHOOK HIS HEAD, had to gather his senses. Everything was upside down. The whole world was flipped over. He looked up to the ceiling, now the floor. The row of torture tables, which would have been bolted to the floor under normal circumstances, now hung from above. Rogan was still cuffed to one of them facing directly down and whimpering like a child. His hair dangled around his face. The scythe weapon now lay directly below him.

Speaking of the scythe weapon, where was Ravekk? Where was that big narse-hole?

A noise to the left yanked Ben's attention toward the corner. A pile of debris sat there, pealing itself away one big chunk at a time. Ben squinted at it.

It turned out to be Ravekk unburying himself.

"Awe, jeez—" he grumbled, preparing himself for the worst. He got to his feet, poised.

Ravekk sloughed the wreckage off and stood over the pile, heaving. His shoulders rose and fell, lacerations left little rivers of green blood falling down his body, two-toning his pale, beryl-colored lizard skin. His eyes lazered onto Ben with the look of crazed anger. "You. Worm. Dog." He growled, and charged forward.

"What? I didn't do—*glak!*"

Ravekk snatched him up, flung him down like a doll. The man-thing straddled him, both hands around his neck, strangling the life out of him. Ben couldn't fight him off. The thing was too strong for any humanoid.

Mind. Use your mind, Ben.

He scanned the room through desperate eyes. Couldn't breathe. Needed a weapon.

There!

The scythe. It was way across the room sitting beneath Rogan.

Ravekk released him. Ben inhaled big. The man-thing grinned, showing exaggeratedly large teeth. "You like dying, wormdog?"

Ben thrust his hand to the side saying, "Particularly, no." He felt something soft and squishy. He grabbed it. It was Zelit's arm—elbow, wrist and all. It included Zelit's cuff release bracelet.

Yes! Now free Rogan!

He smashed the button, looked over at Rogan. The cuffs didn't release.

Whaaa?

Ravekk clenched down on Ben's throat again—*Gluk!*

Ben clawed at Ravekk's thick arm with one hand and mashed the cuff release button with his other hand desperately. Again. Again. The cuffs still wouldn't release.

Gah!

A thought!

The device was programmed to react to Zelit's finger, not his own.

Ravekk let his throat go making him gasp for breath. The man-thing was teasing Ben with his own death. He leaned down close, and whispered, "Now ..."

Ben jammed Zelit's severed hand into his own mouth, found the narrowest knuckle with his teeth and chomped like a crusher machine. The finger snapped off resting on his tongue.

"You..."

He spit the finger out. It landed next to his free hand.

"Die."

He yelled with hardly any breath, "Rogan, get the damn scythe—*gluk!*"

Ravekk squeezed down on his throat one. Last. Time.

Rogan looked over blind as a bat, his hair still dangling around his face, and said, "Huh?"

Ben articulated Zelit's severed finger into his hand, found the button on the cuff and mashed it as his eyes bulged out of their sockets.

Rogan's cuffs released. He dropped straight down, landed hard—*fwump!* He shook his head, felt the weapon, grabbed it and got to his feet saying, "Oh, got it!" He couldn't see. He was blind. He felt around the room with his free hand, stumbling over loose debris. He swung the blade at nothing. Ironically, he hit his mark perfectly. Nothing. He swung again. Another successful strike.

Ben closed his eyes feeling death encroach upon him. His final thought was—*Why, bi-gods, does Rogan have to be such a bumbling idiot?*

There was the sudden sound of a melon being reared in half, and Ravekk's hands released his throat. Ben gasped, looked up. Ravekk's head dropped heavily to one side, then his body slumped to the other.

Ben pulled one huge gulp of breath after another. He

filled his body with beautiful, re-processed, life-giving oxygen and sat up rubbing his throat. Rogan blindly swung the scythe again clanging the blade off a piece of equipment, stumbling around on his feet.

"Rogan!" Ben yelled.

Rogan froze at his own name, turned toward the sound of Ben's voice. "Huh?"

"You got him—*hack, cough*—you can stop swinging now."

BEN FOUND HIS PLASMA PISTOLS, strapped them back on. He looked at Rogan who was still floundering around, blind as a bat. He started to say something, perhaps a thank you, but he was interrupted.

In a sudden, explosive bang, the entire viewport erupted into pieces. Ben hit the deck, looked over. Rogan screamed. The oxygen atmosphere evacuated in a single, violent gush blowing all around them like a swirl of wind. It seemed loud enough to make the ears bleed. Then, silence.

Ben sat up blinking. REX was parked outside looking at him from a hundred meters away. A pair of headlights beamed into the room. It was Tawny in the ATV. She'd used the winch with its electro-suction device to yank the viewport out of its frame. Now, Ben sat there heaving on helium.

"What in the hells was that!" Rogan screamed. The terror in his voice was made even more comical as the helium pitched his words up a few octaves. He sounded remarkably like a four-year-old.

Ben couldn't celebrate. No time. The helium content was way too high to sustain life. They'd be dead in minutes.

He sprinted over to Rogan, grabbed him by the collar and barked, "Let's go, Rogan!" shocked at the pitch of his own voice. He hauled him from the wreckage through the open viewport. Rogan tried to keep up. He stumbled, hit his knees, got up, took a few blind steps, fell again. Ben kept yanking him toward the ATV like a man on a leash.

Tawny was on her way forward dressed in a bio-suit, her exo-leg whining with each step. They met eyes.

"Tawny!" Ben cried out in that baby crib call.

"Babe!" she called back, but stopped and whipped her blaster up. "Look out!"

Ben waved both hands wildly, dropping Rogan in a puff of dust. "No, no, no. Not this time. He's with us."

"That's Rogan!" she screamed, a snarl in her words.

"Yeah, I know. I'll explain later."

They came together throwing each other into an embrace. She looked up into him. His face was battered like a punching bag—swollen here, swollen there, swollen every-where. "Are you okay?"

"I'm okay." He hated that he sounded like a talking infant. He looked down, recognized the battle-mech exo-suit. "You okay?"

"I am now," she said.

"Gods, I missed you," and he wrapped her into a tight hug.

She pulled away. "C'mon, there's no time." She headed to the ATV and saddled up. She spun the vehicle around kicking up a cloud of moon dust and rock and pulled next to them. "This whole place is about to get blown straight to Wi'ahr."

"By who?"

"The Orbinii."

Ben flinched in disbelief and cried, *"Who?"*

"I'll explain later. Let's get back to REX. You fly. I shoot."

"Yeah— I'm getting dizzy out here."

She regarded Rogan. "And he gets cuffed like a dog, whether he likes it or..." she noticed he was missing a few things. Namely eyeballs. "Bi-gods, what happened to him?"

"Explain later. Let's go!"

Ben dumped Rogan onto the flatbed and stumbled drunkenly into the passenger seat. All together, they skid out, spitting gravel back toward REX's cargo bay door.

The ATV roared to a stop in the cargo bay dumping Rogan gruffly onto the floor. He grunted like a baby. The door lifted shut and a blast of atmo flushed into the room. Ben heaved in the new air shaking his head, trying to bring himself back. This was go time. No time for blacking out. He felt his head start to clear as he stumbled toward the exit, already on his way to the cockpit.

Tawny hopped out of the vehicle, went to the armory and returned with a pair of cuffs. She slapped them around Rogan's wrists and hissed angrily, "Move, Rogan. I dare you." She got up, kicked him once in the gut—*hard*—and followed her husband out.

"Cap, you're back!" REX said.

"Yep, and you know the drill, pal," he responded sliding down into the flight chair. Tawny shot down through the bubble turret passageway.

"We're fired up. Control is yours," REX said.

Ben gripped his guidance gear, looked up. Distantly, bright red streamer bombs rained down from space. Splatter explosions churned the ground headed toward them in a wall of rising earth. Here they came, getting close.

REX lifted vertically.

Now they could hear the bombs.

He spun around.

Feel the impact blasts.

And rocketed forward.

The complex exploded behind them. Clouds of debris spread out. Huge oxygen tanks blew up. Explosions created explosions. The fire ball expanded up and out until it swallowed the entire mountain—and just above it all, tiny little REX hauled serious narse up and up toward the lunar sky.

Ben was already getting multiple readings just above the atmosphere. It looked like a space battle. He blenched at the console, looked up through the viewport. Explosions blinked and twinkled way out there. It *was* a space battle.

"Oh, this is going to be fun..."

He kicked on the retro burners breaking through the atmosphere. As he approached, he saw several huge Orbinii cruisers concentrating their fire on a massive Faction battle cruiser—a type of mother ship. Several other Faction vessels warped away. They were getting the hells out of there with their bright white inner-warp trails stretching toward infinitum.

REX sped toward the battle.

A sudden blast of blue energy emanated from the Faction mother ship's topside cannon with a bandwidth far greater than the average cannonade. It had as much power as an entire battle wing. It incinerated one Orbinii vessel into particles and ripped another into halves. Ben jerked back, squinting against the sharp, sudden brilliance of the beam.

"Tawny!" he yelled.

"I see it," she said from the bubble turret.

"Okay—we're strafing."

He hit the mother ship's upper deck at barely twenty feet, rising and dipping with its terraced design. Tawny's bubble turret laid twin trails of laser blasts stitching across the vessel and pock marking it with blossoming explosions. The cannon tower approached. She concentrated her spinner barrels on it, searing it in half as they sped toward it. The thing broke apart and ruptured, sending a ball of flame across the ship's upper quadrant. The cannon, now ejected from its body, blew apart like a mini-sun.

Ben jerked his vessel away, veered at tremendous speed between two Orbinii battle cruisers and hit inner-warp. He figured the Orbin armada could wipe up the rest. They'd done their part.

BOOM—gone.

EVERYTHING FELL PEACEFUL. He shook his head. The last two days had been quite a ride. He'd been captured, beaten up, dismantled, kicked around. He'd faced torture and death. But worst of all, he'd lost his wife.

Tawny. What had she been through? What trials had she faced without him?

Bi-gods, he could never let that happen again.

She emerged from the bubble turret, both looking at each other. Her eyes said a thousand words. His eyes said the same.

Thank you for saving my life.

Thank you for being there for me.

Thank you for making me better.

Thank you for loving me.

Thank you for trusting me.

Thank you for being my husband.

Thank you for being my wife.

Now... let's do it like colliding stars.

They were in each other's arms in the next moment violently and needfully, becoming a piece of each other's body, being in love like this quadrant of the cosmos rarely knew.

CHAPTER TWENTY

____

REX HAD SEEN BETTER DAYS. He'd been bruised and battered over the ordeal at Mortus. He'd even lost his mag-spire attachment. But Ben and Tawny had returned to Orbin to honor their agreement. To that end, the Orbinii had gotten right to work affecting repairs. They'd even set out to retrieve REX's great mag-spires from the Mortus moon.

As Ben and Tawny moved away, they took a hesitant glance back at their home sitting under *Orbiter 1*'s vessel repair platforms. Vacuum crews worked on him diligently. Repair bots hovered around him like little, silver bees. He looked to be in good hands. They could only hope.

The Royal Council had been called for an immediate congress. It was the second time they'd done so in as many days, both on the Dash's behalf. They were beginning to get impatient.

Ben stood precisely where Tawny had the day before. They were now side by side looking up at the great dais panel where the Royal Council sat glaring down at them.

The opening orator proclaimed, "Benjar and Tawny

Dash, you have come before us to resolve the agreement made in confidence concerning the Menuit-B resolution. Are you ready to begin?"

They looked at each other and both declared, "Yes."

The king said, "Our resolve toward you has only grown. You were merely vigilantes before. Now, you are indebted to us. To that end, you are prisoners, until such time as your servitude is complete."

Ben said back, "We made a deal. We'll see it through."

The Administrator of Military Commerce gave his characteristic, one-sided scowl and murmured, "You did not make the deal." He pointed a slow finger at Tawny. "She did."

"*We*," Ben said sharply, "made the deal."

He snuffled. "Where once before you failed."

Ben turned his gaze to King Oto offering a humble grin. "It was different circumstances, your Highness—ness."

The king took a big breath and said, "You have this chance and this chance alone, Benjar and Tawny Dash, to earn our good graces."

Ben agreed, "Fair enough."

Tawny added, "Yeah. Fair. Right."

"One point of warning," King Oto said. "If you betray your word again, your names will be put to the interplanetary death list. You will not only be an enemy to the Orbin state. You will be an enemy to the whole of the Imperium. Even the Guild will hunt you down. For mercy on yourselves, do not fail again."

Ben said conversationally, "So in other words, the status is quo. Sounds good."

King Oto looked down the row to General Ona'Oona. The general, wearing his usual critical glare, said, "The subject vessel is being equipped as we speak. The download process is complete," he tilted his head untrustingly at Ben and said, "yet again."

The king nodded to the bailiff core, which had been doubled, and they moved in. But Ben took a step forward calling, "What about the other guy?"

Rogan...

He heard Tawny sigh in frustration. They had discussed Rogan's fate beforehand, but he allowed her, her disdain. He held his fair share toward the man, too.

The king said, "The one called Rogan. He is a Guilder. He is a mongrel. We would have him put to a palace cell ... but we have no charge against him. Yet he is lame. We have very few options but to make him a ward of the Orbin state."

"Then what?"

"We will inform the Guild we hold one of their own and have them send for him."

Ben nodded. Fair enough. He said, "They'll execute him for his crimes against a Guild member. Namely my wife and me."

"That is not our concern," King Oto said.

Ben inhaled big and glanced at his wife. She gave him a patient *go ahead and get it over with* look.

Ben cleared his throat and said, "He saved my life, Highness. I'm here to fulfill our bargain only because of him. If you're willing and just, my wife and I have a better idea."

WHEN THE ORBINII jail guards shoved open the door, Rogan looked perfectly pathetic sitting in a dark corner on the floor in his holding cell. The medical swath was still wrapped over his eyeless head. He had obviously not detected the cot sitting on the opposite side of the room. Or perhaps his own self-loathing drew him toward the dark and lonely corner. It suited him.

Ben stepped in. Rogan looked up looking puny, frightened. Ben clicked his tongue and said, "Congratulations, Rogan, you've earned the honorary title of *mongrel* from the Orbin Royal Council."

"They're going to put me away aren't they?" he said as a three-year-old might who had been relegated to his bedroom for poor behavior.

Ben said, "No. They're putting you on a jail boat."

Rogan plopped his head back against the wall looking miserable. He groaned, "Jail boat ..."

"What'd you think was going to happen, Rogan?"

He gave him a hopeless smile and said, "I thought I'd be at *Nubbie's* right now."

Ben shook his head with a condemning look and said, "*Nubbie's?*"

"You never been to *Nubbie's?*"

"No. I can honestly say I've never been to *Nubbie's.*" He accentuated the word with a shot of revulsion.

Rogan smiled in deep, needful reflection. "It's a real high-class joint. Molta-Danora. Brew their own, you know. And the dancing girls—shew-wee. There's this one, she's from Golotha, she does this thing where ..."

"Yeah, sounds real classy," Ben interrupted completely uninterested. "Look, you can forget *Nubbie's.* They're sending you back to Speculus."

"The Guild?" he said sounding shocked and puny.

"Yep."

He groaned, "Sympto's going to want his money."

"Yep."

"I don't have his money."

"Nope."

He dropped his head between his knees. "I'm so booster-boofed."

"Maybe not," Ben said.

Rogan's head came back up as if to see him. He said, "Huh?"

Ben said, "You'll be making a stop on the way, and if you're smart you'll never see Sympto again."

"Stop? Where to?"

Ben smiled at him, couldn't refute the irony. He said, "You'll see."

Rogan scoffed, "Oh, ha ha—that's funny."

"From there, you'll be free to go."

Rogan said, "Great," sounding deeply petulant.

Ben shook his head grinning sadly down at him. He sighed, "This deal went raw for you didn't it?"

"Raw as meat," Rogan said.

Ben looked back at the guards who stood at the entrance watching the transaction. He squatted down next to Rogan, got close, and said, "You almost got my wife killed, Rogan. So I'm only going to tell you this one time. Are you listening?"

Rogan reacted to Ben's sudden closeness, looking up blindly, and said, "That's all I can do."

"Good," Ben said. "If you ever see me coming around the corner, it means I'm coming for you, Rogan, and I'm coming to take more than just your eyeballs. So, buddy ... you better run. You better run far and fast. You got it?"

"Yeah," he said, defeated. "There's only one thing. How am I going to see you coming?" He yelled, *"I ain't got no eyeballs!"*

Ben came to his full height still looking down. With a final word, he said, "I know it's not your strong suit, Rogan, but ... *think* about it." He turned and walked out, the cell door slamming behind him.

It left Rogan frowning in the dark, sitting on Ben's last words.

Think about it.

Okay, so an Orbin jail boat was coming to collect him.

But they weren't delivering him to the Guild.

Instead, they were taking him to some mystery stop.

Then he would be free to go.

Rogan tilted his head like a dog putting a riddle together.

Then he'd be free to go?

And if he was smart, he'd never go see Sympto again?

See Sympto.

See!

Rogan grinned.

They were taking him to an out-of-the-way med colony.

He smiled big.

He was going to get new eyeballs!

He tilted his head the other way, confused—*wait a minute!*

How was he going to afford new eyeballs?

New eyeballs cost a lot of yield.

Plus they'd have to bribe the flight crew.

Bribe the med colony.

That takes at least ...

Rogan grinned, whispered, "Half a million."

THE REPAIR CREWS WERE FINISHED. REX looked good, as good as Ben had ever seen him look. He was patched, polished and whole—ready for space flight. They also reattached his mag-spires, turnstile and all, and fitted him with new cargo containers. They were uniform in color, shape and size. They even replaced a few shorted circuits, replenished the armory, even loaded a full capacity into the bubble gun. He no longer looked like a big discolored patch-up job. Everything was painted a suitable light gray with fresh, dark russet highlights. Even the viewport was clean, pristine and mean. The Orbinii obviously didn't want them carrying out this task against the Cabal looking suspect. It only suited Ben's needs. He swam in the view momentarily. He liked what he saw.

Boarding REX was a breath of fresh air. He paused with his face to the ceiling, eyes closed, taking a full breath. Then it was off to the cockpit where Tawny awaited him. She'd removed the exo-suit legging and replaced it with a proper fitting to begin her healing process. She smiled at him as he entered. He smiled back and took his pilot's chair.

"So what about Rogan?" she asked.

"He's—"

"Never mind," she said.

"Right. Disengaging," he called, and REX lowered from the platform, spun about and faced irrefutably toward one tiny moon three inner-warp hours away.

Menuit-B.

Ben emitted the download information on the 3-D pad. Everything zipped up—bullet-pointed information, schematics, a holo-image of the moon.

"There's the plan," Tawny said.

"Yeah. Looks pretty simple," he said. "We go in. Do the drop. Get out. What could go wrong?"

"Absolutely nothing," she said. "So, let's do it."

Ben took a concerned breath and sat back in the chair. It caught her attention. She looked over, said, "What?"

"Tawny, are you sure about this?" he asked.

She gave him an interested look. "What do you mean?"

He cringed in thought and said, "Delivering war technologies. Escorting weapons grade material. Getting involved in espionage. What we're about to do steps across every rule we ever devised to avoid the war. Plus, we're about to foil the Cabal's plans, big time." He paused, said, "That's your war effort. Those are your people."

She put a hand on his cheek, made him look at her. "You're my war effort, baby. You're my people."

Her words choked him up, made him smile. To the two gods of the solar twin system (and he didn't care which one) he'd swear to either one of them, he loved this woman. He loved her more than anything.

More.

Than.

Anything.

He said, "REX?"

"We're set and met, Cap."

He took her hand and squeezed. "I love you, wife."

She squeezed back. "I love you, husband."

They shared a moment looking into each other's eyes.

Ben said, "Burn!"

And *BOOM*—they were gone.

***

Hi. I'm Ian. By reading this book, you have just qualified my existence. Not to mention, I can do things like eat food now. But my biggest hope is that you simply enjoyed the story. If you did, let me know! Hearing from readers makes my day. You can email me or even subscribe at the link below. Also, I'll be including information on any events and future releases. And I won't drop any spam, I promise. I hope to see you there.

My author website
www.IanCannonAuthor.com

* * *

Also, remember to leave a review of the book on Amazon. It makes a HUGE difference in sharing your opinion and getting more eyes on my work. Thanks again for giving me a few hours of your valuable time. Believe me, it means a lot. Let's talk soon!

~ Ian Cannon